Here's what *Romantic Times BOOKreviews*
has to say about

RHYANNON BYRD's

**BLOODRUNNERS series from
Silhouette Nocturne**

Last Wolf Standing
"4-1/2 stars…Fast paced and exciting, Rhyannon Byrd's
Last Wolf Standing is hard to put down."

Last Wolf Hunting
"Top Pick. 4-1/2 stars."

Last Wolf Watching
"Top Pick. 4-1/2 stars…Rhyannon Byrd's
compelling, sexy characters and exciting story
make *Last Wolf Watching* a must read."

RHYANNON BYRD

EDGE *of* DESIRE

HQN™

Recycling programs
for this product may
not exist in your area.

ISBN-13: 978-0-373-77423-4

EDGE OF DESIRE

Dear Reader,

I'm thrilled to present *Edge of Desire,* the third book in my new PRIMAL INSTINCT series with HQN Books. Set within a world where paranormal creatures live hidden among an unknowing humanity, this provocative trilogy continues with the story of the dark, dangerously sexy Riley Buchanan and the one woman he's always wanted...but known he could never have.

Despite his "saintly" reputation as a hardworking sheriff, Riley understands the pain and frustration of hell. He's been living in it since he was a teenager, when a mysterious ceremony revealed to him the horrors of his future. Believing he'd one day become a monstrous killer, Riley turned his back on the life he wanted, ending his relationship with a girl named Hope Summers and breaking her heart. But he's never forgotten her. Caught in the middle of a growing war against a sadistic evil that's returned to this world, Riley can't believe that fate could be so cruel as to bring Hope back into his life after all these years, taunting him with the ultimate temptation. A temptation he must do everything in his power to resist, while doing his best to protect her from the monsters that have followed him to the quaint seaside town of Purity. But Hope wants more than the rugged sheriff's protection. She wants what she never had before...and she isn't going to take no for an answer.

I'm so excited to be sharing Riley and Hope's tender, wickedly seductive romance with you, and hope you'll look forward to future adventures as the PRIMAL INSTINCT series continues. As the war between good and evil intensifies, the sexy shape-shifters who have fought beside the Buchanans will finally have stories of their own, along with a few surprise characters I'm hoping you'll come to love as much as I do!

All the best!

Rhyannon

To my awesome agent, Deidre Knight!
I'll never be able to thank you enough
for all that you've done...and for making this wild,
wonderful ride possible.
You're brilliant and amazing,
and I'm so thankful to have you as an agent
and a friend.

EDGE *of* DESIRE

Some desires can be deadly...

CHAPTER ONE

Some desires can be deadly...

Saturday morning

HE NEEDED A WOMAN. In the worst possible, gut-wrenching way. And yet none of the women Riley Buchanan passed on his way through the quaint seaside town of Purity, Washington, fit the bill. None were quite what he wanted. What he craved. The redhead watering plants outside the floral shop was too thin, the blonde swishing her miniskirt-covered ass in front of him too tall, when what he needed was someone...

He searched, trying to place a mental hold on the words, but they failed him.

Or you're just too stubborn to admit who you really want. Even to yourself.

"Shut up," he muttered to the annoying voice in his head, hunching his shoulders against the blisteringly cool breeze blowing in off the Pacific. The salt-scented air—so different from the dry mountain winds he called home in Henning, Colorado—filled his head, and for a moment he caught a flash of scent that stabbed at his insides, striking him like a physical blow. It was familiar and yet mouthwateringly different, and he stopped in the center of the sidewalk, his narrowed eyes scanning Purity's bustling Main Street, struggling to discern its source. He stood there gripped in a knot of panic, stunned, while his chest heaved from the force of his breaths. But there was no sweet, surprising face from his past. No big, luminous eyes blinking back at him in stunned recognition. No tender mouth curved in a shy, soft-focused smile. No one that he could pick out in the chaotic swarm of townspeople that nudged his memory, taking him back to a time he'd done his best to forget.

Blowing out a rough breath, he accepted that it was just his mind playing tricks on him, which seemed to be happening more and more these days. He thought he'd shoved that period of his life into an impenetrable mental vault, locking it away forever, but the damn awakening was screwing with his sanity, making him remember things, *and people,* that were best left forgotten.

And yet isn't she the very thing that you crave?

"Not going there," he rasped under his breath, pissed at himself for letting his imagination get the better of him. Forcing the wave of unwanted memories from his mind, he set off again down the crowded sidewalk, while the edgy, restless need continued to slither beneath his skin. He knew its source—knew from exactly where it sprang, but there wasn't anything he could do about it. The ancient Merrick blood within his body was coming alive inside him, and that meant only one thing:

His days were numbered.

Darkness was knocking on his door, but it wasn't Riley's life that hung in the balance. It was his soul.

Not that he'd done anything so stupid as to make a deal with the devil—though there'd been times over the years when he'd been tempted. At one point, he'd have been willing to do anything for a chance, the opportunity, to rid himself of the blackness festering within him. A toxic, destructive darkness that had formed the shape of his entire life since the age of seventeen, sculpting the years like an artist manipulating clay.

You're so full of bullshit. It's not the darkness twisting you up inside—it's your weakness. It's knowing that you won't be able to handle it when it hits.

Choking back the graveled curse that threatened to erupt from his mouth, Riley shoved his hands into the pockets of his jeans, while the gusting bursts of sea wind whipped his hair around his face. Despite the violent weather, Purity, Washington, was a beautiful place, caught between the rugged, majestic beauty of a towering autumn forest and a sheer rock face that looked out over the thrashing fury of the Pacific Ocean. On any other day he'd have been captivated by the town, but then this wasn't any other day. He and Kellan Scott had just arrived in Purity that morning, their purpose to retrieve the Dark Marker they believed was buried here in the sleepy little seaside community. His sister, Saige, had only just finished deciphering the ancient, coded map that gave directions to the Marker's location the day before, and Riley had immediately insisted that he be the one to go after the powerful cross. His brother and sister had argued like crazy, but in the end Riley had won with the sheer stubborn force of his will, as well as the threat that he'd simply leave. Just drive out of Henning without telling them where he was headed, if they didn't shut up and let him get out of there.

He couldn't have stayed. His awakening was coming on too strong, which meant that he was, more than likely, already being hunted by a monster. A Casus. One of the ancient enemies of the Merrick, and the very things that were causing the awakenings to begin. With each Casus who escaped from the holding ground that had imprisoned the vile race for over a thousand years, it was believed that the primal blood would awaken within a descendant of the Merrick clan. And though he'd fought it, Riley's turn had finally come. Now he would join the fight against an unholy evil, and hope like hell that he was able to take at least one of those bastards down before he…

No, he didn't want to think about that. About where he was headed. He needed to focus on the coming battle, so that he could destroy the Casus coming after him. That was why they needed the Dark Markers— beautiful ancient crosses that could be used not only as a talisman for protection, but which were the only known weapons capable of killing a Casus's soul and sending it straight to hell. God only knew how many of the things were already on his trail, and Riley had no intention of hanging around Henning, where they could pick off the locals one by one just to mess with his mind. That was how the bastards worked, and he'd seen just how evil they could be when the first escaped Casus had gone after his brother toward the end of the summer. It had killed four women in Henning alone, two of them women Ian had dated. Ian had finally used the first Dark Marker that Saige had found to kill the sadistic son of a bitch, but Riley knew his brother was still learning to cope with the unsettling fact that he was now more Merrick than man.

Riley wished he could accept the primal blood that flowed through his veins as easily as Saige had, but he was too much like Ian. A wry smile twitched at the corner of his mouth with the thought. He could well imagine Ian's reaction to the comparison. Whereas his brother had mostly lived a hard, dangerous life, Riley had done his best to keep himself on the straight and narrow, like a goddamn Boy Scout. And yet they were more alike than Ian realized.

Though his brother and sister didn't know it, Riley had lived in fear of his awakening for years. Since he was seventeen. Since he'd turned his back on the life he'd wanted, casting it aside. That was why, from the moment he'd realized the awakenings were actually coming, he'd been consumed by thoughts of the past. It was pointless and stupid, he knew. Regret wasn't going to save him, and it sure as hell wasn't going to ease the seething, visceral hunger scraping him raw, tearing at his insides like so many claws. But the two events went hand in hand, impossible to separate. Facing his awakening inevitably made him think about the things that had happened so long ago. The circumstances that had changed his life.

That had shaped him into the man he'd become.

But there was nothing to be done. He couldn't avoid his future, and he couldn't go back and change what had come before. The very fact that he was awakening was proof that he'd made the right choices all those years ago, no matter how painful they'd been. No matter how angry they'd made him. No matter the cost. Or how they'd hurt the people who'd cared about him.

Still, he lifted his nose to the air, searching for *that* scent again, but the violent wisps of the sea-scented breeze were too strong, and he finally gave up.

"It wasn't real," he grunted to himself, shaking his head as if to clear it of an alcohol-induced fog. Spotting Kellan coming from the opposite direction, he side-stepped a group of mothers chattering around a circle of strollers, and made his way beneath the awning of a brick-faced hardware store, stepping out of the harrowing wind as he waited for the Watchman to reach him. They'd split up not long after arriving in town, Riley heading to find out what he could about the land where they believed the cross was buried, and Kellan to check the local news database to see if any strange happenings or disappearances had recently been reported. They were almost positive that the Casus, who had briefly held possession of the mysterious maps a few weeks before, hadn't been able to decode them. But they weren't taking any chances. Though they didn't understand why, they knew the Casus were as desperate to get their hands on the Dark Markers as they were.

"Find anything?" he asked the Watchman as he neared.

The younger man shook his head, the sunlight glinting like copper off the deep, auburn strands of his hair, his blue-green eyes glittering with an ever-present spark of mischief. Kellan Scott was a brawny, muscular bastard, which was why he'd been sent along with Riley to find the Marker. As one of the Watchmen—shapeshifters whose job it was to watch over the ancient nonhuman clans—Kellan and his unit had broken with tradition and stepped in to help in the Merrick's fight against the Casus. Like his brother, Kierland, Kellan's inner beast was a wolf, and though Riley had yet to see him shift, he had no doubt that the twenty-six-year-old lothario could be lethal when he needed to be.

"What about you?" Kellan asked, while two early twentysomethings strolled past, their bright gazes eyeing them with obvious appreciation. Kellan flashed the blonde a wicked, come-and-get-me smile, before Riley glowered them both away.

"The land where Saige told us to search is owned by the same woman who owns that café we saw when we came into town, out by the cliffs. Her name's Millicent

Summers," he said, when Kellan finally took his odd-colored gaze off the blonde's ass and looked back toward Riley's scowl.

"Millicent. Mmm…sounds sweet. Let's go meet her," the Watchman murmured, grinning as he waggled his brows.

"I think Millicent might be a little old for you," he grumbled, trying to reroute the direction of Kellan's thoughts. The guy's mental compass seemed to be permanently pointed toward sex.

Kellan's smile twitched at the corner as he lifted his shoulders. "Women are like wine, Ri. They only get better with age."

Riley narrowed his eyes. "Do you remember one word of the lecture Kierland gave you before we left the compound?" he demanded in a gritty slide of words, while Millicent Summers's name kept looping through his brain, driving him mad, same as it'd been since he'd first heard it from the "Chatty Cathy" at the land registry. Millicent had been the name of Hope Summers's aunt, but he knew it was just coincidence. One more thing to mess with his mind. Fate couldn't possibly be *that* cruel. Jesus, he needed to get a grip before his useless obsession with the past made him lose his focus.

He couldn't afford to be distracted, damn it. He needed to stay sharp. Alert. Not walking around in a daze, searching for things that weren't even there.

"Yeah, I remember the lecture," Kellan offered with a tired sigh, pulling Riley's mind back to the conversation. The Watchman lifted his right hand and crossed his heart. "Will it make you feel better if I solemnly swear to keep my filthy paws off the lady, no matter how tempting she is?"

Shaking his head at the idiot's teasing, he grunted, "Come on. We might as well go check the place out." They headed down the crowded sidewalk, and though Riley was aware of the female attention they were drawing, he ignored it. He could honestly say that he'd never had trouble finding a woman when he wanted one. He wasn't being arrogant about it—it was just the way that it was. The only difference was that now, when he *needed* one, he…couldn't. Couldn't act on the offers. Even if a miracle occurred and he found what he craved, he wouldn't be able to do anything about it. Not with at least one Casus on his trail, hunting him down, looking for ways to hurt him, while waiting for him to fully awaken…and more Casus most likely on their way. Until Riley had fed and the Merrick blood within his body had gained full power, they would bide their time. Feed from his flesh too early, and he wouldn't give the monsters the power charge they needed to bring back more of their kind from the holding ground they'd named Meridian.

"If you don't want to draw more attention than we already are," Kellan drawled, "then you need to loosen up, Ri."

"Not gonna happen," he muttered, scanning the crowd, bitterly aware that he was subconsciously searching for a thick, healthy fall of long, chestnut-colored hair. The flash of bright, topaz-colored eyes. He struggled to let go of his tension, to find the smooth, easy well of calm that he'd mastered over the years, but it wasn't there.

"Seriously," Kellan rumbled, slanting him a worried glance. "I can feel the vibes pouring off you, man. It's getting bad."

"I'll handle it," he shot back, unsure whether Kellan was talking about his awakening...or his growing sexual frustration, not that it made a difference. He had no intention of discussing either with the cocky Watchman.

A smiling brunette strolled across their path, flashing a lip-glossed smile in his direction, and Riley looked away. Again. Same as he'd been doing for weeks now.

"Look, it's obvious you don't have trouble attracting women," Kellan murmured, while they turned left at the next corner. "So just pick one and get laid already. And I'm not the only one who's thinking it. Everyone back at Ravenswing is saying the same damn thing."

"It's not a case of just picking one," he said, slipping one hand beneath his jean jacket to readjust his shoulder holster. He'd been out of uniform since finally taking some long overdue leave the week before, and it felt strange. Like a part of him was missing. Thankfully his job as a sheriff enabled him to travel with his piece, so he hadn't been forced to leave his gun behind when they'd left Ravenswing, the Watchmen compound where his brother and sister were now living. And where

Riley had recently been staying, only because they wouldn't take no for an answer. "Believe it or not, Kell, some of us are actually more discerning than you."

The Watchman muttered something under his breath, raked one hand back through his hair, then sent him a look of frustrated confusion. "Honestly, man, I don't know what it is about you Buchanans. Why do you always have to make everything so bloody difficult?"

Riley grunted, knowing exactly what Kellan meant. Ian's awakening had been far from easy. But unlike his brother, who had been afraid of feeding from the woman who would soon be his wife, worried he'd take too much blood and accidentally kill her, it wasn't the feeding part of his awakening that terrified Riley. He knew, after seeing Ian and Saige go through the change, that he could take what he needed without harming the woman beneath him. But that didn't change the fact that he would still have to find a woman willing to let him sink his fangs into her throat, which was pretty damn unlikely. And then there was the issue of the Casus, who would no doubt hunt down anyone he singled out.

Not to mention, you still haven't found the one that you want....

He knew that, damn it. And he also knew that he wasn't going to find her. Not when *she* was on the other side of the country, probably settled down with a brood of children and an adoring husband who worshipped her the way she'd deserved to be worshipped. Hell, even if he did find the balls to track her down, he knew damn well just how Hope Summers would react if she saw him again. He'd either get her hand across his face, or her fist in his eye, and that would be that. No more than he deserved, and no less than he expected.

Gritting his teeth, he jerked his chin toward the gray two-story, wood-shingled café that sat up ahead, nestled between the breathtaking, fenced-off cliffs and the thick, towering forest. "That's the place up there."

Kellan read the wooden sign that swung on a post down by the road. "*Millie's*. Cute name."

They set off up the winding stone path that led to the café's front door, and Riley said, "I heard there are some cabins on the grounds that they rent out, so hopefully we'll get lucky and be able to take one." Then they'd be able to search in the woods that lined the café's back garden, where they believed the Marker was buried, without drawing suspicion.

Thunder boomed out over the churning ocean waters, heralding a coming storm, while the watery sunlight that painted the gray shingles of the café in an ethereal glow disappeared behind a bevy of swollen clouds.

Opening the door of Millie's, they stepped inside, and Kellan's rumbled reply was lost beneath the buzzing in Riley's ears as he drew in a deep breath…and damn near died. There it was again. *That scent.* Familiar, like something he'd known before…but different. Richer. Sweeter. Deeper than he remembered.

He looked, searching, trying to find the source, his heart hammering like a freaking drum, and then the kitchen door swung open at the edge of his vision. "Hope?" he breathed out, unable to believe it could be true. It was…*impossible*.

As though she'd heard her name whispered on his lips, the woman now standing behind the gleaming wooden counter slowly turned his way. She blinked a pair of big, luminous, topaz-colored eyes, her chin quivering, as if she'd seen a ghost. As if she couldn't believe he was standing there, in the middle of the crowded café. She opened her soft, pink mouth, and he took a step forward, accidentally bumping into another customer. She swallowed, staring…her heavy breasts rising and falling beneath a long, baggy sweater.

And then she suddenly let out a bloodcurdling scream of rage.

"What the he—"

Before Kellan could finish his startled curse, Hope Summers took aim and hit Riley smack in the center of his forehead. But it wasn't a punch she'd thrown at him. No bare-knuckled wallop or open-handed slap. No, he thought, grimacing as the hot, melting mess she'd chucked with deadly accuracy dripped into his eyes, blurring her flushed, furious expression. The woman had slammed him with warm, homemade apple pie.

And fate, it seemed, had found one last way to screw him after all.

CHAPTER TWO

RILEY WAS IN TROUBLE.

Serious, neck-deep, quicksand kind of trouble, and he was sinking deeper with each second that passed by. He'd thought it was bad, wanting Hope Summers and not having her near. Not being able to see her. Not being able to breathe her into his system, gulping down that rich, mouthwatering scent as if he needed it to live. Needed it to get through each day. Not knowing where she was, assuming she still lived in North Carolina, where he'd heard she'd gotten married not long after she'd set off for college. Not knowing what she was doing, wanting to punch his fist through a wall whenever his imagination supplied a sickening, nauseating montage of images of her with a husband. *Her husband.* The man whose right it was to want her…touch her. Take her beneath him and do the things that pulled Riley out of the night's darkest, deepest hours of sleep, his body hard, sweat-soaked…shaking, wanting her so badly it was a physical pain in his gut.

After he'd ended things between them, it'd been hell, seeing her at school, around town. Watching her get older, slowly growing more mature, blossoming into a person he would never know…never be close to. Unable to take it, he'd finally gotten as far away from their hometown of Laurente, South Carolina, as he could, hoping the distance would help him deal. And then he'd made it a rule, whenever he was home, that he discussed her with no one. Ever.

Yeah, he'd thought the craving had been bad before. Self-destructive. Stupid.

But this was worse. And her damn "dessert assault" wasn't helping the situation.

Before he'd even managed to wipe the sticky remnants of apple pie from his face, she hit him with another pie that smelled like cherries. The noisy café had erupted into muted chaos, everyone struggling to dodge the line of fire, their rapt attention focused on the bizarre spectacle, while Hope's low, breathless muttering could just be heard beneath Kellan's choking, snuffled cracks of laughter.

"The nerve…coming here…bastard's lucky I don't take off his…"

Using his arm and shoulder, Riley wiped his face on his sleeve as best he could and lifted his head in time to see her taking aim with what looked like a mountainous froth of lemon meringue. A low, aggressive growl lashed out from his chest. "Enough!" he barked, taking a step forward. "Damn it, Hope! What the hell are you doing?"

"I want you out!" she screeched, hurling the pie.

"Gone! This instant!" He ducked to the side just in the nick of time, the lemon meringue zinging by his ear like a missile, until it exploded against the front door, sloshing to the gleaming hardwood floor in a slippery, sunshine-colored mess.

"Christ, Riley," Kellan called out from behind him. "You really bring out the soft side in people, don't you?"

He turned his head to glare at the snickering jackass, which was a mistake. Hope took aim again, and a blueberry pie joined the others, her target lower that time, hitting him square on his chest, chunks of dark blue pie covering his T-shirt, jacket and jeans. Snarling, he finally shook himself out of his stupor. Lifting his right hand, he held it palm-out, fingers splayed, and the sailing chocolate cream she'd just thrown stopped in midair, dropping to the floor five feet in front of him. The air was filled with murmured remarks like *"Damn, she aimed too short that time!"* and *"That one didn't have enough weight behind it!"*—but he knew his action hadn't gone unnoticed by Kellan. The guy's laughter faded, and Riley swore he could feel the heavy weight of Kellan's stare burning into the back of his skull. He'd deal with the silent torrent of questions blasting from the Watchman later, after he'd handled the screaming, pie-hurling banshee.

Flicking more filling from his eyes, Riley narrowed his gaze on Hope as she searched behind the counter for new ammunition. Before she moved on to anything more lethal, like a knife, he stalked across the pie-splattered floor and quickly moved behind the counter. She shrieked, trying to rush past him, but he latched on to her arm, growling, "We need to talk. *Alone*."

She fought his hold, her eyes blazing as she quietly swore in a low, steady stream of inventive phrases. Undeterred, he pulled out his badge and flashed it at the room, thinking to slow down anyone who might come rushing to her rescue. He doubted Hope even noticed what he'd done, she was so focused on escaping his hold, her free hand pulling ineffectually at the fingers wrapped around her bicep. Replacing his badge in the back pocket of his jeans, Riley released her arm as soon as he'd latched on to her wrist, locking his fingers around the fragile bones in an unbreakable hold. Then he started dragging her past a pretty middle-aged woman he recognized as her aunt. Millicent Summers stood at the register, her bright gray eyes round with surprise, mouth open in a look of stunned astonishment as Riley pulled Hope through the swinging door. Instead of leading to the kitchen, as he'd thought, they entered a small service area that sat between the front and back of house, another doorway located on the opposite wall.

"Let go of me!" Hope shouted, and he glanced down, his gaze instantly clashing with hers, the currents of anger and hurt and shock sparking between them so strong, he was amazed there wasn't smoke. Riley could see that she hated his guts, almost as much as he wanted to eat her alive. From the top of her head down to her

cute little Doc Marten–covered toes. He took a slow
visual inspection, noting the baggy sweater and jeans
that did little to hide her killer curves, before reconnect-
ing with her glittering gaze. Then he just stood there,
lost…staring, so wound up he wondered how he didn't
just snap. His eyes felt hot, his chest tight, his skin two
sizes too small for his body, while the primal part of
his nature was in full roar, struggling to fight its way
to the surface.

Forget it, he silently grunted. *You're never getting
your hands anywhere near this woman. So back off.*

The Merrick's visceral fury clawed through him, but
he pushed it down, mentally slamming it into submission. His instincts told him to retreat, but he couldn't
turn away from her. Couldn't stop staring…soaking it
all in, gorging himself on the flesh-and-blood woman,
the reality so much better than the fantasies that had
tortured him over the years.

And yet those fantasies had been centered on a girl
who was gone. Forever. The woman standing before
him now was a stranger. One he didn't know. Couldn't
read. And one he sure as hell couldn't predict. The Hope
he'd known would have never lost her temper. She'd
been quiet. Timid. Shy. The woman before him, vibrating with fury, was anything but. And yet he'd have recognized her from nothing more than a glance.

Jesus. What in God's name was Hope Summers
doing in Purity, Washington? If you'd asked him five
minutes ago, he'd have sworn that such a thing wasn't

possible. The proof, however, was staring right at him. Or glaring, as it were.

He was screwed, and he knew it, because in that moment Riley realized that the only thing worse than wanting something that wasn't there, was having it stand before you, knowing damn well that you couldn't have it. And no matter how wrong it was, he *did* want her. Wanted her soft, womanly body beneath his, penetrated and stretched, her husky cries filling the air while he filled her with his cock. Wanted the Merrick's fangs buried deep in her pale throat, while the hot, provocative rush of her blood spilled over his tongue. He'd been thinking about her since his awakening had begun, but then thoughts of the Merrick had always gone hand in hand with Hope.

Hell, if he were completely honest, he'd just shuck the tough-guy routine and admit that he'd never *stopped* thinking about her. She'd always been with him, all these years, hovering at the edges of his awareness. Always there, impossible to shake. Her scent. Her laughter. Her smiles. He could see shades of the girl in the woman. She'd been beautiful at sixteen, but she was heart-stopping at twenty-nine. Not like the superficial beauties plastered across glossy magazine covers. She was more real than that. More... He struggled to put his finger on it, but couldn't.

Hope, on the other hand, apparently had no problem coming to grips with what she thought about him. The evidence was still covering him, clumped in his hair, on his clothes. He probably had pie in his friggin' ears. And on that point, he snarled, "What the hell was that about?"

She growled. Actually growled at him, looking around as if trying to spot something else to throw at his head.

"Damn it, woman!" he raged, grabbing her shoulders as she reached with her free hand for a thick, sturdy peppermill, probably thinking she could crack him upside the skull with it. It was a jarring thought, considering his teenaged Hope had been the most calm, gentle person he'd ever known. The one standing before him now was a goddamn she-cat, with her claws extended, ready to draw blood. "Calm down!"

She glared up at him, her topaz-colored eyes narrowed to furious slits. "I want you out!"

His fingers tightened, just enough to hold her in place. "Well, I'm not going anywhere, so you might as well settle down."

"Get your hands off me!" she seethed, the energy blasting off her hot and feral and sexy.

"Gladly," he growled. "Just as soon as I know you're not going to try to brain me with anything."

"You know, Ri," Kellan drawled from somewhere off to his right, obviously having followed them into the small room, "I'm usually not all that great at reading the female mind. Too damn complicated, unless we happen to be in bed at the time. But I get the feeling this one isn't all that happy to see you."

At the sound of the Watchman's voice, Hope's eyes

went comically wide. She froze, then peeked around Riley's shoulder, gasping when she realized they had company. Very slowly, she closed her eyes, took several deep, shuddering breaths and finally relaxed in his hold. "Okay. All right," she whispered, her voice soft and thick, the lashing intensity of her rage somehow melting away. It left her with a haunted look on her beautiful face—one that jabbed at him, stabbing at his conscience. "The last time I saw you, I was still numb from the shock of what you'd done, but…I've had years to think about what happened between us. To think about the way that you treated me. And I guess…I guess it all just came roaring out. But I'm…fine now. You can let go of me."

He made a low sound under his breath, and she lifted her long eyelashes, looking back up at him, her golden-brown eyes shadowed by embarrassment. "Really, Riley." She touched her tongue to her upper lip, and he had to fight not to go hard as his blood rushed south, thickening in his cock. "You…you just caught me by surprise."

"I'd love to see what you could do with a little time to plan an attack," Kellan rumbled, and from the corner of his eye Riley saw the good-looking Watchman give her a wink.

"Are you going to introduce your friend?" she asked, smoothing her hands down the front of her shapeless sweater as he forced himself to take a step back. His palms itched to track the same path, and he fisted his hands at his sides, feeling as if he'd slipped into a dream. Or better yet, a freaking nightmare.

"Kellan," he growled. "His name's Kellan Scott."

"Please tell me you're going to be our new landlady," the flirt drawled, one hand pressed against his heart as he flashed her what he probably considered his most charming smile. "Say yes and I'll be willing to step in and sacrifice my body for the cause."

Apparently not immune to the Watchman's teasing, Hope's face turned pink. "What cause?" she asked, her confusion obvious.

Riley turned, glaring at Kellan, who lounged with his shoulder propped against the wall, his blue-green eyes lingering on Hope in a way that tested Riley's control. And he hated to lose control, damn it. "Don't even think about it," he warned in a quiet rasp.

Kellan blinked, his brows raised in a look of wounded innocence. "What?"

"Don't 'what' me. And no one invited you back here," he muttered, just as a clump of crust dropped out of his hair, plopping onto his shoulder. Scowling, he grabbed a nearby hand towel and ran it over his face and head.

"I'm not about to miss all the fun." The Watchman's white teeth flashed in a smile. "Tell me, Ri. This kind of thing happen to you often? Getting assaulted with pastries?"

"Pies aren't pastry," he said, slanting a narrow look toward Hope as he tossed the towel onto the counter.

"Is that so?" Kellan murmured, scratching at the dark bristles covering his chin.

Hope nodded. "They're desserts."

The teasing idiot winked at her again. "As well as ammunition."

"We do have wonderful pastries, though," she told him, returning the guy's grin, though Riley could see the strain lingering around her eyes. "You should try the pecan ones. They'll melt in your mouth."

Kellan appeared riveted, and Riley knew damn well that it wasn't food the Watchman was thinking about as he practically purred, "You can bet I will, sweetheart."

"That's enough," he ordered, struggling to get control of himself. He focused his attention on Hope, who had managed to put more distance between them, so that she now stood with her back pressed up against the counter behind her. "First things first. What exactly are you doing here?"

Crossing her arms over her chest, she arched one slender brow. "Considering this is my business, maybe that's what I should be asking you."

"You own this place?" Kellan asked.

She nodded. "Along with my aunt. We're partners."

"I meant in Purity," Riley persisted, interrupting them for the second time. "What are you doing in Washington?"

He could see her calculating how much to tell him, and how much to keep to herself. Finally, she said, "Millie had a friend who left her this land after she died from breast cancer. I went in with her, and we converted part of the house into a café."

As he looked around, there was a belligerent bite to his words as he said, "And where's your husband?

Work?" He'd noticed she didn't have on a wedding ring, but knew that wasn't unusual for people who worked in restaurant kitchens.

A bitter sound that wasn't quite a laugh caught in her throat, and she lifted one soft, feminine-looking hand to push her hair back from her face. Though some of her angry flush had begun to fade, her skin still glowed with a healthy, fresh-faced vitality, the rosy color in her mouth and cheeks completely natural. "Try the state penitentiary in North Carolina."

He stared, thinking he *had* to have heard her wrong. "What the hell does *that* mean?"

"Watch it," she warned him, suddenly bristling again at his tone. "This is my place, Riley. Not yours. You have no right to come in here barking at me."

"State penitentiary?" he echoed, struggling to wrap his mind around the jarring idea. It didn't fit. Not in the rose-colored, white-picket-fenced life he'd always envisioned for this woman. She had to be jacking him around, screwing with his mind. "Are you seriously telling me that the guy you married is in prison?" he rasped out of a dry throat.

She gave a low, tired-sounding laugh. "Yeah, you know. Nasty places where they lock up creeps and keep 'em there. Don't they have prisons where you live?"

He kept staring, trying to read behind her closed expression and forced sarcasm, but her walls were too thick, blocking him out. "What exactly did he do?"

"What does it matter?" she asked, shrugging one

slender shoulder. The sweater slipped a little, revealing smooth, pale skin along with a slender bra strap, and his muscles tightened in reaction. "We're divorced now. He's no longer my problem."

His eyes started to burn, but he just kept staring, trying to make sense of what she'd said. It was as if the words wouldn't compute in his head. Divorced? Oh, God, that wasn't good. Was even worse than her being married. Being divorced meant that she was…

No way. Whatever you do, do not follow that train of thought. She's still off-limits.

Right, right. Of course she was. Hell, even if she wasn't married, there had to be a serious boyfriend. And even if there wasn't, Riley couldn't touch her. Not with the rain of chaos he'd bring down on her head.

"So you're single?" Kellan murmured, breaking the awkward silence that had settled in the fragrant room like a fourth presence.

"This is your last warning, Scott," he barked, cutting her off before she could give a response, not wanting to hear it. "Don't even think about her that way."

"You can snarl orders at me all day long, Ri, but I'm afraid my mind is a powerful thing," the Watchman replied, lifting the dark slash of his brows, a cocky tilt to his mouth. "Has a will of its own, I'm afraid."

"Yeah, well, get a grip on it, or it's going to have my fist shoved up its—"

"Okay, okay. I get it." Kellan laughed, holding up his hands. "She's off-limits. Same as Millie."

Hope's golden eyes went wide. "My aunt is off-limits?" she asked, sounding fascinated.

The Watchman grinned. "'Fraid so, sweetheart."

The corner of her mouth twitched, and Riley could tell that she was trying to hold back one of her infectious smiles. Like the ones that had brightened up his miserable adolescence. Made him feel like a god whenever she'd looked at him with that soft, sensual curving of her lips. "How sad. She'll be crushed to hear it."

"I'm feeling pretty crushed right now myself," Kellan said in a low, teasing rumble. "Riley's ready to kill me for even talking to you."

"Exactly how do you two know each other?" she asked, her curiosity so thick he could feel it.

Riley's common sense told him to turn around and get the hell out of there, but he couldn't move. Whether he stayed or left, Hope was now in danger. The cross had to be unearthed, before it fell into the wrong hands—and he was too much of a realist to hope they wouldn't be followed to the town. They'd done their best to cover their tracks, but it wouldn't stop the Casus and their psychopathic buddies from finding them…and fast. Riley knew all about how a Casus could tune in to the Merrick and know exactly where they were, as if the demonic creatures carried some kind of metaphysical tracking device. And now that they knew he'd come to Purity, it didn't take a genius to realize they'd think he was there to find the third Marker. Hell, even if there were some way he could mask his presence—which he knew damn well there wasn't—with a little searching, they'd learn that he'd asked about this property…and the trail would lead them right to Hope.

With the Marker buried on her land, Hope was going to be caught in the crossfire whether he was there or not. Which meant that until the Dark Marker was found, she needed protection, and he was more than qualified for the job. And yet the last place in the world he needed to be was this close to her. He didn't even know her anymore, but the girl she'd been was too wrapped up in the woman she'd become, and it was messing with his head. God, he could still remember the taste of her mouth. The softness of her skin. The way her eyes went heavy when he touched her.

Don't go there. Bad road, man. Just step back and get it together.

"Well?" she asked. "Is it some dark, juicy secret?"

Kellan seemed to have found his brain for once, and remained blessedly silent until Riley finally said, "How we know each other isn't important."

"Whatever," she breathed out, quickly losing her patience, her anger still simmering just beneath the surface. "So are you going to tell me what you're doing here in Purity? Or is it another dark, dirty secret?"

He drew in a deep breath, studying her guarded expression, while his mind worked, searching for a way to explain. But he was too fogged up with lust. Anger. Frustration. "Were you in town earlier?" he suddenly asked, his voice a quiet, gritty rumble.

He could see her confusion as she nodded. "I had to run in for some more milk. Why?"

He shook his head, knowing that it *had* been her scent he'd picked up while on Main Street. Scrubbing his hands down his face, Riley wondered how he was going to say what needed to be said. God, he didn't even know where to start. "Look, I know this is…" He faltered, searching for the words. "Awkward as hell," he finally growled through his clenched teeth, "but we need access to your land. Out in the forest. We were hoping to talk to the owner here about renting one of the cabins, so that we could search for something out in the woods."

What are you saying? You can't stay here now.… Are you crazy?

"Search for what?" she asked, interrupting the argument in his head, her gaze moving suspiciously between him and Kellan.

Riley closed his eyes. Tried to think. "You remember Saige?" he said, scraping one hand back through his hair as he lifted his lashes. "Well, she thinks there's something buried out there. A family heirloom of sorts, and we've come to find it for her."

She looked at Kellan. "Is he serious?"

The Watchman nodded, and Riley cleared his throat, saying, "I know it sounds strange, Hope. But this is important."

"Why?" she asked, her mouth flat as her gaze found his again.

Because my life is falling apart. Because if we don't find it, something else will. Something that could hurt you, just to get to me.

Instead of muttering the pathetic, melodramatic words, he simply said, "You're just going to have to take my word for it."

"Not likely." She laughed, tightening her crossed arms over her chest, the position doing interesting things to the shadow of cleavage revealed by the V-neck cut of the sweater. "This is mine and Millie's land, Riley. You're not going to just dig it up without telling us what's going on."

Obviously trying to help, Kellan lifted his shoulders and said, "It's not an easy kind of thing to explain."

She narrowed her eyes. *"Try."*

"Damn it," Riley snapped. "Suffice it to say that there are lives at stake. And that's all you need to know at this point."

"Lives?" Her brows drew together, her expression a blend of frustration and wary disbelief. "Whose?"

He silently cursed, painfully aware that he was botching the explanation with every friggin' word that came out of his mouth. "I don't have time to go in to details, and you're better off not knowing them. But we're not the only ones who want what's out there. Because of that, people are in danger."

She gave him a baffled look. "And it's your job to protect them?"

"Actually, it is," Riley explained with a hard sigh,

pinching the bridge of his nose, while a hell of a headache started knocking around inside his skull.

"Wow, that's some pretty serious responsibility," she said, lifting her brows. "Did you suddenly become God in the past thirteen years?"

Kellan snuffled another laugh under his breath, while Riley just ground his jaw. "I'm a sheriff," he muttered. "In Colorado. That's where I live."

"Huh," she breathed out. "Well, I guess that would explain the gun."

He paused, realizing she must have seen his Beretta in the holster beneath his jacket. Shoving his hands in his pockets, he said, "I know there's a helluva history between us, Hope, but my family's safety is on the line. If it wasn't, you can damn well bet that I'd already be out of here and we wouldn't be having this conversation."

Another low, bitter laugh left her lips and she turned her head, staring through a long, narrow window at the distant storm rolling in over the ocean. "Are your mother and Saige in danger?" she asked after a moment, her voice quiet…controlled. "I never really knew Ian, but I always liked your mom and your sister."

"Saige is involved, but Elaina…she passed away at the beginning of the year."

He could see her shoulders stiffen with surprise, though she still didn't look toward him. "I'm sorry about your mom." She drew in a deep breath, then slowly let it out. "And even though I know I should tell you to get lost, my stupid curiosity seems to be getting the better of me, because I'm dying to know what you're really doing here. The cabins are all empty right now because we were getting ready to do some redecorating, so if you want, I'm willing to let you rent one."

"Thanks," he rasped, while inside there was a voice shouting, *Idiot! Fool! Jackass!*

"Don't thank me yet," she said, snagging his gaze. "I still haven't told you how much I'm planning to charge you for your stay."

"Something tells me that we won't be getting the going rate," Kellan offered wryly, sounding as if he still thought the entire situation was hilarious.

She lifted one hand, rubbing at her forehead as if she were in pain. "We'll hash out the rental agreement when you come back."

"Come back?" Riley echoed.

She gestured toward the door he assumed led to the kitchen. "I was right in the middle of getting prepped for lunch. I need to finish and—"

"Probably bake some more pies," Kellan cut in with a lazy drawl.

The corner of her mouth twitched, though she didn't quite smile. "That, too. I can get the paperwork together for the cabin and show you out to it later this afternoon. They all sit on the trail that leads out from the back garden, winding its way through the forest, so you'll have plenty of privacy for whatever it is you're going to be doing out there."

Riley watched her from beneath his lashes, wanting to argue that they needed the cabin now, but knew that putting some space between them for a while was a good idea. Maybe, if he got lucky, she'd panic and leave town. Which was exactly what he wanted.

Yeah, sure it is.

Ignoring the words, he said, "We'll be back around three, then."

"Fine," she sighed, and turning, she headed through the swinging kitchen door.

"Hope," he called out.

"Yeah?" she asked, looking back at him over her shoulder, one hand holding the door pressed open. He stared at the thick, glossy sheet of her hair for a moment, having never seen it so long. The tips curved against the base of her spine, the sight unbearably erotic, even though she was hardly dressed for seduction.

Her voice snapped with impatience. "What is it, Riley?"

"If anyone asks, you don't know me. You only—" he gestured with his head toward the front of the café "—reacted like that because you thought I was someone else. Understood?"

She rolled her eyes. "Whatever."

He locked his jaw, knowing she didn't have a clue how important this was, wishing like hell that he'd never set foot in Purity. "I mean it, Hope."

"I heard you the first time, Sheriff Buchanan." She held his stare, then slowly shook her head. "Let's be honest. It won't be such a lie, because I never really knew you to begin with."

Riley watched the door swing shut behind her, and just stood there, still pulling in lungfuls of that mouth-watering scent, his head in a freaking daze. In so many ways, she was a stranger—but he still wanted to go after her, lay her down, strip her bare and study the changes in her body. Not that he'd ever seen her in the raw. He'd been too bloody terrified of losing control. Even at seventeen, his physical appetites had been...*hard*. Harder than a virginal girl like Hope should have had to handle. So he'd choked them back, waiting for her to get older

And then he'd lost her.

Shaking his head, he finally turned, surprised to find Kellan still standing there, quietly waiting for him. Silently studying his expression, no doubt seeing far more than Riley wanted to reveal. He was too stripped down at the moment. Too shocked open. Without saying anything, Riley headed back into the bustling café, where a busboy was mopping up the remnants of pie from the floor. Ignoring the curious stares sent their way as they walked out, they stepped into the rainy mist now drifting down from the sky.

"So," Kellan said lightly, as they made their way down the path, "are we going to talk about it?"

"Talk about what?" he asked, pulling his jacket up around his ears, his heart still beating painfully hard.

"What you're going to do about the woman," Kellan

murmured, while the bristling wind grew stronger, whipping at their hair, the thunder rolling in hard and fast. "Who she is. Why she hates you. Why you can't take your eyes off her. Not that the last one needs an explanation, considering she's some serious eye candy, though she doesn't flaunt it. And we can't forget the way you damn near fainted when you set eyes on her."

"I've never fainted in my life," he growled. "And it's none of your goddamn business."

Kellan made an obnoxious buzzer sound and smiled. "Wrong answer, man. I'm on babysitting duty, remember? Everything you do right now is my business."

"Babysitting duty my ass," he grumbled, heading back toward Main Street. "Everyone back at Raven-swing just wanted you out of their hair."

Shaking his head, Kellan made a low sound under his breath. "Now that's just not nice. Especially coming from ol' Saint Riley. What would your brother say if he heard you being so rude?"

Riley grunted in response, his lip curling at the mention of the ridiculous nickname Ian had given him. Yeah, he'd done his best to make a difference in his life—to fight for things that were good and just and pure—but that was only because he knew what lay ahead. Knew just how messed up things were going to get. Knew he needed to score some decency points while he still could, racking them up before it all went to hell.

They moved along the crowded sidewalk, Kellan

quiet at his side, while Riley's thoughts churned around and around. "We need to head back to the truck so that I can get some clean clothes. Then we can grab some food at that sports bar near the parking lot. What was the name?"

"Shorty's."

"Yeah, that's the place," he murmured, fighting the frustrating urge to turn around and head straight back to Hope, hovering over her like a protective shield. With each step he took away from her, his agitation rose, cranking tighter, making him sweat. The back of his neck began to tingle, and Riley lifted his hand, rubbing at the odd sensation, almost as if he could feel the press of a stare against his skin. Running his gaze over the crowded street, he searched for the source, but couldn't find anyone that snagged his attention. No one with pale, ice-blue eyes. Not that it mattered. He might spot a Casus's icy, unusual gaze, but the Collective soldiers working with the monsters were human. They could be anywhere, anyone.

A militant organization of human mercenaries, the Collective Army was devoted to purging the world of all preternatural life. Thanks to an unlikely ally—a Collective lieutenant colonel named Seth McConnell—Riley and the others now knew that the Casus and the Collective were working together to acquire the Dark Markers. According to Seth, a mysterious man named Westmore was behind the bizarre alliance, though his motives were still unknown. But whatever Westmore's goal, Riley and the others knew it wasn't going to be good.

Still feeling as if he were being watched, panic nearly had him turning and rushing back to the café, but he fought it down. He didn't need to do anything to make Hope stand out. Though he would be searching on her land, he knew that the more distance he could keep between them, the better. Which meant that he didn't need to be hovering over her like an overprotective lover.

At his side, Kellan suddenly said, "What's going on?"

Riley sent him a dark, questioning look.

"You're blasting vibes like a psychic firecracker. What gives? Are your Spidey senses tingling?"

Though he didn't like it, Riley had to admit that it was impressive, how good Kellan was at reading him. "I have a feeling we've already got company," he said in a low voice, before adding, "So I think it would be smart if we stay as close to Millie's as we can. I don't want to take any chances."

"You'll get no arguments from me," Kellan replied, casting his own gaze out over the crowd of people filling the sidewalks. "You know, if one of them is onto us so quickly, it could be Gregory."

Riley nodded, the panic in his gut turning to dread at the mention of the Casus who had seemed to make it his personal mission to go after Buchanan blood. The first Casus to return to this world had been Gregory's brother, Malcolm. Ian had killed Malcolm with a Dark Marker, and upon his own return, Gregory had gone after Saige for revenge. Though they hadn't heard anything from him since the day they'd all rescued Saige from Westmore's clutches, they knew he was still out there, no doubt waiting for an opportunity to strike. Because of that, Saige was all but under lockdown back at Ravenswing, her soon-to-be husband, a Watchman named Michael Quinn, unwilling to take any chances with her safety. Riley had expected his footloose sister to have been champing at the bit, but he'd been wrong. Instead, she practically glowed, her blue eyes shining with happiness…with a peace that he'd never expected to see in her. And it was the same with Ian, who was set to marry his own fiancée in just two weeks' time back at the compound.

"So if we can't talk about the woman, how about the other?" Kellan asked, pulling Riley from his internal thoughts as the first drops of rain finally began to fall.

"Other?"

"What you did," Kellan said, lowering his voice, "stopping that last pie in midair. Don't think I didn't notice it. We've been wondering at Ravenswing what your weird little Buchanan gift would be. Looks like we found it."

Riley knew exactly what Kellan was referring to. His brother and sister each had special…*talents,* though Ian was still trying to come to grips with his unusual dreams and instances of precognition. But unlike Saige, who had discovered that she could communicate with physical objects when she was still in her teens, it seemed that his and Ian's "gifts" had been brought on by their awakenings. Or simply unlocked, as Saige had explained it, believing the unusual powers had always been there, lying dormant because of his and Ian's unwillingness to accept that they were anything more than human.

"I'm guessing some sort of telekinesis," Kellan added.

"I have no idea what it is," Riley muttered. "And I sure as hell don't feel like talking about it. I just need some peace and quiet right now. I need to be able to think."

"Think all you like. But it isn't going to change anything."

"What are you talking about?" he demanded in a gritty rasp, just as the Watchman's cell phone began to ring.

Instead of explaining, Kellan just smiled and answered the call.

CHAPTER THREE

An hour later...

GREGORY DEKREZNICK SAT at the bar of a crowded local hangout in Wellsford, Washington, just up the coast from the quaint, cliff-side town of Purity. Despite the verdant feeding ground provided by a local college, his mood was sour. He missed Brazil, where he'd spent the first weeks of his freedom stalking little Saige Buchanan. Missed the hot, searing burn of the South American sunshine. Missed his brother, Malcolm, whose life had been taken by that son-of-a-bitch Ian Buchanan.

What he didn't miss was Meridian, the stinking hell-pit where the Casus had been imprisoned for centuries, cursed to a fate worse than death. Where he'd slowly rotted away, year after year, until Anthony Calder had finally sent him through the gate and back to this world. The first Casus to successfully organize their race into a cohesive force, bringing rule to the anarchy, Calder was the one who'd finally offered the Casus hope, as well as the chance of freedom. But it didn't come without a price.

Calder wanted the liberated Casus to avoid human kills. To feed only from the Merrick, so that they might bring more of their kind across the divide. To find the Dark Markers, though he still hadn't shared why they were so important to their freedom. Yeah, Calder wanted a lot of things, not that he cared.

All Gregory wanted was power. He liked the taste of it. The smell. The way it filled his head, his body, making him feel like a god. And he would use his power to strike down the Buchanans, one by one. They'd taken his brother, and now he'd made it his mission in life to take away everything, and anything, they cared about.

Then, once his thirst for revenge had been quenched, he would set his sights on new prey. On finding a new rival. Someone to push against, to keep himself entertained. Calder was ideal, since Gregory had never cared for the sanctimonious prick, and for that reason he was already planning on keeping any Markers that happened to fall into his lap. Calder was desperate for the Dark Markers, promising significant rewards to any Casus who handed a Marker over into Westmore's possession. Instead, Gregory thought it would be fun to collect them himself, just to screw with whatever ol' Calder had planned for the crosses.

But first he would finish the job here, then track down his own little Merrick—the one he'd caused to awaken when he'd returned to this world—and get it out of the way. Though he wouldn't use the power he took from the feeding to bring another Casus back from

Meridian, the idea of letting someone else take what was his grated against his pride. And now that Malcolm was gone, his pride was all that he had left.

Scrubbing his hands down his face, Gregory stared at the image reflected back at him in the mirror behind the bar. The human host he'd taken wasn't bad for something that was no more than food. A long, well-muscled body, topped off by a chiseled face that drew women to him with ridiculous ease. The chin-length, sun-streaked brown hair worked well with his tanned complexion, but there was a gauntness to the compelling features that hadn't been there before, and he knew he needed to feed. He'd been so busy watching, and waiting, that he hadn't seen properly to his needs. Now he was hungry, the craving for a warm, lush body grinding him down. A male could satisfy his need for nourishment—but only a woman could give him what he really required to feel whole...*powerful*. Only a woman—spread and pinned and bleeding beneath him, screaming in terror as she saw her death reflected in his eyes—could fully slake his dark, insatiable hungers.

He still wasn't happy about losing his chance to get at little Saige, but now that Riley Buchanan had headed off with only one Watchman for protection, things were definitely looking up.

To celebrate, he'd decided to treat himself to a good meal. The scent of warm, female flesh surrounded him, a carnal banquet of fresh-faced college girls steadily streaming in as they gathered with their friends on a lazy

Saturday afternoon. He watched them in the mirror, searching for the one who most appealed to him. The one he'd charm away from her friends, getting her alone, where he could throw off this pathetic human mask and show her what he was really made of.

The door opened for another customer, allowing the biting wind to whip through the heated interior, and he scowled. *This place is too bloody cold,* he thought, taking a drink of his beer, noting that a strange, new energy suddenly seemed to be spilling through the room. Looking over his shoulder, he had to fight down the urge to snarl as he watched the newcomer heading straight toward him.

"What the hell are you doing here?" he stormed, the instant the woman eased onto the stool at his left. She was stunningly gorgeous, but then he knew Pasha well enough to know that she'd never take an unattractive body. She was too vain. One of the most beautiful Casus females when in human form, she'd been renowned for leading unsuspecting men to their doom, taking them to the heights of sexual ecstasy, before taking them to pieces.

She was tall, probably around five-nine, her body one of provocative valleys and swells that drew every male eye in the bar. Deep, pale green eyes—the shocking color only made more striking by the dark, glossy tendrils of ink-black hair tumbling around her perfect features—stared back at him with a bold, aggressive air of confidence, which was why Casus females held so little interest to the males. Instead of screaming when you hurt them, they just laughed…then begged for more, which ruined the mood, as far as he was concerned.

"Well, well, well, if it isn't Gregory DeKreznick," she purred, running one perfectly manicured nail down the muscled length of his arm. "Wow. You've finally got a little meat back on your bones. I take it freedom is sitting well with you?"

He stared, recognizing the sensual tilt of her mouth, the glittering calculation in her gaze. Even though she was wearing the body of a host, he knew precisely who she was. "What do you want, Pasha?"

"Can't I come calling on an old friend?" she asked, leaning closer, as if she were sharing something intimate.

Forcing the words through his clenched teeth, he said, "We were never friends."

"But we could be," she murmured, smiling at the bartender as she gestured toward Gregory's beer, silently asking for one of her own. "We're all on the same side here, you know. Freedom of our kind and all that."

A rough, husky bark of laughter jerked from his throat. "I could give a shit about our kind, and you know it. I'm in this for no one but me. As others have already discovered."

She crossed her legs, the black miniskirt she wore rising along her slender thigh, revealing far more skin than was decent. Holding his stare, there was a knowing edge to her words as she said, "From what I hear, Gregory, you're in it for revenge."

"Is that right?" he asked, forcing a bored tone to

his words, though he couldn't help but wonder what she was after.

"Mmm," she purred. "Heard the oldest Buchanan took out Malcolm. Dear big brother is rotting in hell now, no?"

His eyes narrowed, a low, feral snarl surging up from his chest, but he fought back his temper, focusing on keeping his fangs and claws from releasing. Now wasn't the time to rip the stupid bitch to shreds. "Last time, Pasha. What the fuck are you doing here?"

She smiled at the burly bartender as he approached with her beer, his brown eyes glazed with lust. "They're so pathetically easy," she murmured with a casual air, when the guy reluctantly moved away to take an order at the far end of the bar. "And in answer to your question, Gregory, I think you know exactly why I'm here." Her smile was sly as she met his stare. "Doubt I'll be the only competition you have coming into town."

Yeah, he'd known that competition was on its way, simply because Riley Buchanan wasn't *his*. Wasn't the Merrick that Gregory's release had caused to awaken. And then there was the issue of the Marker, which the other Casus knew the Buchanans would be going after, now that Saige was once again in possession of the maps. It was going to be a battle to get his hands on the Merrick and the Marker, but he had no intention of turning tail. No, he wanted this too badly. Wanted to take the Buchanans apart, piece by piece. But they had the other two in lockdown. The only one to venture out of the safety of Ravenswing was the lawman, and Gregory knew exactly what the bastard was after.

"You want the Marker," he said to Pasha. "The one he's come here to find."

"That would be nice," she drawled. "But I want the sheriff, too."

Gregory snorted. "Well, you're not getting him. He's *mine*."

She ran her finger around the top of her glass, and softly said, "Actually, Gregory, he's mine."

"Shit," he muttered, understanding exactly what she meant. In an effort to promote order among the newly escaped Casus, it'd been decided that since only a fully awakened Merrick could provide their kind with the "ultimate" feeding, each escaped Casus would be allowed exclusive rights to the Merrick their return to this realm had caused to awaken. It was an important rule, as only a Merrick could provide the power charge needed for the Casus to "pull" another one of his kind back from Meridian, bringing them across the divide. It was also a rule that Gregory had no intention of following.

"You knew someone would be coming for him," she murmured. "That someone's me. And the others, well, they know he's here for the Marker. They'll wait until he's found it and reached full power before striking, but the competition is only going to get worse. If you'd listen, I can guarantee you'll be interested in what I have to say."

"Better yet," he growled, "why don't you just get the

hell away from here and forget you ever even heard the name Buchanan."

She shook her head, which sent the dark, silky curls tumbling over her shoulders. "I can't do that, and you know it. But," she said, watching him carefully, "I was hoping we could make a deal."

Shifting so that he faced her on the stool, he asked, "And what exactly did you have in mind?"

She leaned forward, keeping her voice low to ensure they weren't overheard by the customers crowding in, some kind of college sporting event getting ready to play on the multitude of televisions situated throughout the bar. When she was done with her explanation, she straightened and took a drink from her glass. Gregory rubbed a hand over his bristled jaw, unable to deny that he was intrigued. He wanted Riley Buchanan, but Pasha's proposal was tempting. And the conniving little bitch knew it.

It would mean waiting, but for the prize she was offering, he could stomach holding off. And in the meantime, he'd do his best to screw with the sheriff's mind. Twist the knife until he had him jumping to his tune. It would be so easy. And, hell, maybe even a little fun.

"Just think about it," she said, smiling as she slipped a piece of paper in front of him. She took another drink of her beer, laid a ten-dollar bill on the polished bar, then winked at the blonde who suddenly pressed up close against Gregory's other side, the giggling girl obviously in the mood to flirt. Pasha was right, he thought. They really did make it too easy.

Slipping off her stool, the beautiful Casus leaned in close to his ear. "I'll let you go and enjoy your meal now," she whispered, allowing her lips to brush against the side of his throat. "But be a good boy and give me a call when you're ready to talk."

CHAPTER FOUR

10:00 p.m.

HOPE DIDN'T KNOW how long she'd been standing at the deep bay window, staring out into the thick fall of darkness at the faint, flickering glow of light just visible through the trees. Someone was out there, smoking a cigarette. She watched as the tip moved with a slow rhythm each time the person lifted it to their lips, took a drag, then lowered it again. She could just make out the shadow of their body leaning against the trunk of one of the thick, massive maple trees that lined the back garden. The form was decidedly male. Tall. Broad. Rangy and lean.

Riley.

A flurry of startled, disquieting emotions took flight inside her, and she pressed one trembling hand to her belly. It seemed so surreal now, and yet she knew she hadn't imagined the things that had happened earlier that day. Her high school sweetheart showing up in her café, walking back into her life after all these years, blasting her with his sharp, potent energy. God, her skin was still tingling in the places he'd touched her, a wild heat still blooming beneath her skin that made her press her cold hands to her cheeks for relief.

She should have never stopped throwing pies at him that morning, because once she had, she'd had to breathe…and look at him. It'd been impossible not to stare, her heart beating so hard it'd been a physical pain. He'd been gorgeous as a boy, but the man. God…the man was stunning, with a drop-your-jaw-and-stare-at-him-on-the-street kind of masculinity that no doubt got him noticed wherever he went. He was animal beautiful. Like something…something feral and wild. Predatory and dangerous.

She wasn't buying the story he'd continued to spill when he'd come back that afternoon, but then he never had been able to lie worth a damn. In clipped, graveled tones, he'd explained how Saige had become an anthropologist, claiming that she'd been in search of a family heirloom that some dangerous people were working to get their hands on. An heirloom they had reason to believe was buried out in the woods, because of a map that Saige had found. When she'd pressed him for details, he'd refused to tell her anything more, saying again that the less she knew, the better. And while she found the whole story incredulous—the idea of something that belonged to the Buchanans being buried there in Washington…on *her* land—Hope knew there was something bad going on for Riley to still be there. Something was up. Something that was important to him, though God only knew what it could be.

But his frustration at having to deal with her had been obvious. She knew, if he'd had the choice, that he'd have turned and gotten out of Purity so fast he'd have left a trail of smoke behind him. And while she'd tried to tell herself throughout the late morning and early afternoon that she didn't care if he came back or not, there had been a strange sense of panic in her chest until he'd finally walked back through the front door of the café at three o'clock.

The feelings rioting through her were a bad sign, but who knew? Maybe having him there would be a good thing. Help her to move on. Find closure. It was the only reason she'd given in that afternoon, pretending that she bought the load of drivel he'd given her, allowing him and his too-handsome-for-his-own-good friend to take one of their cabins.

Yeah, sure it was.

She blew out a shaky breath, and argued with the voice in her head. After all, allowing him to stay was exactly what her therapists would have told her to do. Closure, she reminded herself. That was what she could get out of this. Finally, after all this time.

The only problem was the way he made her feel, as if she'd crawl out of her skin if she didn't get her hands on him. It was a strange, startling sensation, after going for so many years without feeling anything even re-motely sexual. It was as if that part of her had shut down, only to be zapped back to life, and now she was hungry. Starving, actually. And nothing in the café's kitchen was going to ease the craving that churned through her veins like a molten burn of fire.

But she had to face the facts. She was one pathetic puppy. Even if she weren't furious with him, she wouldn't know how to get what she needed. From an early age, she'd been lectured on what good girls do and don't do. Her mother had gotten pregnant by a married man at the age of seventeen, and left a newborn Hope with her devastated grandmother, then hit the road in search of a new life. Desperate to make her grandmother happy, Hope had allowed the woman's lectures to form the framework of her personality, and it had led to disaster.

Good girls married the men they had sex with.

Good girls didn't walk out on their husbands.

Good girls put up with whatever was forced down their throats.

And in the end, good girls paid for being such pathetic wastes of space.

She almost wished she could just forgive Riley for the pain he'd caused her all those years ago, shovel it off her chest, and for once in her life act on pure, gut instinct. Just open the door, sink her bare feet into the cool, damp blades of grass as she stepped out into the silvery moonlight, and go to him.

And when she reached him, she'd place her hands on that hard, wide chest, lift up onto her toes, and cover the grim, beautiful shape of his mouth with hers. And maybe, just maybe, he'd have the power to breathe some life back into her.

"Hope?"

Gasping, she jumped about a foot when Millie called her name as she came through the doorway that connected their house to the industrial-size kitchen they shared with the café.

"Christ," she wheezed, pressing one hand to the center of her chest as she stared over her shoulder. "You scared the hell out of me."

"Sorry," Millie said, the gleam in her eyes warning that she was up to something. "I was just thinking that you should run up to the cabin and see if there's anything those boys might need."

"Stop," she murmured, turning back toward the window to press her forehead against the cool glass. It surprised her that the heat in her skin didn't leave condensation on the icy panes.

"Stop what?" her aunt asked with just the right amount of calculated innocence.

"I know what you're doing, Mil," she said with a shaky sigh.

"Oh? And what's that?"

God bless Millie, she thought. After things had gone south with her ex, it had been the recently divorced Millie who had stepped in and saved her. Who had somehow put the broken, jagged pieces of her back together and kept her from just slipping away. "Nothing is going to happen between Riley and me, so you might as well get those crazy thoughts out of your head."

"Well, if that's the kind of attitude you're going to

have, then of course nothing is ever going to happen. Happiness isn't something that comes easily in this world, Hope. You, of all people, should know that. If you want it, you have to be willing to work for it, to take risks."

"Some risks are just too much. I still have too much toxic damage from how things ended before. There isn't enough left to risk a second time around."

"There's always enough," Millie insisted. "You're just being stubborn."

Looking back over her shoulder, she struggled to keep her tone even as she said, "He isn't here to stay, Millie. He lives in Colorado and I live here. So what are you suggesting? That I try to have some kind of hot, sordid affair with him before he walks out of my life again?"

Millie's gray eyes gleamed with a womanly knowledge. "When that boy walks out your door, you're going to regret it one way or another. Might as well get what good you can out of it while he's here."

"He isn't a boy, Mil."

The older woman waggled her brows. "Noticed that, did you?"

She pressed her forehead to the cool glass again, her sigh leaving a fogged patch. "Of course I noticed. My eyesight works just fine."

"And?" Millie pressed her, making Hope want to groan.

"He's gorgeous, I'll give you that. But I have too much self-respect to make a fool of myself over him for a second time in my life. Like I said before, I'm still stinging from the first time."

Millie gave a ladylike snort. "Nonsense. You're letting your experience with Neal color your attitude toward men. And you've been doing it for too long now."

"You know what I think?" Before her aunt could answer, she straightened her spine and forged ahead, saying, "I think you should stop lecturing me, and start taking your own advice."

Eyeing Millie's reflection in the window, she watched as a frown tipped the corner of her aunt's mouth. "What does that mean?"

"You still haven't jumped Hal's bones, and I know you want to." Hal Erickson was a retired widower who lived in town and worked part-time as a local carpenter and handyman. He and Millie had become friends the year before, when he'd done some beautiful work remodeling the kitchen for them. And while Hope knew there was a mutual attraction between them, Millie had led Hal to believe that she was only looking for a platonic relationship.

"Hope!" Millie gasped, sounding flustered. Ha. As if the idea hadn't occurred to her aunt. She wasn't buying it for a second.

"Well, it's true. You've been stringing that poor guy along for months now."

"I've been doing no such thing," Millie argued, crossing her arms over her chest. "He's only interested in being friends."

This time, it was Hope who snorted. "Yeah, and I

only torture myself with diets because I'm addicted to the mouthwatering taste of lettuce. Go on, Millie. Feed me another one."

"You're awfully feisty tonight," her aunt murmured, while Hope eyed her own reflection in the window. The familiar image should have provided a measure of stability to the frenzied, chaotic swarm of emotions twisting through her, but instead it felt as if a layer of protection had been peeled away, like an X-ray, everything she tried so hard to conceal suddenly exposed…revealed. All her embarrassing emotions laid out on display for everyone to see. "I like it," Millie went on to say. "You've been too closed down for too long. It's good to hear you get some spark back in your voice. I've been worried about you."

Hope knew her aunt was right, just as she knew how much the woman cared about her. "I'm sorry for worrying you," she offered, the words halting…subdued. "But I'm fine. Really. I've just been tired."

Millie finally took mercy on her and said good-night, heading up the staircase that hugged the far wall. Hope moved through the warm, inviting room with its off-white walls and comfortable, coffee-colored leather sofa and love seat, checking the locks on the windows, same as she did every night. It was a ritual, as if each sturdy, protective bolt could somehow shelter her from the darkness and the quiet hours of solitude, when she felt too vulnerable. When she didn't have work to occupy her time. That was when her barriers were at their thinnest, allowing in thoughts and memories that were best left forgotten.

When she reached the bay window again, she stopped. Staring through the glass, Hope realized the flicker of the cigarette was even closer now, as if drawn nearer to the house by the sheer force of her longing. Without giving herself time to think about it, she suddenly threw open the back door and headed out into the night, down the cold wooden porch steps, until her feet were buried in the damp blades of grass. The sharp chill made her gasp, but she refused to turn back. She couldn't. Once she'd started moving, there was too much adrenaline to do anything but see it through.

Though his face was still in shadow, she could feel the power of Riley's stare, the touch of that hot, darkly sensual gaze making her shiver more than the damp chill of the air. And then the clouds moved, revealing the ethereal glow of the moon, and her breath locked in her chest as the details of his face were illuminated by the hazy, lavender beams of light. It was so hard to believe that she was staring at Riley Buchanan—at the boy who'd given her her first broken heart. Not that she'd ever had much heart left to offer another man, once Riley was done with it, which Neal had blamed for their problems. But then her ex had enjoyed laying the blame for his failures on anyone's shoulders but his own. Hope had often questioned how she'd ever let herself get involved with a man like Neal Capshaw. But then, he'd played her perfectly during their whirlwind courtship, and she'd let herself be fooled by his act, too naive to know better.

In a way, she knew that much of Neal's appeal had been the fact that he was the polar opposite of Riley. Fair to Riley's dark looks. Social to Riley's quiet intensity. And determined to keep Hope at his side, like something he owned, when Riley had just tossed her aside like yesterday's garbage.

God, she could still remember how badly it had hurt when Riley had broken up with her. She'd had a crush on him forever, worshipping him from afar, and then, at the beginning of her sophomore year, she'd experienced one of those fairy-tale moments when he'd done the impossible and asked her out. She'd almost died, feeling as if she'd walked into a dream. Nervous and painfully excited, she'd gone with him for a milk shake after school, and that had been the start. They'd been inseparable from that point on. Until he'd shattered her heart.

Before today, she'd spent years wondering why she couldn't get over him. Teenaged crushes were transient things, meant to come and go. Stolen moments in time to look back upon fondly, thinking how precious those first rushes of passion and discovery had been. They weren't meant to scar you for life. To imprint themselves on you so deeply, it was impossible for anyone else to ever come close, to measure up.

A few more steps across the dew-covered lawn, and she stopped, no more than a handful of feet separating them. Enough space for her not to feel crowded, but close enough that she could feel the blast of his hot, sharp-edged energy. Pull in the rich, mouthwatering scent of his skin. Her breath quivered in her throat, eyes hot…burning, as she stared through the moonlit night, soaking up the beautiful, breathtaking details. God, he was insanely attractive. Not pretty, in any sort of polished Hollywood kind of way. He was too hard, too rugged, too devastatingly male to appeal to the masses, his rough-edged masculinity sending a nervous shiver down her spine, as if she'd just encountered something beautiful…but deadly. A pitch-black panther roaming the foggy dead of night, or a long, sinuous viper twisting through the damp blades of savannah grass. The bump on his nose that he'd gotten during a varsity basketball game somehow only made him more appealing, as did the firm, sensual mouth that could no doubt induce hot flashes in the most frigid of matrons. And those Buchanan-blue eyes. Dark, intense, beautiful. She still saw those eyes in her sleep, the endless beauty of them making her awaken with her breath jerking in her lungs. Angel's eyes, darkened now by some kind of angry, violent emotion that looked almost like pain. Fear. Desperation. Which was madness. Just her own emotions projected on to him. She couldn't imagine anything in the world that would frighten a man like Riley Buchanan.

He was a mountain. A rock. Something immovable and strong. Completely indestructible.

He stood silent and still beneath her breathless scrutiny, then lifted the smoldering cigarette for another long, slow inhalation that made the tip burn like a tiger's eye in the hazy darkness. "I can't believe you smoke," she finally rasped, her voice feeling strange in her throat, as if the husky sound didn't belong to her. "It doesn't fit with how athletic you were in school."

"Yeah, well, I can't believe you live in Washington."

The graveled blast of his words made her flinch. "Small world, I guess."

He took another drag on the cigarette, the exhaled smoke curling through the damp night, while another storm brewed out over the water. She shivered, pushing her hands into the pockets of her jeans, and he said, "I thought I told you to be careful."

She frowned, recalling the lecture he'd drilled into her that afternoon about the need for her and Millie to be cautious until he and the redhead were out of town. He'd even gone so far as to demand that they not go anywhere alone, especially at night. She'd have scoffed at the ridiculous dictates, except for the fierce intensity with which he'd delivered them, as if he honestly *did* fear for her and Millie's safety. And she supposed the fact that he was a lawman added an authenticity to his warnings that she couldn't ignore, though it still drove her crazy that he'd refused to answer the barrage of questions she'd fired at him. "I know how to be careful, Riley. I always am."

"Speaking of careful, do you have an alarm for the house?"

"We do," she replied, lifting one hand from her pocket to push her windblown hair behind her shoulder. "Two women living on their own, in a place that takes in pretty good money." She shrugged, adding, "Purity is a safe town, but we figured it would be stupid to take any chances."

The grim set of his mouth pulled her gaze, the brackets that lined those sensual lips becoming deeper as he said, "I have some things I'd like you to use on your bedroom doors and windows, just as an added precaution."

"Are you serious?"

"As a heartbeat," he muttered, tossing the cigarette butt into the damp grass, then grinding it out with the toe of his boot.

"What are they?"

Pushing his own hands into his pockets, he said, "Kellan makes them. Behind that irritating attitude, the guy's some kind of genius when it comes to technology."

"And you say he's the brother of a friend," she said, a wealth of questions hidden beneath her casual tone that he seemed to pick up on.

He held her stare, his nostrils flaring as he drew in a deep, searching breath that made her feel somehow exposed, as if he were pulling in her scent. Taking it in. Holding it. Finally, he gave a slow nod, a silky, ink-black lock of hair falling over his forehead. "That's what I said."

"Okay," she breathed out. "I'll accept that, for now.

And I'll take the gadgets. I'm not stupid, and God only knows what kind of trouble you've brought with you. But you can stop lecturing me on the need to be careful, because I always am."

He narrowed his eyes. "Coming out here by yourself at night is not what I would call careful."

"I'm not alone," she argued, lifting her chin. "I'm with you."

He grunted under his breath. Internally debated with himself, she could tell. And then quietly said, "It's not safe for you to be alone with me, Hope. In fact, that's the last place you need to be."

A dry, brittle laugh jerked from her throat, the ragged sound lingering between them with painful, unsaid meanings. "It's not safe in the town. Not safe to go out alone. Not safe with you. Is it just me, Ri? Do you think I'm so weak that I don't know how take care of myself? And just what exactly do you think I'm going to let you do to me?"

His eyes narrowed further at the provocative words, though she hadn't meant them that way. Thick, curling lashes shadowed his gaze, but she could still see the startling intensity of that deep, dark blue. The same fierce, wicked color that had haunted her dreams for years.

When he looked at her like that, she felt stripped. Naked. Bared down to the raw, as if he could see right through the protection of her clothes, her skin, down to the truths she tried so hard to hide. With so little effort, he could peel back the layers and stroll through her mind at his leisure. Through the mangled minefield of her issues and emotions.

Needing a distraction, she lowered her gaze to the shoulder holster he wore over his long-sleeved black T-shirt, the dark handgun like some kind of perfect accessory, as if it were a part of him. "So you're a sheriff, huh? That's an awfully big position to fill at thirty."

He blew out a rough breath. "Yeah, but I'm ages older where it counts."

"You always were," she murmured, and it was so easy to remember how much she'd worried about him when they'd been together. His dad had left when he was little, and after Ian had bailed out on them, Riley had been forced to become the man of the house, which had been a hefty role to play at such a young age. "And now you have the weight of the world resting on your shoulders. Protecting your town. Your family. Millie and me from some unknown danger lurking in the dark. It must be exhausting, Riley. No wonder you look tired."

"The danger is known, and all too real," he grunted. "I don't suppose there's anything I can do to convince you to leave town for a while?"

"Are you serious?" she asked again, lifting her brows, suspecting he just wanted to get her to leave so that he didn't have to deal with her. And considering this was *her* home, and *her* life, she wasn't about to let him run her off.

"Yeah," he replied, his tone grim. "I'm deadly serious, Hope."

"Well, that's too bad then. Because I'm not leaving."

RILEY WANTED TO ARGUE with the hardheaded woman, but choked back the sharp words burning in his throat, knowing she was determined to fight him, pushing against him out of anger and bitter resentment. Not that he blamed her. If she'd dumped him the way he'd done to her, he would have still been hurling nasty insults in her face. Instead, she stood there with her head held high, the epitome of cool, calm composure. It made him crazy just to stand there, so close to her. He wanted to map out those lush, womanly curves with his hands. Taste the pansy-soft texture of her mouth. The soft inner curve of that voluptuous lower lip that could have driven a saint to sin. And despite his annoying nickname, he wasn't feeling at all saintly at that particular moment in time.

No, there was something about the way the ethereal streams of moonlight were hitting the smooth, vulnerable stretch of her throat that pushed him into a dark, dangerous place. Made the night feel too close, as if the heavy weight of the darkness was pressing in on him with crushing force, his temperature rising from the strain of holding himself together, until a fine sheen of sweat covered his body. Memories of the girl she'd been had always tempted him in ways that no other woman ever had. But seeing her all grown up damn near killed him with need. There was a fertile, succulent facet to her scent that cranked his need up to the point where he worried he'd do something stupid. A stinging heaviness in his gums that signaled the release of the Merrick's fangs. He knew that if he wasn't careful, they were going to descend, eager for the chance to sink into that pale, tender flesh. To take her blood into his mouth, hot and sweet against his tongue, feeding the primal darkness within him.

And no doubt scare her to death in the process.

And while the hunger for blood was most definitely the Merrick's doing, Riley knew he had to take responsibility for the violence of his desire. Though his Merrick blood was only just awakening, his physical appetites had always been dark…aggressive. It was just a part of who he was, and he'd always chosen women who could handle it. Handle him. Strong, independent, career-minded women, who had no desire for a relationship, but still needed a sexual outlet from time to time.

Not that he slept with women indiscriminately, or ones he didn't like. He just chose partners who were safe. Who could match his sexual appetites, and enjoy sex for what it was, without involving complicated emotions in the mix. Simple, clear-cut, mutual exchanges of pleasure. That was all he'd ever had—all he'd ever been able to find.

Until now. Already, the cutting edge of desire that Hope brought him to was screwing with his head. They didn't have an emotional attachment. The rational part of his mind knew that. Accepted it. But he also knew that sex with her would be unlike anything he'd ever known, pushing him to levels of need that he'd never come close to experiencing. He'd always suspected that would be the case, but the reality of facing her again after all these years was so much more than he'd been prepared for.

His fictional idea of the person she would become had been based on the girl he'd known, but the woman standing before him now was a stranger. She was all grown up, the product of years that had had nothing to do with him. Unknown experiences that had shaped her personality, like powerful forces of nature upon the planet. Rushing waters that cut through the ground, digging deep, shifting and shaping and molding the earth into something new. It should have made it easier, but instead, he found that the "real" Hope was so much more fascinating than his imagined one. Throwing pies at him. Losing her temper. Hammering questions at him that afternoon with an intensity that would have put even the most seasoned investigator to shame. Facing him barefoot in the moonlight, with the wind whipping through her long hair, unwilling to back down or to let him intimidate her. She was fire and heat and passion, and he just wanted to pull her around him like something warm and soft, until she could melt the cold burn of fear sitting in his gut like a leaden weight. Fear of the darkness inside him. Of the danger closing in around them. Of what he was becoming…changing into.

Despite knowing that the Merrick were the good guys in a fight against one of the most deadly evils the world had ever known, Riley couldn't let go of the bitterness he'd felt for so long. He couldn't embrace the family legacy breathing down his neck like Saige had always done, largely because of what it had cost him. His mother, Elaina, obsessed to the point of mental instability. His brother, Ian, who had finally left home to get away from her. His sister, simply because he hadn't been able to deal with Saige's own ardent devotion to the search for answers about their family bloodline. And then Hope, who had been the crushing blow, nearly doing him in, so violent he was still reeling from its force thirteen years later.

He'd been too shocked for most of the day to really process it—this colossal screwup of fate. But now it was sinking in, soaking into him, and with it came a sharp, piercing rage.

He wanted to know what kind of jackass was looking down on him, pulling the strings, as if some cosmic prankster had taken over the heavens, tossing the dice with his life. And with Hope's.

He'd been putting it off all evening, knowing he needed to have this talk with her, but dreading it all the same. Just being near her threatened his ability to keep himself together. Another chink in his emotional armor. A constant struggle that he knew, instinctively, was going to grow worse with each passing day.

He'd tried to think, to put together a plan, while he

and Kellan had spent the afternoon getting the layout of the town. There was no doubt that the Casus wouldn't be far behind them, if they weren't already there. The best plan was to stay at the cabin, and find the damn Marker as quickly as possible. Then get the hell out of Purity, taking his troubles with him. If he could keep his distance from Hope, then maybe she'd go under their radar. He'd warned her about the danger, but hadn't gone into specifics. God willing, he'd be able to spare her the details. He didn't want her looking over her shoulder for the rest of her life, living in fear. There was still promise for Hope. Happiness. That rose-colored dream. He didn't want to shatter it with death and monsters and terror. Didn't want her jumping at every sound she heard in the night.

And yet he knew she wasn't taking him as seriously as she needed to.

It was both a blessing and a curse that she and Millie actually lived in a section of the house that was blocked off from the café. Having her so close would undoubtedly make watching out for her easier. But it also meant she was more accessible, which presented an entirely different sort of danger in itself. The thought made him want to turn around and haul his ass out of there, but concern for Hope, as well as guilt, kept his feet rooted in place. He couldn't leave her alone with the Marker buried there on her land. And he couldn't go back to Colorado and dump all this on his family. He still felt bad over the way he'd treated Saige when she'd tried to warn him at their mother's funeral that she feared the awakenings were coming. About the way he'd kept quiet when Ian's world had started going to shit, stupidly trying to convince himself that his worst nightmare wasn't coming to life. He'd been wrong, and Ian had damn near paid the price for Riley's stubbornness.

He'd made so many mistakes already, he couldn't afford to make any more. Which meant he had to see this through to the end. Do what good he could for his family, while there was still time. He'd find the Marker, take out as many Casus as possible, then put the issue to rest, once and for all.

He just had to keep Hope safe till it all played out. Then the danger would move on to wherever the next Marker was hidden, and he'd be out of her life. Forever.

Doing his best to ignore the sickening feeling that came with that thought, he leaned his shoulders against the rough bark of the trunk behind him. Breaking the heavy silence that had settled between them like a thick, weighty presence, he finally said, "So."

He watched as her mouth twitched with the shadow of a grin. After a long, dramatic sigh, she said, "Uh-oh."

He quirked one brow. "What?"

"It's just that that 'so' is such a leading kind of word. Tips you off right away that something bad is coming. Something deeply personal. Like, *so, how long have you been into ritual sacrifice?* Or, *so, why did you decide to become a raging lesbian?*"

The corner of his mouth curved, his own grin feeling

foreign on his face, as if the muscles had almost forgotten how to do it. "Huh. So you've become a raging lesbian?"

"Unfortunately, no," she offered with a low laugh, shaking her head. "Though I sometimes think life would be infinitely more simple if I had."

This time he arched both his brows. "How so?"

Rocking back on her bare heels, she said, "The female mind I at least understand."

"Men aren't such a mystery," he countered.

Hope snorted, rolling her eyes. "So says one of the most complicated men I've ever known." A moment of tangible silence settled back between them, the playful exchange fading as their gazes locked into one another. Drawing in a deep, shaky breath, she seemed to force herself to say, "At any rate, I know what you were going to ask and, no, I don't want to talk about him."

There was something in her tone...in that haunted look in her eyes that made the hairs on the back of his neck rise, while a visceral, deadly rage twisted through his insides. "Did he hurt you?"

"No," she said too quickly, and he ground his jaw, struggling to stay calm. Even though Riley knew her answer was a lie, he bought it. He didn't have any other choice. It was either swallow the sugarcoated pill she was shoveling at him, or risk releasing that part of himself that he always struggled to contain.

But inside, under those layers of emotional concrete, he was roaring, ready for blood. To take the bastard apart with his bare hands and make him suffer. He'd seen how much damage a man could do when he wanted, and he knew just how defenseless a woman could be when facing such a prick.

"At least tell me why the asshole is in prison," he growled, struggling to keep his breaths deep and even.

She crossed her arms over her chest and looked away, staring into the thick, impenetrable depths of the forest. "If I wanted you to know, I'd tell you. But I don't even want to think about him, much less discuss him with you."

"Tell me anyway," he growled, the words hard with impatience as he pushed away from the tree and took a step toward her.

Her head snapped back around, the look in her eyes warning him not to come any closer. "Drop it, Riley. It's ancient history. One I've done my best to forget."

He drew in another deep breath, studying her through his lashes. "I could just look into it, find out for myself."

Hope snorted again, rolling one shoulder in a *whatever* gesture, while inside she was recoiling, shrinking into herself, hating that he would eventually learn the whole sordid story and know just how stupid she'd been. "To be honest, I'm surprised you haven't already done it," she snapped, turning away from him with every intention of heading back toward the house. Until he latched on to her arm, spinning her back around.

"How do you know that I haven't?" he asked, his voice a soft, husky rasp of sound, contrasting sharply against the hard cast of his features, his expression one of mounting frustration and rage.

"I just know," she whispered, practically hanging there in his hold, her neck craned back so that she could see his face. "I can tell by the look in your eyes."

He made a gruff, disbelieving sound under his breath, but it was the truth. He didn't have that *look,* the one that said he didn't know how to deal with it. Didn't know what to say. People always got that same uneasy shadow in their eyes when they learned about what had happened to her, and she hated it.

His expression tightened, as if he'd experienced something piercing and sharp, those dark eyes staring down at her, the moonlight giving them an odd glow as they struggled to break through and see inside her mind. He breathed out her name, the hand on her arm clenching, and something electric sparked between them. Something dangerous and wild. Something that made them both stiffen with awareness, just before he quietly said, "You need to go inside, Hope. Now."

Her lips shook, but she didn't argue as he released his hold on her arm. And as she turned, making her way back toward the beautiful, gray-shingled house, she could feel him watching her, every step of the way.

CHAPTER FIVE

Sunday morning

TAKING ANOTHER fortifying sip of her coffee, Hope
leaned her shoulder against the wall of her bedroom as
she watched Kellan Scott install a sleek, expensive-
looking motion detector beside her window. Beneath a
stormy, slate-gray sky, the frothy caps of the Pacific
Ocean could be seen rolling in through the rain-
splattered panes of glass, while a watery thread of pale
sunlight filtered into the room. She didn't want to think
about how much the high-tech device would cost her,
but made a mental note to ask Riley the next time she
saw him, since Kellan had refused to give her a price.
The charming, good-natured flirt had claimed the security devices were free of charge, considering he and
Riley were the ones who'd brought the danger to her
doorstep. And while he had a point, Hope refused to
take anything on charity. Especially from a friend of
Riley's.

After a fitful night's sleep, she'd awakened early and
gone down to do the daily baking, allowing Millie a

chance to sleep in. Not long after opening, her two new tenants had come into the already bustling café, and every female head had turned. Not that Hope could blame them. The two newcomers to Purity were an impressive sight, as well as a formidable one, both over six foot and packed with solid muscle. After Kellan had teased her about whether or not she intended to throw another round of pies at Riley, they'd had breakfast, and afterward Riley had gone outside to make some calls on his cell phone. Grabbing the backpack he'd come in with, Kellan had then told her he was ready to install her extra security. She'd left Millie in charge, along with two of her best staff members, and taken Kellan into the residence part of their house through the connecting kitchen.

They'd made some idle chitchat about the house and the café, but now, as Hope watched him work, she took advantage of the easy silence that had settled between them to collect her thoughts. There were questions she wanted to ask him about Riley, but she knew she had to get the wording *just* right. The last thing she wanted to do was sound too eager…or too desperate. But before she'd even managed to formulate the first one, Kellan beat her to the punch, the faintest trace of a British accent to his words as he said, "So what exactly happened between you and ol' Riley anyway?"

He was hunched down by the base of the window, his attention still focused on the sensor, his back to her, so that she couldn't read his expression. But there was no mistaking the curious edge to his words, no doubt brought on by her embarrassing reaction to seeing Riley yesterday, after so many years of brooding over the way that he'd treated her.

Though a part of her still believed that he'd deserved everything she'd literally thrown at him, Hope couldn't help but feel mortified that so many people had witnessed her violent reaction. With the way that gossip ran wild in a small community, she had to assume that everyone in Purity had probably heard about the infamous "pie fiasco" by now.

Coughing to clear her throat, she set down her coffee and responded to Kellan's question with one of her own. "He, uh, didn't tell you?"

"Riley?" he snickered, fiddling with something that made the device make a low, buzzing sound for a few seconds. "Naw. That guy doesn't tell me anything. But after yesterday, I have a feeling it's gotta be one helluva story."

"I don't normally do things like that," she murmured, her cheeks burning with heat.

He shot her a disarming grin over his shoulder. "The pies? They were a riot, but I was talking about Riley. About how *he* acted."

She blinked, not understanding. "What about him?"

Turning back to his work, Kellan said, "The guy completely lost his cool when he saw you. In the time that I've known him, I've seen Ri in some pretty intense situations, and he's never batted an eye. Never lost control, not even once. He always just pulls it all in, never letting anything out, and then he sees you and *whap!* The guy's been shaking like a leaf ever since."

A shaky, girlish giggle escaped before she could choke it back, and she covered her mouth, wondering where the quiet, detached Hope had gone. The one she'd lived with for so long now. "I'm sorry," she said, "but that's not exactly the imagery I would use to describe Riley. He seems so…intense. Grim, even."

"Yeah, well, it's been a rough time for his family lately. Hell, for all of us."

"How so?" she asked, thankful that he'd eased into the subject on his own.

He hesitated for a moment, as if deciding how best to respond. "It's a long story," he finally rasped, putting his tools back in the pack that sat on the floor beside him. "One that—"

"You won't be telling." Riley's gruff, husky voice suddenly cut in, making Hope jump, as if she'd just been caught doing something that she shouldn't.

"And that's my cue to go," Kellan murmured, flashing her another deep-grooved grin over his shoulder. "I still need to install some sensors in Millie's room, but if you come over here, I'll show you how they work. This one on the window will operate exactly the same as the one I installed on the back of your door."

Without looking at Riley—though she could feel the force of his presence filling the room, sharp and aggressive and insanely male—she moved to Kellan's side and listened as he explained how to set the high-tech gadgetry when she went to sleep at night.

"Wow, that's impressive," she said when he was done with the simple explanation.

Kellan flashed her a killer smile. "I'm more than just a pretty face, eh?"

"And not an immodest bone in your body," she drawled, rolling her eyes.

He stood up and tapped her on the nose. "Let's leave my body out of it, sugar, or I'm going to get myself in trouble."

A soft laugh fell from her lips as Riley looked between the two of them, then slowly shook his head. Kellan grabbed his backpack, winked at her, then headed out into the hallway, turning toward Millie's room as he left them alone. Riley kept his eyes on her face while taking a drink of his coffee, the white mug appearing fragile in his strong, sun-darkened hand, then tore his gaze away, looking around the room. His eyes darkened as they roamed the white wooden furniture and froth of antique white lace on her bed, the fierce intensity of his expression somehow intimate and personal, as if he were looking into secret parts of her heart. That was how it felt as he stood there in her private space, her chest painfully tight while he stared with a quiet absorption at the virginal-looking four-poster bed. Hope had never slept there with a man. In truth, she'd never been with any man but her worthless ex, and Neal had left such a bad taste in her mouth, she'd simply lacked the desire to seek out another sexual relationship. She'd thought Neal had probably killed that part of her, but that theory had been annihilated the instant Riley Buchanan had walked back into her life.

And watching the devastatingly sexy sheriff stare at her bed only confirmed that fact, her body going deliciously warm at the thought of falling onto the snowy expanse of white lace with him, his hard, heavy weight pressing her into the thick feather comforter. Sinking her teeth into her lower lip, she lifted her gaze, and found herself trapped. Not by a physical touch or restraints, but by deep, piercing blue that had always held the power to make her feel wild. Desperate. Out of control. She'd been too innocent to know how to act on those primal, carnal impulses when she'd known him before, but not anymore. If she were brave, she would have simply thrown herself at him. Tackled him onto that mountainous bounty of white linen and lace, his dark, muscular body in stark contrast against the virginal white, and have had her wicked way with him. Peel the T-shirt and open flannel from his broad shoulders, and run her hands over the hard, flat shelf of his chest…his stomach, soaking in the heat of his skin, the breathtaking power of heavy muscle and sinew.

But she wasn't brave enough. There was too much fear inside her. Fear that he'd reject her. Turn away from her. Or worse, laugh at her desperate attempt at seduction. She wasn't a fiery femme fatale. She was just pudgy little Hope, with the cartload of shattered dreams, foolishly wishing for things she was never going to have.

Stop feeling sorry for yourself, because you sound pathetic, a waspish voice snapped inside her mind, and she took a deep breath, knowing that voice was right. Yes, she'd lost the most precious things in her life, but there were still wonders to be seen. She knew that. She might have been broken and scraped and scarred inside, but she could still look out at the world and let the bitterness soften to a dull, gnawing ache when she saw that some dreams survived. Despite everything that she'd been through, she still believed in the miracle. Love. Beauty. Warmth and family. It just…it just wasn't meant to be hers, and that, she thought, trying to choke down the trembling knot of emotion in her throat, hurt worse than not believing in anything at all.

Shivering, she tried to look away from the raw, naked hunger in Riley's eyes, but she couldn't. Her mouth quivered, and she lifted her hand, once again covering her lips with her cold fingers. His dark gaze narrowed, and then he suddenly set the coffee mug on her dressing table and took a step toward her, while the soft sound of Kellan whistling to himself in Millie's bedroom was drowned out by the roaring surge of her pulse in her ears. Riley had a certain look about him, one of purpose and intent, and Hope trembled, wondering if he was actually going to kiss her. And no idea what she would do if he did. Slap him? Kiss him back? Or dissolve into a puddle of emotional overload and completely fall apart?

The air in the room went thick, like a physical thing against her skin, and something dangerous flared up between them, electric and sharp, jarring her with its force. Riley just kept coming across the room, drawing nearer, his expression set in fierce, determined lines. His nostrils flared as he pulled in her scent, so close now that she could see the pattern of sexy stubble that covered his jaw, see the flecks of navy in his beautiful eyes. So close she could almost feel his heat against her skin…and then the shrill cry of the phone rang out through the house. Hope instantly jumped, flinching, taking a shaky, embarrassed step away from him. And then another. Lowering her gaze, she mumbled something about the phone and rushed from the room, into the hall, where a cordless cradle sat on an antique table.

"Hello?" she said, struggling to sound calm as she put the phone to her ear.

"Would you listen to that?" purred a deep, familiar voice over the faint, crackling connection. "Been a long time since I've heard that sweet, husky sound. Did you miss me, sweetheart?"

Hope closed her eyes against the nauseating wave of shock that slammed through her system. Gripping the phone with both hands, she was careful to keep her voice low as she hissed, "How did you get this number?"

"How do you think?" Neal asked with a low, taunting thread of laughter. "My family has connections, Hope. And they never did buy your version of how things went down that night. They still think I'm the poor, betrayed little husband who got blamed for something I didn't do. And you…well, they think you're the same lying little slut that they've always thought you were."

She was acutely aware of Riley standing close behind her, the heat of his big, powerful body somehow giving her strength as she said, "What do you want?"

"Just thought you'd want to know that I'm a free man now."

"That's impossible," she whispered, wondering how he'd managed to get out after only a handful of years. He must have made parole. She'd known it was a possibility—one she refused to let herself think about. It was easier just to picture him rotting away in a cell for the rest of his life, which was what the bastard deserved.

"Nothing's impossible," he drawled, "if you have the money to get what you want."

"What? Did your pathetic daddy bribe the parole board?"

His low, slick laughter made her skin crawl. "Is that any way to talk about your in-laws?"

"We're divorced, Neal. And it's against the law for you to contact me. Do it again and you'll be sorry."

Though she wanted to slam the phone back into its cradle, Hope forced herself to set it down gently as she fought back an angry wave of tears, determined to keep them from falling. Not over a pathetic bastard like Neal Capshaw.

God, this was all she needed now. How much more

crap could get dumped on her head? Riley. Neal. Those ominous warnings that her and Millie's lives could be in danger, accompanied now by the sickening possibility that Neal could be looking to cause trouble. Just one would be a difficulty in itself, but handling them all at the same time was going to be damn near impossible. Not that she had any choice. It was either stand her ground or lie down and let them run roughshod over her, and she'd already had enough of playing the doormat to last her a lifetime.

Bracing herself, she did her best to plaster on a bright smile as she turned toward Riley, intending to just walk around him, when he reached out and took hold of her arm again, his long fingers locking around her bicep in a hold that was beginning to become oddly familiar. Lifting her brows, she said, "Something wrong?"

He stared into her eyes, searching…seeking, and she tried not to flinch, as if he were brushing against emotional scar tissue too sensitive to touch. Slowly, he said, "You tell me, Hope."

Her gaze slid away from his, focusing on a distant point at the other end of the hall. "I'm sure you need to be getting on with your search out in the woods, and I don't really have time to chat right now, Ri. I need to get back downstairs and make sure they're doing okay in the kitchen."

As if he didn't notice her trying to pull away from him, he kept his fingers locked around her arm. "Who was on the phone?"

"The phone? Oh, um, no one important," she murmured, hoping for an interruption that would allow her to go and find someplace quiet, where she could collect herself. "And nothing I can't handle."

Obviously unwilling to play the game, he reached out with his other hand and pulled her chin around, forcing her to meet his heavy-lidded gaze as he said, "You're afraid of him."

"Of Neal?" she scoffed, shaking her head. "He's too pathetic to be afraid of."

He drew in a deep breath, the sexy creases at the corners of his eyes deepening as he grunted, "You're lying."

"And what if I am?" she snapped, just wanting to get away. Neal was not someone she discussed with anyone. Not even with Millie. She'd already hashed out the stupidity of getting involved with a man like Neal Capshaw with a whole slew of therapists, after it'd all come to a crashing end, and felt no better for it when the medical bills had finally been paid.

Of course, Riley wasn't ready to let it go, reminding her of a dog with a bone. "What did that son of a bitch do to you? And this time, I want an answer," he told her, a gritty, graveled edge to his words that revealed so much. His protective instincts. His honor. As well as what he thought of men who tried to bully women.

"You want an answer, huh?" she breathed out with a soft, brittle burst of laughter. "Come on, Ri. Haven't you learned by now that we seldom, if ever, actually get what we want?"

She could tell it'd been the wrong thing to say the instant the words left her mouth. His expression tightened, as if in pain, and the next thing she knew, he was pushing her against the magnolia-colored hallway wall, trapping her there, his long fingers wrapped around her biceps, holding her in place. "What do you think you're doing?" she demanded, staring up into his dark, glittering eyes. Her lips quivered, throat tight, while the searing heat of his gaze pressed against her skin like a physical touch, making her melt and burn in places that had been cold for too damn long.

"Stop trying to run away from me and just answer the goddamn question," he rasped in a low, almost silent growl, the primal sound shivering across her stunned nerve endings. Her body tingled, as if she'd placed her fingertips against a live current, the electricity arcing through her body, vibrant and piercing and warm. It made her shaky. Made her crazed for something that she didn't understand.

She opened her mouth, ready to say God only knew what, but nothing would come out. No explanations. No denials. Just a gasping, breathless silence that somehow seemed to push him further toward the edge of some strange, gripping emotion. It was like a wild, shocking blend of lust and frustration and worry, all jumbled into one seething mass.

"Your heart is racing," he said in a rough voice, shifting his right hand until he could press the callused pad of his thumb against the rapid quiver of her pulse at the base of her throat. "Why are you so afraid?"

She wet her bottom lip, struggling to finally find her voice. "D-didn't you tell me that I should be scared? On guard? Ready for catastrophe?"

"Yeah, I did. And you should be. But you weren't upset until that phone call." The sudden touch of his hand against the side of her face was too much for her, his thumb stroking the shivering corner of her mouth, and she panicked as she felt her grip on the tattered edges of her control begin to slip from her grasp. She made a small, breathless sound of panic, and he leaned closer, pressing the heat of his body against her, anchoring her in place.

"Jesus, Riley," she gasped, acutely aware of the solid weight of his gun against her rib cage as she realized he was wearing a shoulder holster beneath the open flannel he'd layered over his T-shirt. "What are you doing?"

He kept his gaze on her mouth, even as he slowly shook his head. "Damned if I know," he answered. "But it's going to be one hell of a mistake."

"What is?"

"This," he groaned, lowering his head, but she ducked at the last second, and his mouth grazed her cheek.

Oh, God. Sparks of sensation skittered across her skin, and she moaned deep in her throat, the husky, provocative sound taking her by surprise. It hadn't sounded

like her, like the woman she knew, and she had the
oddest sensation that a stranger was taking over her
body. One who wanted to crawl her way under Riley
Buchanan's skin and become a part of him, whether he
broke her heart again or not. Who wanted to strip off
her clothes and pull him into her body, losing herself in
the violent, desperate hunger of his possession.

"Kiss me, Hope," he whispered in a velvet-rough
voice within the sensitive hollow of her ear, and his lower
body pressed against hers, the thick, enormous ridge of
his hardened cock leaving no doubt that however else he
felt about her, he *wanted* her in that moment.

She swallowed, struggling to force out a shaky,
tremulous "I can't," when what she really wanted was
to scream "*Yes!*"

"I know it's stupid," he rasped, threading his fingers
through her hair, holding her head in place as he pressed
his lips against the sensitive edge of her jaw, while her
own hands curved greedily around the hard, powerful
bulge of his biceps. "I know I don't have any right to
touch you, not after what I did to you. But I *need* it. It's
driving me crazy, wondering if you really taste as good
as I remember. If your mouth can really be that hot. Your
lips that soft."

She blinked, her eyes heavy, his mouth so close now
she could feel the delicious heat of his breath. Taste it.
And then the sound of the kitchen door opening downstairs broke the spell, jarring them back to awareness.
Riley instantly released his hold on her, taking a step

back as they heard Millie making her way up the stairs. He stared into her eyes, his throat working, looking as if he wanted to say something…but couldn't find the words. A swarm of emotions flashed through his dark, beautiful gaze, stunning her with their intensity, and then he shook his head with a sharp, decisive motion. Grabbing the pen and small tablet for messages that sat beside the phone, he wrote down what looked like a number. Ripping off the sheet, he turned and handed it to her, then walked away, saying a gruff good-morning to Millie as he passed her on the stairs.

Hope watched as her aunt turned right down the hallway, walking away without even seeing her slumped there against the wall, then heard Kellan's deep voice telling Millie hello. She knew she needed to pull her aunt aside and explain about the phone call. Warn her that there might be even more trouble on the way. But her legs were too shaky to support her, much less walk.

Closing her eyes, she leaned her head back against the wall, unable to think about what had almost happened with Riley. It was too dangerous, too fragile, even for the guarded privacy of her mind. She should focus on Neal instead, but she was almost too afraid to think of what kind of stunt he might try to pull, now that he was a free man. It made her blood curl to think of facing him again, but she had to be ready, in case he decided to make an appearance. That was all she needed. One more worry to hang over her head.

It sucked, but she didn't have time to stand there and

wallow in doubts and fear. Opening her eyes, she ground her jaw, determined not to let them control her, and looked down at the note that Riley had given her. She struggled to steady her shaking hand as she read what he'd written.

It was his cell phone number, followed by two brief sentences.

Call me if anything weird happens today, or if you get scared. I'll be close by.

As far as messages went, it wasn't anything to fall apart over. But there was something inherently telling in the simple words that made her chest feel tight, her throat quivering with emotion. Taking a deep breath, Hope pressed the small piece of paper to her mouth for a moment, then quickly tucked it into the front pocket of her jeans and started down the hall.

CHAPTER SIX

Monday morning

TWENTY-FOUR HOURS LATER, Riley's tension had reached the breaking point. Despite their nearly constant digging deep in the forest, he had nothing more to show for it than a grinding sense of desperation in both his mind and his gut. He knew that every minute he spent in Purity put Hope's and Millie's lives in danger, but that wasn't the only thing that had him on edge. Despite his determination, the stubborn woman still hadn't answered his questions about her ex, and Riley was ready to snap.

You could always solve the problem and just make the call. Find out on your own just what kind of prick Neal Capshaw is. Find out why Hope is so afraid of him.

It was true, damn it. But as he glared at the rich, moss-covered floor of the forest, he knew he couldn't do it. To seek out the answer behind her back felt like a form of betrayal, and God only knew he'd already betrayed her enough. He wanted to hear the truth from Hope, and knew that in some perverse way, it was a symbol of his pathetic need for proof that she trusted him. Not that he'd ever given her any reason to trust him with her secrets. Even now, he was *still* lying to her. Still doing his best to sugarcoat the truth. The truth being that he posed an even bigger threat to her safety than her ex, no matter how despicable the man had been.

Drawing in a deep breath of the damp, forest-scented air, Riley tried to clear his mind and focus on his search for the Marker, but he could *not* get the bad feeling out of his gut. The one that said this was all going to end in disaster, with him standing at the center, pulling everyone down with him into the churning slime, like a toxic sinkhole of destruction.

Wiping his face on his sleeve, he gritted his teeth and dug the blade of the shovel back into the rich earth, while bitterly wondering once again if this was all some kind of maniacal cosmic joke. One whose punch line was going to be nothing more than rot and blood and gore. Violence and pain and deception. The last thing in the world that he wanted was to drag Hope into the middle of it all, and yet here he was, sucking her into the nightmare that he'd always known was coming.

He couldn't leave, and yet, when it all crashed down on him, he didn't want to be anywhere near Purity. He could feel his control slipping a little further each day, his gut constantly knotted with fear at what he was sliding into.

Though he did his best to hide it, that cold burn of fear never left him. Not since that night when everything he'd thought would be his had been ripped away. *Bam!*…and it was gone. Taken away from him forever. And since then, the fear had been like a cancer eating away at his insides, slowly scraping him raw. Taking him deeper, bit by bit, into a deep, dark well of loathing.

Ironic, how after all the ribbing Ian had given him over the years—all the wisecracks about that ridiculous nickname—that it was his older brother who had managed to come through all this like the *saintly* one. Ian had killed the Casus who had been hunting him, saved his woman, and was now a part of a fight that would save lives, make a difference, while Riley was the walking time bomb of destruction. He would do what he could, but the simple fact was that he wouldn't be around long enough to truly make an impact. He only prayed that he could find a way to help Hope in the time that he had left by getting the Marker off her land. And God willing, have a chance to face the man who'd put that haunted look in her eyes.

Riley hated that she wouldn't confide in him. Wouldn't tell him what was wrong…what she was afraid of. He'd seen that look on enough faces to recognize it for what it was. The cold, stark burn of *fear.* When he'd seen it in Hope's beautiful eyes yesterday morning, it'd screwed with his head, and damn near caused him to make the mother of all mistakes.

It had been madness for him to try to kiss her. He didn't know what he'd been thinking, but then that was the problem. He hadn't. There'd been no rational thought, his head overloaded with the savage, visceral need to get her mouth beneath his. Her body…her flesh. To feel the provocative slide of her blood down his throat, warm and thick and impossibly delicious, at the same time she pulsed around his cock in a long, wet, mind-shattering release.

If you'd try…she'd let you take what you need. You know she would. If you told her you were in pain…that you needed it, she would never tell you no. Not Hope.

The dangerous, tempting words came from a dark, seething place buried deep inside him, and Riley knew it was the Merrick. The creature was conniving, he'd give him that. Its hunger was growing stronger…wearing him down, his body aching like an addict going through the brutal symptoms of withdrawal. It wanted satisfaction. Completion. It wanted power and sustenance and the feel of a soft, womanly body beneath it as it buried its fangs into tender, succulent flesh.

And for some goddamn reason which was going to be the death of him, it seemed to have fixated on Hope.

Riley swung his hand through the air in a sharp, cutting motion, as if he could swipe away the dark, destructive images burning through his mind, of him and Hope together, her pale thighs spread wide as he powered into her, shoving deeper…and deeper. The sound of something heavy colliding with a nearby tree made him flinch. Looking up at the sound, he found himself staring at the bizarre sight of his coffee Thermos embedded in the rough trunk of a towering Garry oak.

Holy shit. When he'd cut his hand through the air, he must have inadvertently swept up the Thermos without touching it and hurled it at the tree. The realization stunned him, and he scrubbed his hand down his face, quietly freaking out. Christ, what if Kellan had been standing there? Or Hope? He could have hurt someone. Killed them.

The power or telekinesis or whatever it was appeared to be growing stronger, but he still didn't know why. Was it because the Merrick was coming closer to the surface? Or was it simply that his control was slipping? Ever since he'd learned that the awakenings were coming, it had been sliding through his fingers like rushing water, and that's when the first signs of the power had started to show. Since seeing Hope, that control had slipped further from his grasp…leaving the power freer to escape.

He needed to be careful, damn it. Needed to rein in his temper. Needed to learn to control the Merrick until he found that Marker, doing everything he could to master its craving.

Hope, it growled through his head, telling him what it wanted, and Riley choked back a snarl, slamming the shovel back into the ground, wishing that he could just find the bloody cross. Now. Before things got any worse. And yet he couldn't deny that there was a dark, secret part of him that hoped it would take them just a little bit longer. That he could have just a little more time with her.

"Enough," he muttered under his breath. "Get a damned grip."

The sudden sound of someone coming through the trees caught his attention, the scent on the air telling him that it was Kellan. The awakening Merrick was altering his senses, making them sharper…more precise, so that he could now identify people by their smell alone.

"This sucks out loud," Kellan muttered, twisting off the top of his water bottle and taking a long drink as he came into view. They'd mapped out the prime search area based on calculations Saige had given them, with Kellan starting on one end, and Riley working at the other. They would search the area in rows, until they met in the middle, and if the cross still hadn't been found at that point, then the original square would be widened, until they finally discovered the Marker's resting place.

Taking another drink, Kellan wiped the back of his wrist over his mouth and continued to bitch. "I mean it, man. This sucks on so many different levels, I don't even know where to start. It's cold. Rainy. Windy. I thought Saige said the damn Marker would be easy for us to find. That she had an even better reading on this map, after using the first one to find that Marker down in Brazil."

Unfortunately, that Marker was now in Westmore's possession, leaving them with only one, until they found the cross buried there in Purity.

"She said it *might* be easier," Riley murmured, hunching his shoulders against the blistering wind. Despite the crappy weather, he still thought the area was intensely beautiful, the deep, earthy brown of the tree trunks and branches in sharp contrast to the jeweled, mossy green of the leaves. Everything smelled moist and rich and alive, like a primeval Eden filled with blossoming life. He was sure that by the time his sister had finished deciphering the maps, the others would find themselves searching in places far worse than this. "But it's not an exact science," he went on to say, wiping a sheen of sea-scented mist from his face. "Saige warned us we might have to keep expanding the search area."

Using her unusual gift of communicating with physical objects, his sister was still working out just how to understand the strange, encrypted maps that she'd found buried with the first Dark Marker in Italy. They called it the first, or original Marker, simply because it had been the first one that she'd found, and had been buried with the maps that led to the location of who knew how many others. No one knew how many crosses the original Consortium—the organization that governed the ancient clans—had made, and the maps were actually nothing more than an endless set of directions to various locations around the world. The directions bled into one another, the code evolving as it went, which meant you couldn't look at the weathered sheets and say exactly how many Markers they would lead to. The act of deciphering the strange code was a tedious one, and so far only Saige knew how to do it. Her fiancé, Quinn, was trying to help her, but who knew how long it would take to work through all of them. Weeks? Months? Years?

Although it'd been proven that the maps were a valuable aid, when Saige used the first one to finally unearth the second Marker in Brazil, it had not been an easy process. The maps were anything but specific, and she'd had to search a substantial area of rain forest before she'd found the cross. She thought she'd gotten a more exact read on this second map, narrowing down the search area, but Riley wasn't holding out much hope. With the way his luck had been going lately, he wouldn't be surprised if they ended up excavating a good half-acre or more before they found what they'd come for.

Leaning his shoulders back against one of the thickest trunks, Kellan bent his right knee, braced his foot on the tree and took another drink of his water. "Do you think Westmore and his men made copies of the maps?" the Watchman asked after a moment, while a low, ominous rumble of thunder accompanied his words. Westmore had actually had possession of the maps for a few days, until they'd gotten them back with Seth Mc-Connell's help.

"I'm sure they did," Riley replied, shoveling aside a layer of soil. "But who knows how long it will take for them to learn how to read them. Hell, without Saige, they might never be able to decipher that series of codes."

Kellan grunted under his breath, jerking his chin toward Riley's spade. "Well, if we don't hurry up and find this thing, I'm going to start thinking they've already been and gone."

Riley shook his head, working the shovel back into the moist earth. "If that was the case, we'd know. I don't think Gregory, if he's here, would be holding out, waiting for me to feed and fully awaken before trying to kill me. From what Quinn and Saige said, he's more interested in revenge than he is in getting enough power to bring more Casus back from Meridian. Which means he must be waiting for us to the find the Marker, like the others will probably do, and then he'll make his move."

At least he hoped that was the case. It made him uneasy as hell, not knowing what the Casus were up to. What they had planned. With every minute he and Kellan spent searching that verdant patch of forest, the monsters were out there, waiting. No doubt watching them. As the sky cracked open with a thundering jolt of lightning, Riley looked toward the cloud-scarred horizon and shivered. He couldn't explain it, but it felt as if something bad was coming in on the weather. Something ugly and dark and destructive. And when it hit, all hell was going to break loose.

God, he *needed* that damn Marker. If he didn't find it soon, he would have to get Hope out of there, whether she was willing to go or not. It couldn't just drag on, the danger…the not knowing when it was going to hit.

Kellan yawned again from his resting place against the tree, sounding as if he were ready to drop. Riley buried the shovel back into the ground, resting his hands on the handle as he studied the Watchman through narrowed eyes. "Just what were you up to last night?" he asked. Kellan had headed into town, saying he needed to blow off some steam after they'd grabbed dinner in the café. He hadn't gotten back before two, which was when Riley had finally managed to fall asleep.

"What do you think I was doing?" Kellan laughed, dropping his head back against the tree as he closed his eyes.

Knowing he sounded like a lecturing father, Riley said, "We're in the middle of a war, Kell, and you're still out every night getting laid. Your brother's terrified that sooner or later you're going to end up in bed with the wrong woman."

"There's no such thing," Kellan drawled, opening his eyes. "And this one was definitely *right*. Long black hair. Big green eyes. And legs that go all the way to the floor. Amazing."

"You do realize that you could end up getting the poor woman killed, don't you? If the Casus see you with her, she'll be an easy target. One they'll use against us."

"You think I don't know that?" Kellan muttered, his laughing expression replaced by a tense scowl. "I'm not an idiot. We left the bar separately and then met up later at a motel. No one saw me enter, and no one saw me leave. I made sure of it."

"You better hope so," he grunted. "Because if not, you're going to have one helluva burden on your conscience."

"You know, Ri. Maybe you'd be a little less pissy about my sex life if you were getting some of your own."

"Shut up, Kellan."

"The hunger's wearing you down, man. You can't hold out forever."

Slanting the redhead a look of serious warning, he said, "I've got it under control."

"Like hell you do," Kellan shot back, pushing away from the tree. "I still don't know what the deal is between you and Hope, but I'm not blind. It's obvious you want her. So either take care of it and 'fess up to Hope, or you're going to have to go with option two."

"And what the hell is option two?" he growled.

Lowering his voice, Kellan said, "We'll find a female Watchman. Like we tried to do for Ian."

"Oh, Christ," he muttered, pulling his hand down the lower part of his face, the bristles of his stubble scratching against his palm. Ian had told him about how Kierland Scott, Kellan's brother, had arranged to have a female Watchman named Morgan come down from Reno so that Ian could feed from her. But since a Merrick feeding for males consisted of taking blood *during* sex, Ian had refused, knowing that he would lose Molly, his fiancée, if he took what he needed from another woman.

Glaring at the younger man, he said, "You know, something tells me this Morgan woman isn't going to like being offered up as the Watchman whore again."

Something shifted in Kellan's odd-colored eyes, like a flash of rage, hinting at a side that he rarely showed. Despite being a kick-ass fighter when the situation called for it, Kellan always played the clown. The easygoing prankster who enjoyed riling everyone around him. But in that moment, it suddenly occurred to Riley that there was more going on with the irreverent Watchman than he'd guessed, and he felt like an idiot for not seeing it earlier.

With a gruff bite to his words that Riley had never heard before, Kellan said, "Don't talk about Morgan like that. She didn't have to come down to Colorado to make that offer to your brother, but she did. And she damn well didn't do it because she's a whore. Though she'd rather die than admit it, the truth is that she'd do anything that Kierland asked her to do."

Riley lifted his hand, rubbing at the knotted tension in the back of his neck as he thought over what Kellan had said. "Huh. So is there, like, a history between those two?"

Kellan rolled his shoulder in a frustrated gesture and pressed his lips together, obviously knowing better than to start gossiping about his brother's private life. He muttered something foul under his breath, then shoved his water bottle beneath his arm and pushed his hands into his pockets. "At any rate, I wasn't thinking of Morgan. But we could go to one of the other compounds, see if there's anyone there who you're interested in. At least a female Watchman will know what to expect from bedding down with a Merrick."

It soured his stomach to think of it—the idea of finding some stranger and nailing her…taking her blood. But even as he thought about it, Riley knew the problem wouldn't be the woman. No, he'd spent his life sleeping with women who didn't touch him any deeper than his skin. The problem was with *him,* because at the end of the day, there was only one woman he could imagine doing something that intimate with. Only one woman who could truly give both the man and the Merrick what they needed.

Clearing his throat, he said, "What do you think the others are doing?"

Kellan lifted his brows, the surging wind blowing his dark red hair into his face. "What others?"

"The other Merrick," Riley grunted, not quite meeting the Watchman's gaze. He felt too open…too exposed, as if his longing for a woman he could never have was plastered all over his face, etched into his hot eyes like a blinding neon sign. "The ones who are awakening and need to feed the hunger."

"Those who have wives or girlfriends are probably doing okay," Kellan murmured, "so long as they aren't partnered up with a bitch. But the single ones, they're in the same boat you are. Hopefully they'll be smart about what they're doing, or we're going to have a helluva time keeping the stories of bloodsuckers out of the news."

Riley nodded, thinking that he didn't envy the Watchmen and the Consortium—the governing body of officials the shifters worked for—their jobs. In today's world, it had to feel like a constantly losing battle, trying to keep the existence of the remaining ancient clans out of the media spotlight. Keeping the tales relegated to superstitious folklore. Though very few of the species actually attacked humans, there were still those who preyed upon innocent victims. If the Collective didn't get them first, it was sometimes left to the Watchmen to take them out, under special command of the Consortium—but most often there would be a special extermination unit brought in by that specific race. The main objective of the Watchmen was to act as the Consortium's eyes and ears.

"So, anyway, about finding you a woman," Kellan rumbled.

"I'm fine." Riley's tone was hard…flat, somehow devoid of the emotion twisting him up inside.

Kellan snorted. "Fine, huh? You know, that's one *F* word that I get damn tired of."

"Yeah, well, here's another one," he sighed. "*Forget* about it. If it gets to the point that I can't handle it, I'll figure something out. Until then, I don't want to talk about it. Understood?"

"Whatever you say, old man," Kellan drawled, and with a mocking salute, the Watchman turned and headed back the way he'd come.

Riley watched Kellan's retreating back until he was out of sight, then lifted the shovel and dug up another patch of ground. He supposed he should be thankful that the area Saige had marked for them to search was deep in the forest, where they weren't drawing the attention of townspeople. And while he was certain the Casus knew he was there, he figured the bastards would just keep watching them for now.

Waiting for him to find the Marker.

To feed.

To awaken.

Riley could hear the hands of the clock ticking down in his mind, slowly working their way toward destruction, and the Marker was the only thing that could stop it.

He had to find the cross. For his family's sake. For the safety of the town.

But most of all, for Hope.

CHAPTER SEVEN

Monday evening

LEANING HIS SHOULDER against the rough bark of a gnarled, majestic maple, Riley stared through the thickening lavender shades of twilight, watching through the bay window as Hope sat in her living room. He supposed most would call him a Peeping Tom, or worse. What he was doing could probably even be classified as stalking, but he didn't give a damn. He needed to be there, standing guard, assuring himself that she was okay.

She'd been sitting and reading for the past half hour, drinking from a mug that sat on the gleaming surface of an end table, the hazy wash of light from the lamp casting a golden glow over her luminous skin. She looked ethereal, surreal. Lush and womanly and warm. A sensual Madonna. The image struck a chord deep inside him, and for a moment Riley could only marvel at the fact that she'd never had any children. But then that probably had more to do with her bastard ex. He was positive Hope would have wanted a baby, and a wrenching image of what could have been—of her swollen and round with his child—flashed through his mind, bringing a searing pain to his chest. Hissing through his teeth, he pressed one hand against the bizarre ache and breathed through the piercing sensation, wondering what in God's name was wrong with him.

Get a grip, Buchanan. You're slipping off the deep end.

True, but no matter how wrong it was, there didn't seem to be anything he could do to stop it. He felt dirty watching her, as if she could be tainted by his mere presence. And yet he couldn't just walk away. He could sit and make useless, lame-ass excuses until the end of time, claiming that he needed to stand there and watch over her…guard her, but the hardcore truth was that he *couldn't* stay away from her.

Despite how badly it hurt, he was stuck there, subjecting himself to this internal hell. Watching her like this was perverse. Insane. Like jabbing a needle under his fingernail again and again. Pouring acid into a raw wound. Self-inflicted torture that he couldn't protect against, simply because this was Hope. She was his ultimate weakness. Forbidden temptation that would drive him beyond reason in his final days of life, before it all came to a crashing, resounding end.

And the end *was* coming closer. His hunger was rising…mounting. If he didn't find the Marker soon, he would have to figure something out. And despite what he'd told Kellan that morning, he still didn't have any idea of what he would do. Of how he would handle it.

Her telephone rang, his already heightened sense of hearing allowing him to pick up the shrill sound, and he watched as she set the book aside and reached for the handset that rested in a cradle beside the lamp. She lifted the receiver to her ear, her head turned to the side, the thick fall of her hair making it impossible for him to see her expression. He marked the passage of time in his head, and no more than a minute had gone by before she slammed the phone back in the cradle. Surging to her feet, she quickly checked the lock on the back door, then walked out of the room, through the doorway that he knew led into the kitchen.

Without any conscious direction from his brain, Riley found himself moving across the damp grass that stretched out from the back of the house to the beginning of the woods, the pebbled path that curved through its center snaking into the trees, leading to the cabins that lay farther within the forest. Taking a deep breath, he climbed the shallow porch steps and lifted his hand to knock. A moment later, Hope peeked through the panes of the bay window to see who was there, her shoulders sagging with a subtle gesture of relief when she saw that it was him.

"Riley," she murmured, opening the door, her warm, mouthwatering scent instantly filling his head, making him feel dazed.

The silence was already stretching out to uncomfortable proportions and he knew he needed to say something, but his throat was too locked up. He just stood there, staring, feeling like a hungry dog caught begging at the back door for a scrap of attention. A bone. A friggin' scratch behind the ears before he got kicked away.

Only, Hope didn't kick him or slam the door in his face. Instead, her head tilted a fraction to the side as she studied him with those big, soulful eyes, her soft gaze lingering on the burning heat in his face. "Do you, um, want to come inside?" she finally asked.

He nodded, his throat working as he stepped into the warm, inviting room, while she closed the door behind him. As Riley moved farther into the quiet house, the weight of his guilt was staggering, weighing him down, until his legs felt leaden, his shoulders and chest tight with strain. He felt as if he was dragging a trail of slimy, festering destruction in his wake. One that would ruin the clean, beautiful floorboards beneath his feet, rotting the wood until there was nothing but a black, sopping maw opening beneath them, waiting to swallow them whole. And yet he couldn't make himself leave.

Standing in the middle of the room, Riley turned to find Hope leaning back against the door, just watching him, waiting to see what he would do, what he wanted. He ran his gaze over her body in a quick, visual feast. With an inner smile, he noted the loose sand-colored pajama pants and long-sleeved baggy T-shirt, knowing it was a wasted effort, the way she tried to hide that beautiful body with the shapeless clothes. As far as he was concerned, the shadowy, fleeting glimpses of her figure that were revealed by the softly draping fabric were as erotic as any skimpy, revealing piece of lingerie. They made you work for the details. Made you long to rip the teasing cover of cotton from her body, piece by piece, until you'd reached the warm, womanly treasures hidden beneath.

His hands flexed at his sides, as if ready to reach out and grasp hold of her, until he spotted the knife she held in her right hand, the lamplight glinting off its wicked-looking blade. Lifting his gaze, Riley stared into the flickering shadows in her eyes. "Something going on?"

"Nothing I can't handle," she slowly replied, casting a wry look down at the knife. "I guess I just believe in being prepared."

"Did your ex call again? Was it him on the phone?"

She shook her head, the sharp movement sending her thick, lustrous hair tumbling over her shoulders, making his fingers itch with the need to bury themselves in that warm, burnished silk. "I'm just nervous," she murmured. "They found a college girl up in Wellsford who'd been murdered over the weekend."

"They what?" He went completely still, not even breathing. "When? Where did you hear about it?"

A shiver ran through her body. "It's been all over the news tonight. They're saying that she'd been mutilated, torn to pieces. I guess she was missing some fingers on one hand, and had been clawed up pretty badly. They'd think it was a bear attack, except that there was enough of her left to tell that she'd been raped. It's crazy, isn't it? I mean, who would do something like that?"

Turning away from her, Riley stared through the window into the ever-thickening shades of twilight. He should have been keeping his eye on the local news, but he'd been so wrapped up in his search for the Marker and worrying about Hope that he hadn't even turned on a radio or a TV all day.

Shit, they were so screwed. He knew, just from the little that Hope had told him, that the kill belonged to Gregory. The twisted Casus had a thing for fingers, which they'd discovered when he'd gone after some friends of Saige's during her awakening. And Riley himself had handled the investigations into the murders committed by Gregory's brother, Malcolm, back in Colorado. He'd seen exactly what a Casus could do to a body. Knew exactly how evil they could be.

"Where's Millie?" he asked, hating the cold, bleak sliver of fear in Hope's eyes as he turned to catch her gaze. It made him want to hold her, wrap his body around her until he could shelter her from anything and anyone who ever tried to cause her harm.

"She's in the café with Hal, a friend of hers. He's going to do some remodeling to the front counter and she's showing him the design she wants."

"You need to talk to her, tell her to be careful. I can't stress how important this is, Hope."

Her brows drew together in a dainty *V* of surprised confusion. "You don't actually think there's some connection between that girl and the people you said would be coming here? The ones who will be looking for whatever the hell it is you and Kellan are searching for out there in the woods, do you?"

Locking his jaw, he said, "All I'm saying is that whatever killed that girl is still out there. You and Millie can't take any chances."

Her gaze slid away from his, focused sightlessly on some unknown place on the floor. She swallowed as she wrapped her arms around her middle, the knife still clutched in her right hand.

"Promise me, Hope." There was a guttural edge to the words that Riley could easily attribute to the Merrick, which was seething beneath his surface at the idea of another Casus kill. It wanted blood…wanted to make that son-of-a-bitch monster pay.

Hope finally nodded, straightening her shoulders as she reconnected with his gaze. "I'll talk to her," she rasped, "but not right now. I don't want to interrupt her and Hal's alone time."

He quirked a brow, and there was the faintest shadow of a smile playing at her lips as she said, "I think something could get started between those two, if Millie would just give it a chance. I'm hoping she uses the opportunity tonight to make her move. That's why I've been lying low and was getting ready to head upstairs to watch a movie."

"I'll get out of your hair, then," he told her, making to move toward the door, until she stopped him with his name.

She hesitated, then made a nervous gesture toward

the kitchen. "They'll still be a while, if…if you'd like to have a cup of coffee before you go."

The look on his face must have been so telling, she actually laughed, the soft, husky sound like something delicious and sweet that he wanted to taste on her lips. "Just coffee, Riley. That's all," she teased, her topaz-colored eyes shining with mirth. "You don't have to look as if I just asked you to strip naked and give me a lap dance."

He grunted under his breath, the provocative image invoked by her words hitting him low in the gut. "Damn it, Hope. You didn't use to be so open with your words."

The mischievous fire in her eyes deepened as she said, "Am I embarrassing you?"

He gave her a stern look for asking such a ridiculous question, and she laughed again, saying, "Well, I'm a woman now, not a child. You can't expect me to be that same girl that you used to know. I grew up, and now you have to deal with it."

Riley held up his hands in a sign of surrender. "Hey, I'm not complaining. It just takes some getting used to."

"Hmm," she murmured, heading toward the kitchen. Following behind her, Riley took a seat on one of the sturdy wooden stools positioned along the edge of a massive, beautifully crafted butcher's block, a bowl of clove-studded oranges sitting in its middle. Despite being a working kitchen, the room still had that warm, homey feeling that blended perfectly with the beautiful house.

"You must close pretty early for dinner," he commented, noticing that the kitchen had already been cleaned and shut down for the night.

"The majority of our business is breakfast and lunch, so on the weekdays we only do an early dinner service," she explained, setting the dangerous-looking knife in the sink. "The hours are perfect for me and Millie, since neither one of us has any desire to be a slave to a full-time restaurant. The café pulls in great money and gives us a creative outlet, which we both love, while still allowing us some downtime. The weekend is actually the only time we stay open a little later."

She washed her hands, then began setting up the coffeemaker, putting in a new filter…grinding some aromatic beans. Riley sat on the stool, simply watching her move about the kitchen, wishing he could think of something to say, but casual conversation seemed impossible. Completely beyond his scope at the moment. Still, he had to admit that she eased something inside him, as if she were a cool, cleansing balm for his tainted soul. And yet, at the same time, she ignited him to a fever pitch of desire, his cock already thickening with lust just from watching her make coffee, for God's sake.

Since she didn't seem in any hurry to break the silence, either, he used the time to simply enjoy watching her, soaking up the details that were revealed by the recessed lighting spilling from beneath the cupboards, illuminating the room with a warm, golden glow. He could sense, on an instinctual male level, that she honestly had no concept of how beautiful she was…how sexy. So soft and lush and endlessly feminine, it made him crazed, as if he could bruise her tender surface with nothing more than a look. And, Christ, he didn't even want to think about the damage he could inflict if he lost control and gave in to the visceral pangs of hunger that clawed through him every time he set eyes on her…or so much as thought about her.

Riley had hoped that he'd be able to hold it together, at least long enough to enjoy a cup of coffee with her before he hightailed his ass back to safer territory—but he'd been wrong. Already, his control was slipping. Pulling in a deep breath, he choked back a groan as her mouthwatering scent filled his head, his body going hot…muscles clenching from the strain of holding himself in check.

The coffeemaker began to gurgle and hiss, and she pulled down two mugs from a cupboard, sliding him a nervous look as she moved to the fridge, and he knew that she'd finally recognized the animal in the room with them. The wild, primal beast that had risen up, and was now charging the air with a thick, warm spill of desire. One he couldn't fight. One he didn't even want to. Not until he'd finally gotten the taste of her in his mouth. Until he had at least that much to hold him over. That much to cling to until it just didn't matter anymore.

"Do you take milk or cream in your coffee?" she asked with a husky catch to her voice, looking over her shoulder as she opened the refrigerator door, and her eyes went wide when she saw that he was no longer sitting down.

Was, in fact, heading straight for her. There was some kind of argument going on inside his head, but he tuned it out, no longer able to wait. Need was punching against his insides with vicious, destructive force, his skin too tight to contain it. If he didn't get her mouth under his, and soon, he was going to self-destruct before he'd even had a chance to make a goddamn difference.

"Riley?" she breathed out, closing the door as he reached her. One second she was staring up at him with wide, startled eyes, and in the next, her back was pressed against the stainless steel door, the damp, delicious heat of her mouth dominated by his. She gasped, and he stroked past her silken lips with his tongue, thrusting inside with a dark, hungry aggression, nearly dying as her taste spilled through him, sinking into his blood…into his veins.

"What are you doing?" she whispered, the breathless words soft against his lips as he lifted his hands, tangling his fingers in the warm silk of her hair, holding her still as he nipped and teased and tasted.

"Damn it," he growled, leaning into her, grinding his denim-covered cock into her lower belly, wanting to be inside her more than he wanted to breathe…to live. "Hope, I'm starving," he groaned, the graveled words scraping against his throat. "For your taste. Your scent. Your heat. I can't…I can't stop."

She stared…trembled, and then her eyes slid closed as she finally kissed him back. All it took was the first stroke of her tongue against his—that first curious,

questing glide—and the kiss turned explosive…
savage, the angle changing again and again as they
tried to feed the demanding hunger that rose between
them.

"Are you seeing anyone?" he suddenly rasped, pulling his mouth from hers just long enough to scrape out
the husky words.

She blinked, her eyes going round. "Me?"

"Yeah, you," he growled, wondering why she
seemed to be so completely unaware of just how incredible she was. How beautiful and tempting and sexy.
"Do you have a boyfriend?" he rasped, holding her face
in his hands, his thumbs stroking the sensitive skin
beneath her eyes…the wild bloom of heat in her cheeks.
"Some jackass I should know about, who's going to
come after me for putting my filthy hands on you?"

She shook her head within the hold of his hands,
the glazed look in her glowing eyes one of nerves and
fear and excitement. If he'd thought she was afraid of
him, he'd have forced himself away from her…but
the fear wasn't of him. At least not yet. And hopefully
not ever, if he could just get this *one* taste of her
without losing that last tenuous hold he had on the
dark, predatory side of his nature. The one that wanted
to tilt her head to the side, exposing that tender curve
of flesh, and bury his fangs deep in her throat, at the
same time he ripped her clothes from her body, spread
her legs and drove himself into her with a hard, hammering thrust that would force the memories of every

other lover she'd ever known right out of her beautiful little head.

Fighting against the violent demands of the Merrick to do just that, Riley kissed his way back into her mouth, losing himself in the petal-soft texture of her lips. They were so smooth and tender, luscious and sweet and impossibly warm. And her taste. God, it nearly killed him. He touched his tongue to hers, sliding it inside her mouth...stroking...devouring, intoxicated by the mouthwatering flavor that made him tremble. His hands shook, his cock so hard and aching that he could feel each pulse of his heartbeat through the taut, swollen flesh that wanted so badly to become a part of her.

Too soon, his gums began to sting, feeling heavy... hot, and he tore himself away from the wildly erotic kiss, too afraid that he wouldn't be able to hold back the release of the Merrick's fangs. Hope panted as she leaned against the door, swiping her tongue against the shiny swell of her lower lip, and he growled a deep, rumbling animal kind of sound that made her shiver. Her heavy-lidded gaze focused on the hard, savage intensity of his expression...seeing too much, too deeply, and he took his hands from her hair, curling them over her shoulders as he quickly turned her around, so that she faced away from him. She gave a questioning murmur under her breath, but he was already pressing her forward, trapping her against the chilly metallic surface of the fridge as he pulled her hair to the side.

"Lift your arms and brace them against the door," he

whispered in her ear, before scraping his teeth along the sensitive cord that connected her throat to her shoulder, the dangerous caress prompting the Merrick to claw at his insides, furious that he wouldn't give it what it wanted. What it needed.

She whispered his name, lifting her arms exactly as he'd told her to do, and Riley ground his jaw, desperate for just a few more stolen moments with her. Moments that would no doubt torment him every waking hour of every day as he played them through his mind again and again, but he didn't give a damn. He *had* to have them. Had to at least have this much of her.

Unable to wait any longer, he slid his left hand inside the loose neckline of her shirt, beneath the stretchy camisole she was wearing, until he cupped the naked heat of her right breast in his hand. Her heartbeat pounded against the inside of his wrist as he memorized the lush, perfect shape of her, stroking the soft, swollen nipple with his thumb. She choked back a startled cry of pleasure, resting her forehead against the cool surface of the metal door, her breath hitching as he quickly slid his right hand down the front of her pants, inside the cotton panties, and burrowed possessively between the damp, velvety folds of her sex. She was already swollen there as well, drenched with hot, slippery juices, warm and soft like silk. Fighting the Merrick into submission, Riley swirled his fingers through that hot, rich cream, learning her, burning the feel of her into his brain. Her folds were exquisitely tender and smooth, her clit a knotted little kernel of flesh that he wanted to taste with his tongue…tease with the gentle scrape of his teeth. God, he wanted to bury his face in her delicate little sex and take every part of it into his mouth. Wanted to penetrate her with his tongue. Lick and suck and swallow until he lost count of how many times she came. Until she was boneless and drifting in a perfect state of bliss, slippery and soft enough that he could work himself inside, sinking deep, until she'd taken every thick, demanding inch of him.

Unable to wait any longer, Riley thrust two fingers into the tight, tender opening of her body, and pushed deep inside, gasping at the feel of her strong, cushiony muscles clutching onto him, sweet and hot and slick to the touch.

"Oh, God," she whispered shakily, and he could hear the shyness in her voice as he began moving his fingers in a slow, provocative rhythm that made them both tremble and moan and gasp.

"Don't be embarrassed." He breathed the husky words against the smooth, creamy curve of her shoulder, while grinding his painfully rigid cock against her lower back, wishing he could rip open the confining denim and just shove inside her. "You feel so good, Hope. So hot and wet and tight. You have no idea how badly I want to be buried inside this part of you, thick and hard and deep enough that you can feel me everywhere. Until you can't feel anything *but* me."

A CHOKED SOB BROKE from Hope's chest as those deliciously erotic words melted into her system, adding a deeper level of intensity to the stunning, breathtaking pleasure he was creating, and she sank her teeth into her lower lip, acutely aware of just how close by Millie and Hal were. No matter how badly she wanted to scream from the blissful, scorching swirl of sensation spiraling through her, she had to hold it back. But it wasn't easy. He was insanely good, taking her apart with devastating skill, as if he were inside her head and knew just where to touch and stroke and rub. His long, talented fingers felt so incredible, she could already feel the tiny pulses of pleasure that signaled the rushing rise of release. Only…this orgasm didn't feel like anything she'd ever experienced in the past. Not by a long shot. It was too powerful. Too strong.

As if sensing the cues from her body, Riley shifted his hand, thrusting his fingers deeper while his thumb pressed down on her clit, rubbing it…stroking…circling, and she crashed, her body seized by a thick, devastating wave of ecstasy that slammed through her so hard, she couldn't breathe…couldn't see. She pulsed around his fingers…drenching him, clutching at him, while the wild, provocative heat of it swept through her—and she could have sworn she felt his teeth scrape against the sensitive curve of her throat, the erotic caress somehow deepening the shocking crests of sensation. Each hard, violent pulse slammed through her with a stunning surge of power, until her legs finally gave way.

He had to hold her up with his left arm banded about her waist, while his right hand continued to stroke and thrust inside her body, prolonging the wrenching orgasm, ensuring she got every last drop of pleasure that could be had.

Hope collapsed against him, her head resting on his chest, eyes squeezed tight as she concentrated on keeping herself together, instead of shattering apart in a million fragmented pieces. She was covered in a fine sheen of sweat, her face hot, lips parted as she struggled to draw in a deep enough breath, while his rich, woodsy scent filled her head, drugging her senses. Riley cursed something hot and gritty and sexy under his breath as he pulled his fingers from the tight, liquid suction of her body, and she opened her eyes just in time to see him putting his glistening fingers inside his mouth. She gasped, a fresh wave of heat scaring through her veins at the carnal sight of him tasting her on his skin. His eyes slid closed while a low, guttural sound of pleasure vibrated deep in his chest, and then he lifted his lashes, his dark, oddly glowing gaze connecting with hers with a crackling force of emotion that practically sparked on the air.

The moment spread out, rife with tension…with hunger and need and carnal, explicit desires that demanded satisfaction, his chest rising and falling beneath her head with the ragged cadence of his breaths. And then she suddenly heard Millie and Hal moving into the small service area that sat just beyond the swinging door to the right of the refrigerator, her aunt saying something about having a measuring tape in one of the drawers that they could use. Hope's eyes went wide with panic, but before she could move, she heard Hal's deep, rusty voice say, "I hear Hope caused quite a scene the other day with some pies. What was that all about?"

"Well, I don't blame her," Millie murmured. "The man she was throwing them at is none other than her childhood sweetheart. He broke her heart, and to tell you the truth, I don't think she's ever gotten over him."

"He didn't hurt her, like that other bastard, did he?" Hal asked, sounding endearingly protective. Hope would have been touched by his concern, if it weren't for the fact that her blood had turned cold at what he'd just revealed. She had no doubt that Riley had heard every word and it made her feel sick.

Hunching her shoulders, she wished that she could draw in on herself like an oyster. Just hide away inside her shell and block it all out. The pain and fear. Riley and Neal and the feeling that her entire life was spinning wildly out of control.

And the terrifying sensation that there was nothing she could do to stop it.

CHAPTER EIGHT

KNOWING SHE NEEDED to interrupt Millie before she accidentally revealed any more of her secrets, Hope started to call out, but Riley covered her lips with his hand, whispering "Shh" in her ear. He listened intently as Millie said, "No, Riley never physically abused her. But I think that in a lot of ways the emotional scars he left behind did more damage than the ones Neal put on her body. That is, if it wasn't for the loss of her and Neal's child. Hope never recovered from that. She's always been the sweetest person I've ever known, so much hope and faith in the world, but something died inside her when she lost her baby. And she's never been the same since."

Riley's breath was coming harder, faster, his body burning against her back, fever-hot and rigid with tension as he listened to her aunt's words. Growling low in his throat, he ignored her attempts to stop him as he forced his hands beneath the hem of her T-shirt, running his palms over the jagged scars that crossed her midriff.

"Son of a bitch," he snarled, loud enough that she worried Millie and Hal would hear, but they were al-

ready walking back into the restaurant. The minute
Hope heard the outer door swing closed behind them,
she wrenched free of Riley's hold and headed straight
for the living room on unsteady legs, putting as much
distance between them as she could.

Of course, he followed right behind her. She stopped
at the bay window, keeping her back to him as she
wrapped her arms around her middle, holding herself
together. Her stomach felt ill at what he'd learned…at
the fact that he'd felt her scars—not out of any mis-
placed sense of vanity, but because of what they sym-
bolized. Her failures, her weaknesses, as well as the
most painful loss of her life. She struggled to stay calm,
but the shivering that had started deep inside her slowly
spread outward, until even her teeth were chattering. "I
th-think it's time for you to l-leave now."

"Like hell it is," he shot back in a low, hard voice that
crackled with fury. "We need to talk."

She shook her head and tried to take a deep
breath…mellow out, but it was impossible. The night
had been too much, starting with that infuriating phone
call from Neal, followed by the mind-shattering episode
in the kitchen…and now this.

"You should have told me," he said in that same
intense tone, coming up behind her, so close that she
could feel the fevered warmth of his big muscular body
blasting against her, helping to ease the violent shivers
that were trembling up from inside her.

"What, Riley? What should I have told you?" she

asked, staring at his reflection in the window. "That my ex-husband's an ass? That he's one of the most worthless human beings on the face of the planet, and I was actually stupid enough to marry him? To stay with him?"

"You *lied* to me," he growled. She could only be thankful that he wasn't shouting at her, which would have no doubt brought Millie rushing in. "Christ, Hope. You actually told me that son of a bitch hadn't hurt you!"

She shrugged, her gaze sliding away as a brittle laugh jerked from her throat. "You're one to talk. God, Riley. You've lied about everything. In the past, when you told me you cared about me…that you were going to marry me…spend the rest of your life with me. Now, every time you try to feed those stupid lies about what you're searching for. Why you think we're in danger. I doubt you've ever told me the truth, not once, in your entire life," she finished wearily.

"Damn it, Hope. Stop turning this around. I asked you if he had hurt you, and you told me no."

Turning around, she lifted her chin and stared him right in the eye as she said, "Please, Riley. If this was something I wanted to discuss with you, I would have. But I don't. I just want you to leave."

He stared down at her for a long, agonizing moment, a devastating blend of emotion swirling through his eyes and reaching deep inside her, squeezing painfully around her heart. "Millie mentioned that you lost a child," he finally said in a strained, halting voice, the bleakness of his tone breaking her heart, as though he mourned the loss of that little life as much as she did.

She stumbled back, wishing that she could somehow distance herself from the painful truth of his words. Shaking, her face began to tingle with tiny pinpricks of sensation, her breath coming in harsh, jerking pants, as if there wasn't enough air in the room. "If you care for me at all," she whispered, "you won't make me talk about it."

He locked his jaw, and she could see the rage he was trying so hard to control, as well as the grief. "I just want to help you, Hope."

A sound jerked from her chest, too painful and stark to be a laugh. She'd have cried, but her tears had dried up when she'd lost her baby. She'd cried for days, weeks, and then Millie had come and taken her away, and the tears had dried up. The pain that lingered stayed inside, unable to make its way out, bottled up and slowly eating her alive.

"Help me?" she burst out, the words jagged and raw with hurt. "Why would you want to help, Riley? I meant nothing to you before, and I obviously don't mean anything to you now."

"That's not true," he argued, his massive body trembling with a violent wave of emotion, one strong, dark hand raking his hair back from his forehead as the words tore out of him, choppy and hoarse. "Damn it, Hope, I was insane about you! I know it doesn't make any sense, and I know you're not going to believe me, but I turned my back on you because I *did* care about you. Because

I knew you didn't deserve to deal with the shit I'm going through now. So don't stand there and tell me that I never cared about you. I cared more about you than I've ever cared for any goddamn thing in my entire life!"

She stared, stunned…wondering if she dared to believe him. It would be madness, but then, that was how he made her feel. Mad. Wild. Reckless. If there was so much as an ounce of truth to his words, then why couldn't she just do it? Just be crazy. Take Millie's advice and get her fill of Riley Buchanan while she could, before the opportunity had passed her by and he'd walked right back out of her life.

"Did you mean it?" she asked, the words thick on her tongue, her body going heavy, pulsing with excitement. She took a deep breath and finally allowed herself a moment to look him over, soaking up the physical beauty of him in a way she'd been too afraid to do before, knowing he'd be too much of a temptation. His tall body was wrapped up in a clean pair of jeans and an untucked, navy-blue, long-sleeved T-shirt that revealed the lean, powerful muscles in his shoulders and arms, while bringing out the navy flecks in his eyes. He had on the same pair of big, sturdy hiking boots that he'd been wearing on Saturday, when she'd thrown the pies at him, and the corner of her mouth twitched at the thought. Every part of him was a thing of dangerous, provocative beauty and rugged, masculine power. She loved the arrogant angles of his face and the windblown, spiky mess of his ink-black hair. Loved the lines that fanned out around his eyes and the hollows of his cheekbones. The strong, corded column of his throat. The sexy, shadowed shape of his jaw and chin, as well as the midnight slash of his brows.

God, she loved it all. Every single breathtaking, mouthwatering detail.

She wondered if he was going to stand there and let her stare at him forever, when he finally rolled one shoulder in a frustrated gesture and broke the silence.

"Did I really mean what?" His voice was low… breathless.

She rolled her lips together, painfully aware of the wild flush burning in her cheeks. Of the butterflies swarming through her belly. The crazy, frenetic rhythm of her pulse. "What you said about wanting to help me. Did you mean it?"

SPELLBOUND…FASCINATED and wary as hell, Riley watched the change in her. Watched as her anger and hurt shifted, bleeding into something that made his heart race, his muscles going hard, tight, as if he were facing an unknown threat. Something snapped in her changing expression, the crack deafening, as if it'd been an actual blast through the room, and he flinched, his hands fisting at his sides. "What's going on?" he asked, unable to shake the feeling that he'd somehow stumbled into someplace he shouldn't be. Someplace that was going to land him in a world of trouble.

"You want to help, Ri?" she whispered, taking a step closer to him. "Then help take my mind off my troubles."

He jerked back, sensing a trap looming before him, one that was yawning and deep, capable of swallowing him whole. "What the hell, Hope?"

She came closer, her shaking fingers spreading out over his chest, kneading and pressing as they curved over his shoulders, her topaz-colored eyes wild and bright with a carnal hunger that made him want to roar, because he knew there wasn't *any* chance he could feed it.

"You know what I want, Riley?" she asked in a breathless, shivery rush. "I want what I never had before. What I've always wanted. I want to finally get my fill of you. I want you to cover me. Want you inside me. And I want it right now."

There was a rough, desperate edge to his words as he grabbed hold of her wrists, saying, "Damn it! Don't do this. Scream at me. Throw things at me. Be pissed at me."

She lifted her gaze to his face, staring into his eyes. "Why should I?"

His breath jerked from his chest, so hard that it actually hurt. "Because it made it easier," he rasped, wondering if this was one more cosmic prank being played on him, just to see how much torture he could take. He felt like the proverbial child being offered candy from a stranger. The helpless fish that caught sight of the juicy, wriggling worm in the water. Here he was, with the woman he wanted more than any other being dangled in front of him, telling him she wanted him, and he couldn't take what she was offering. Couldn't touch her, lose himself in her warmth and goodness and light, for the simple fact that he wasn't the man that she thought he was. She didn't know what he'd want from her…didn't know what he would become. Not to mention the monsters he'd brought to her town, lurking out in the night, who would be all too happy to use her to get to him. God, he shouldn't have even been in her house. Should have stayed away from her!

He could feel her pulse racing beneath his fingers as he held her wrists, her mouth full with sensual promise, face flushed with a wild, radiant bloom of color. "I hate to break it to you," she said in a low voice, "but I'm not looking to make anything easy for you, Ri."

"What do you want from me?" he demanded, the guttural words fractured and raw.

"I want to feel alive. To do something wild, for the first time in my life, before I'm too old to enjoy it. If I even live that long."

"Don't say that," he growled, while fear slithered through his insides, painful and cold. "Nothing's going to happen to you, Hope. I won't let anyone hurt you. And I'm not going to use you. That's not the life you deserve."

"The life I deserve?" She laughed and shook her head. "You mean the one with a husband and white picket fence, in a soccer-mom neighborhood? I tried to live that life, and look what it got me. For once," she told him, tugging at her wrists, "I'm going to follow my instincts and see where they lead."

"And what would Millie say?" he rasped, letting go of her wrists as he grabbed onto her shoulders, towering over her while he glared into her bright, beautiful eyes.

She lifted her right hand, cupping his cheek, her thumb stroking the shadow of bristles. Staring at his mouth, she said, "Millie already told me that I should have a hot, torrid affair with you."

God, he wanted to accept what she was offering so badly, but the only way he could take that kind of risk was for love, like Ian and Saige had done. A commitment where he'd be by her side forever, protecting her, watching over her, which was impossible. He wouldn't be around to protect anyone in the long haul. Which meant that touching her would be the biggest prick thing he'd have ever done.

No matter how badly he wanted her, he couldn't do it.

"This argument or whatever it is is pointless, Hope. Because it's not going to happen."

She fluttered her hand toward the kitchen. "Then what the hell was that about in there?" she questioned, a tremulous edge to the words that tore at his heart. Made him feel like the biggest jackass alive.

Shoving his hands deep into his pockets, Riley worked his jaw. "It was a mistake," he rasped, forcing the words through his clenched teeth.

She flinched as if he'd struck her. "That's cold, Ri. Even for you."

"I'm sorry." His voice was strained…rough. "It shouldn't have happened. Won't happen again."

She pressed her hands to her face. Closed her eyes. "I don't believe this. What kind of head games are you playing, Riley? I'm trying to understand, but you aren't making any sense."

"I know, damn it. But I can't explain."

Her eyes flew open, a volatile blend of anger and hurt and frustration brewing in the burnished depths that made his chest ache…his face burn. "If you don't want me," she snapped, "then just say it!"

He vibrated with tension, his gut knotted with too many emotions to name or control. "I didn't say that."

"Then what's the bloody problem? I'm not asking you to save me or marry me or even take care of me. All I want is to take what you've no doubt given to so many other women. Why should I be the one who misses out? Why should I be any different?"

He made a sharp, thick sound in the back of his throat. "Damn it, you've always been different!"

She stared, shaking, clearly not believing him.

Muttering a foul stream of words under his breath, he locked his hands behind his head and began pacing, from one side of the room to the other. Slanting her a dark look from the corner of his eye, he said, "I want things with you that I've never wanted with another woman."

"And that's bad?" she asked, her words soft with confusion.

His laugh was low, pained. "Yeah, honey. It's bad."

"Why?"

"Because I don't want to hurt you," he muttered. "Emotionally...or physically."

"You won't," she argued, lifting her chin as though he'd just insulted her.

Riley shook his head, lowering his arms as he came to a stop on the far side of the room, staring at her across the distance. "You're right, I won't. Because I'm *not* doing this. I won't be the thing that destroys you."

"You didn't let that bother you before." She wet her lips, cleared her throat. "God, it almost killed me when you told me we were over, and then, within the blink of an eye, took Amee Smith to the prom. She couldn't wait to get to school on Monday, so that she could tell everyone how you'd nailed her in the backseat of your car."

Guilt burned beneath his skin, making him sweat. He tried to swallow the knot in his throat, his chest tight...body clutched in a grip of self-loathing. "I had my reasons," he finally managed to rasp. "They had nothing to do with you." Which was a lie, because they'd had *everything* to do with her. He'd been so sure of himself, thinking he was going to be the white knight who took her away from Laurente and gave her the life she deserved, only to discover that all he'd end up offering her was a life of hell. He'd known he needed to sever the connection between them, and he'd done a damn good job of it. So good that they were both still reeling from the pain.

She took a deep breath, then slowly let it out. "If you

don't want me, fine. But don't tell me lies, Riley. Don't keep making excuses. Just be a man and say it."

Before he could stop himself, he'd closed the space between them, grabbed her hand and pressed it over his bulging fly, where his cock was throbbing hard and long and thick beneath the confining denim. "Does that feel like I don't want you?" he growled, pulsing against her hand. "All I ever have to do is set eyes on you and I get like this. Even after all these years, just the thought of you makes me burn. Makes me harder than any woman I've ever had under me. No matter how beautiful they are or how eager, I'm always left wanting when it's over, unable to get away from the ugly knowledge that the one woman I want, I'm *never* going to have!"

She breathed his name on her lips, staring back at him in startled, stunned amazement.

Riley knew he should cut his losses while he still could and shut the hell up, but the gritty words just kept pouring out of him. "Christ, Hope. You have no idea how hard I have to fight it when you walk into a room. I sat through eleventh-grade history hard as a bloody spike every goddamn day, just from staring at the way your hair fell across your shoulders, imagining it draping over my chest, my stomach. And now…now it's even worse, because you're not that innocent, big-eyed little girl anymore. You're a beautiful, breathtaking woman, and I'd give a limb just for the chance to spend one night with you. Hell," he confessed with a bitter, jagged laugh, releasing his hold on her hand as he stepped back, moving away from her, "you don't want to know what I'd be willing to do for just an hour with you. A handful of minutes."

"But you're still rejecting me, aren't you? I don't understand," she whispered, wrapping her arms around her shivering body. "It doesn't make any sense, Riley."

His voice was hard...grim. "I know."

"Then explain it. *Please*."

He shook his head again, forcing out a hoarse "I can't."

She took a step toward him, vibrating with emotion. "You'd better damn well try."

"I'm not what you think I am. I...I'm..." His voice cracked, and he gave another bitter laugh, shoving his hands back in his pockets.

"What?" Her tone was soft...pleading. "What are you trying to tell me, Riley?"

The sudden ringing of his cell phone made them both jump, and he swore softly under his breath. Pulling the phone from its case, he looked at the number and swore again. "I have to take this," he muttered, turning away and answering the call.

"What's going on?" he asked, knowing that Seth McConnell, their unlikely Collective ally, wouldn't be calling unless there was a problem.

McConnell's deep voice crackled over the crappy connection. "It looks like there's some serious trouble headed your way. We've got a good lead, but I can't go into it right now. Just wanted to let you know that there's a lot of movement headed in your direction."

"Casus?" he grunted, aware that Hope was listening to his every word.

"Along with some of Westmore's personal unit and a group of Collective soldiers," McConnell rumbled. "I think word's gone out about you, but it's more than that. Sounds like they might be coming after Gregory from all sides. I'm going to finish up here, then head your way. I'll call if I get anything else."

McConnell didn't say where "here" was at the moment, but Riley knew the guy couldn't tell him over the phone. "Thanks for the heads-up. And I'm pretty sure Gregory's already in town."

"How many victims?"

"One so far."

"Shit," McConnell cursed. "And the Marker?"

"God only knows," Riley said with a tired sigh. "But we're looking."

Voices started shouting in the background, and McConnell said, "I gotta run, but stay sharp."

"You, too."

The instant Riley disconnected the call, Hope said, "Is there a problem?"

"Yeah." He slid the phone back into its case, then pulled one hand down his face as he turned back around to face her. "Just one more to add on top of everything else. This whole situation is going to shit."

Needing to get the hell out of there before he did something stupid—like touch her—he turned and started to head toward the door, when her words stopped him in his tracks, the soft, shivery sound reaching into his chest and taking hold of his heart. "Neal… He… killed our baby."

Riley waited, his shoulders hunched, hands fisted at his sides while he stared at the floor, giving her the privacy he could sense she needed for the telling.

"He'd gone to law school, graduated top of his class, set to be the next brilliant Capshaw in one of those old-money Southern families. You know the ones I mean. But as his career started to take off, he…wasn't able to handle the stress. So he began drinking. Heavily. And as the drinking worsened, so did his jealousy. His rages. He'd always been…possessive, but suddenly I couldn't so much as smile at another man without him accusing me of having an affair. He began to get violent, even though I was seven months pregnant. Hit me a few times. Bloodied my lip, blackened an eye. I…I started making plans to leave him. But I wasn't fast enough."

She paused for a moment, and he turned his head to find her standing at the window again, staring out at the darkening sky. Finally, she said, "On the night when it…happened, he'd gone out with some friends, hitting the local bars. Doing God only knows what. The temperatures were freezing, and there was a problem with our heating. I couldn't get anyone to come out to fix it, but we had a neighbor across the street who owned a local contracting company, and when I asked, he was more than happy to come and see if he could help. When Neal came home and found the man there, he went into a rage about the fact that I'd let him into our house, and he…attacked him. Picked up a wrench from the man's toolbox and started beating him with it. I was trying to call 911 when Neal knocked the man unconscious and turned on me." She pressed her hands to her belly, as if she might still somehow protect the life that had been growing inside her. "I tried to get away from him, but he grabbed me, and we struggled. I was clawing and kicking at him, doing everything I could to get away, terrified that he was going to try to kill me. Though he later claimed in court that he was simply trying to push me away, feeding them some pathetic story about how my so-called lover and I attacked him when he came home and found us together, that wasn't the way that it happened. Neal… He deliberately shoved me through the living-room window. The glass shattered, cutting me, slicing through…my abdomen. And the baby died."

It scared him, how calm and level her voice was. How even, as if the emotion had just drained away, leaving a lifeless shell in its wake. That was obviously how she dealt with the pain, pulling in on herself…shutting down, and it made him want to get his hands on Neal Capshaw and beat the ever-loving hell out of him.

"So you see, Ri? I tried to tell you," she said in a quiet, hollow voice, "but you wouldn't listen. Any starry-eyed dreams I ever had died a hell of a long time ago. I don't need you to protect me from reality. To shelter me from the truth."

She was right, and it killed a part of him to know that he hadn't been there when she'd needed him. He thought he'd been sparing her pain by leaving her, and yet she'd still suffered. Worse than he could ever have imagined.

She shivered, lifting her hands to push her hair back from her face, then carefully said, "So anyway, that's what happened. And if you ever cared anything about me, Riley, then you won't make me talk about it again." She turned and walked past him like a ghost, to the bottom of the staircase, then looked back over her shoulder as she added, "Do me a favor and lock the door behind you."

Riley stood rooted to the floor, his face feeling like a rigid mask as he watched her silent ascent, until she finally went out of sight.

CHAPTER NINE

SLIPPING HIS CELL BACK into its black leather case, Kellan set the phone on the dresser, then turned back toward the woman waiting for him on the king-size bed. He'd already had her twice, but his cock hardened a third time as he took in her sultry pose, her long hair falling over one shoulder, dusky-colored nipples peeking through the silken tendrils. For the moment, her long legs were folded demurely to the side, but he knew if he could have stayed, they wouldn't remain that way for long. Despite being kind of quiet and shy, she was a hellcat in the sack, which fit his mood perfectly these days. He wasn't looking for a lot of conversation. He just needed a way to work out his tension, and she had been like a blessing from heaven when he'd met her at one of the local hangouts.

They'd met back up at the motel where she was staying, since she'd only just arrived in Purity and was still looking for a place to rent. Kellan had mentioned the cabins that Hope and Millie rented out, but she'd said she was looking for something a little closer to the north side of town, seeing as how she was going to be doing some student teaching at the college up in Wellsford.

That had been the extent of their conversations, other than some idle chitchat, the brunt of their time together spent doing things that made them too damn tired to talk.

"Is something wrong?" she asked, her big green eyes dark with lingering satisfaction, a curious smile playing softly across her full mouth.

"It's nothing I can't handle," he told her with a grin, grabbing his jeans off the floor and slipping into them. "But I need to be getting back." His grin turned wry as he had to work his cock inside the denim—a difficult task, considering the size of the damn thing—and she gave a throaty laugh, the sexy sound shivering down his back, making him wish he could ignore the outside world and just hide away with her for a few more hours. But he knew that if he didn't get back, there'd be hell to pay with Riley. Seth's phone call had put the guy on edge, and to be honest, it freaked Kellan out, as well. Before this all came to an end, it seemed as though Purity was destined to find itself at the center of one major bad-ass showdown, with all of them just fighting to survive.

Pulling on his shirt, boots and leather jacket, he grabbed his phone and headed for the door.

"When will I see you again?" she asked as he placed his hand around the door handle.

Kellan looked over his shoulder, suddenly struck

with an odd, uncomfortable sensation that jolted him all the way down to his toes. For a split second, he'd thought about walking to the bed and kissing her goodbye, then immediately reeled back from the impulse. Kisses were for lovers and friends, and while they'd had a helluva time messing around together, there was a glaring lack of intimacy to their encounters that he couldn't ignore.

Not that it was her fault.

No, the problem was with him, and he was struck with the unsettling realization that all his sexual exploits had been leaving him with this same taste in his mouth lately. Not bad. Just…lacking, as if he knew, instinctively, that there was something a lot better out there, if he would only make the effort to go and look for it.

Whoa. What universe did that just come from?

Mentally stumbling over the staggering thought, Kellan felt as if he'd slipped into some kind of alternate reality, because those were *not* his kind of thoughts. At least not until recently. He liked sex for sex's sake. Liked the way it felt. The sweat and the heat and the crazy release of pressure. He didn't know why his brain was suddenly wandering into unsavory territory he normally wouldn't have touched with a ten-foot pole. All he knew was that he didn't like it. It made him too aware of the emptiness in his gut that he'd been doing his best to push away…to ignore, unwilling to look at it too closely. The feeling had been coming on stronger, day by day, and it was starting to piss him off. That little

voice in his head whispering that he could screw his
way through a stream of beautiful women until the end
of time, and it still wasn't going to make him happy He
might get his rocks off, but it wasn't going to give him
what he needed. Wasn't going to fill that hollow, aching
void that had settled in the center of his chest, growing
deeper…and deeper.

"Hey, are you okay?" she asked, sitting up in the bed
with the sheet clutched against her chest, and he
blinked, realizing that he'd been standing there for a full
minute, one hand on the doorknob, staring at her while
his mind had floated a million miles away.

Thinking of the murdered college girl that Riley had
mentioned on the phone, he pushed his free hand back
through his sweat-dampened hair and said, "There's
been a murder up in Wellsford, near your school."

Her eyes went round, and she clutched the sheet tighter
against her body as he added, "So, uh, just be careful.
Don't go out anywhere alone if you can help it." She
nodded, and he said, "I'll call if I'm able to get away."

Before she had time to pout or argue, Kellan walked
out the door, feeling like an ass for just nailing her and
hitting the road. But at least he could say that he'd been
honest with her from the start. Pulling the door shut
behind him, he stepped out into the foggy night and
curled his lip at the misty drizzle of rain coming down
from above. He could have taken Riley's truck into town,
but he liked walking along the picturesque streets, enjoying the sound and scent of the nearby ocean. He just

wished the rain would ease up for longer than an hour, but knew there wasn't much chance of it happening. At least not anytime soon. The weather forecasters were predicting that a violent storm front would be moving in over the next few days. The lightning showers brewing out over the Pacific were just the precursor to what they were calling one of the worst weather systems to hit this part of the country in a hundred years, and Kellan could only shake his head and laugh. He didn't know why, but it seemed that lately, if it weren't for bad luck, he and the others wouldn't have any friggin' luck at all.

Thinking about the digging that would start again in the morning, Kellan lifted his hand to rub at the knotted tension in the back of his neck, when a strange sensation of being watched suddenly slithered through his system. Moving down the foggy street at a steady, even pace, he carefully sniffed the nighttime air, but the rainy mist made it impossible to pick up anything and he scowled, not liking the feeling creeping around the backs of his ears. The one that said he was no longer alone…and that trouble was coming.

Cutting through a small alleyway that connected to Main Street, he'd made it halfway down the shadowed road, when a voice behind him shouted for him to get down. Everything that happened afterward seemed to play out in slow motion, even the sounds distorted as he swiveled round to see a bulky, fair-haired man emerging from one of the shadowed doorways, the lethal-looking Glock in his right hand aimed low at

Kellan's legs. As the man fired, Kellan dropped, rolling, barely avoiding the deafening spray of bullets. With only seconds to react, he took the knife tucked inside his jacket pocket, lifted his arm and hurled it through the air. It sank into the blonde's throat with a sickening, slick kind of sound, and the guy's eyes went round with shock as he dropped to his knees, the gun sliding from his fingers to smack against the wet asphalt. Instead of falling, he just swayed there, the rain misting against his face, while a crimson wash of blood poured from the wound in his throat.

Moving toward him, Kellan knocked him back on the ground by placing one booted foot against the guy's right shoulder. "Who sent you?" he demanded.

Blood bubbled on the man's lips as he growled out a garbled "Go to hell!"

"Wrong answer," Kellan offered dryly. Then he lifted his foot, placed the bottom of his boot against the hilt of the blade, and shoved down. The man's body contorted, a choked, gurgling scream tearing from his throat as the rain washed away the pink froth that bubbled at the corners of his mouth.

Reaching down for his knife, Kellan pulled it free, then grabbed the Glock as well, tucking it into the back of his jeans as he headed toward the end of the alleyway, looking for the man who'd shouted out the warning. Finding nothing, he cursed the thick fog that made visibility—as well as smell—impossible, and turned back toward the alleyway…only to discover that the man he'd just taken down was gone. "Shit," he breathed out, slicking his wet hair back from his face.

"You'll never kill Westmore's men with bullets or steel."

Turning, he watched as a man emerged from the shadows. Thick, rain-wet hair the color of coal was plastered to the stranger's skull, his ice-blue eyes piercingly bright through the thick fog that had prevented Kellan from being able to scent him. "Who the hell are you?"

"Someone who's trying to help," the stranger rasped, "if you're willing to listen."

Staring into the man's pale gaze, Kellan slowly smiled. "And since when are the Casus interested in helping the Watchmen?"

Arching one midnight brow, the man said, "Compared to the dangerous game you're playing, shifter, putting your trust in me is the smartest thing you'll do tonight."

Kellan assumed that by "dangerous game" the man was referring to his unit's fight against the Casus, and was about to tell him exactly what he could do with his offer, when a chorus of howls cut through the silent night…drying up the smart-ass comment on his tongue. The stranger gave him a sharp smile, saying, "I'd shed that human skin of yours if you want to live, Watchman. Otherwise, you won't last two seconds against the Casus. I think there are at least three of them headed your way."

"Wait!" he shouted as the man turned and started to walk away. "Why the hell did you help me?"

"I'm not what you think I am," the stranger said over his broad shoulder, before disappearing into the fog.

Looking back toward the street, Kellan could feel the evil drawing closer and knew his only chance was to fight, which meant that the jackass was right. He was going to have to shift. He hesitated for a split second, hating the idea of shredding his clothes, but it couldn't be helped. Grimacing at the loss of a five-hundred-dollar leather jacket, he allowed the change to flow over him as he ran toward the coming howls, his body instantly expanding, musculature and bone altering their shapes as he transformed into the deadly, terrifying shape of his beast.

And then Kellan answered the bone-chilling howls with one of his own.

HE WAS SO ANGRY his blood was boiling.

Riley had heard the expression often enough in life, but he couldn't see the truth in it. Not at that particular moment in time, because there wasn't anything hot about the fury swelling through him, thickening in his veins, in every cell of his body. It was too desolate and bleak for heat. An arctic, icy tundra. Barren and cold and brutal.

He couldn't believe what that bastard had done to her. Couldn't believe what Hope had suffered. But most of all, he couldn't believe that he hadn't been there to protect her. That he'd turned his back on her, thinking it would keep her safe, and she'd ended up suffering anyway.

Snarling, Riley turned and punched the stone face of

the fireplace that covered one side of the cabin, cursing at the crushing blow of pain that radiated up his wrist, into his arm. Looking down, he scowled at the bruised, bloodied mess he'd made of his hand.

"Smooth move, asshole." He gave a weary shake of his head, disgusted with himself for acting like such a prick. Smashing his hand to pieces wasn't going to solve anything, and it sure as hell hadn't made him feel any better.

Footsteps sounded on the porch, and he turned his head at the sound of Kellan coming through the door. The bedraggled Watchman took one look at his bloody hand and quirked his right eyebrow. "Whoa. What happened to you?"

Eyeing Kellan's blood-streaked, nearly naked body, the tattered remnants of what looked like the Watchman's leather jacket wrapped around his waist, Riley muttered, "I think I could ask you the same thing."

"You first," Kellan snorted, heading for the duffel bag he'd left sitting on the end of his bed.

"Hope. She…" He blew out a rough breath, then forced the words out past the knot of emotion in his throat. "She told me what happened with her ex. Bastard threw her through a window in a jealous rage. She was pregnant at the time. Lost the baby."

"Son of a bitch," Kellan rasped, grabbing a towel from the end of his bed and using it to wipe the smears of blood from his legs, before pulling on a pair of jeans. "The prick should still be rotting away in prison."

Riley grunted his agreement, then said, "What happened to your clothes?"

"They got shredded when I had to shift," Kellan explained with a wince, but Riley couldn't tell if it was from what he'd been through, or the fact that he'd had to destroy his designer duds. "So I guess Seth was right. Not only are the Casus in town, but it looks as though we've already got some of Westmore's guys here as well, probably hoping to cover up any messes their psychotic buddies leave around. I had a run-in with one of them, and it wasn't pretty."

"Who won?" he asked, watching as Kellan used the towel to wipe away the streaks of blood that covered his torso.

"I'm still in one piece, so I think the point goes to me. But I gotta tell ya, we were right about those bastards not being human. I took his throat out with my blade, and the next thing I know he's gone."

"No shit?"

"It gets weirder," Kellan warned him, sitting down beside his bag. "I don't think he was trying to kill me, so much as injure me, which begs the question of just what they were planning on doing with me. And he probably would have gotten in a good shot, too, if I hadn't been warned he was there."

Leaning against the stone fireplace, Riley said, "Warned by who?"

"No idea," Kellan muttered. "It just seems to be one of those nights where things don't make any sense. I thought the guy must be Casus, since he had that whole freaky ice-blue eye thing going on, but he gave me another warning that a group of Casus were coming. I had to shift just to fight my way out of there."

"Are you sure the man wasn't Gregory?"

Kellan nodded, having heard the same description that Riley had of Gregory from Saige and Quinn. "This guy's hair was short and as black as yours."

"Then who in God's name is he?" Riley muttered, growing increasingly uneasy at the thought of another unknown element being added to the equation. "And why did he help you?"

"Who knows," Kellan said with a groan, rolling his head over his shoulders. "And you know what else I'm wondering? Why, if we have all these Casus running around, haven't there been more killings? I went up against three of them tonight, and Gregory would make four."

Pushing away from the wall, Riley paced his way across the floor. "Either Westmore and the Collective are doing a good job of covering up for them right now, Gregory's kill up in Wellsford aside, or they're not feeding like before. Maybe they've even been warned. If the ones planning this war have any brains, they'll know how dangerous it is for the Casus to keep killing at the rate Malcolm did. It'll draw too much attention."

Pulling on a pair of socks, Kellan said, "Do you really think it was Gregory who killed the girl?"

Still pacing, Riley struggled to hold on to his seething frustration. "Considering that her fingers were bitten off," he grunted, scraping one hand over the bristled surface of his jaw, "I'd say it was Gregory's way of letting us know he's here. But it still makes me wonder where the others are and what they're doing while waiting for me to find the Marker and reach full power. What the hell are they up to?" he snarled, cutting his hand through the air, the same way he'd done in the forest. And like before, his power was accidentally unleashed, sending the nearest lamp crashing into the wall.

Kellan whistled softly under his breath. "Whoa. Remind me not to piss you off," he offered in a low, choked voice, obviously trying not to laugh.

"It isn't funny," Riley snapped, shoving his hands into his pockets as he glared at the grinning Watchman. "And just so you know, I don't think you should keep going into town on your own."

Kellan tugged a sweatshirt over his head and scowled. "What the hell?"

"It's too dangerous," he grunted, knowing that Kellan's ego wasn't going to like what he had to say. "You got lucky tonight, but who knows what will happen next time. If they went for you once, they'll go for you again."

"I'd like to see them try," the younger man snarled, sounding thoroughly insulted as he pulled on a pair of trainers.

Shifting his gaze to the broken pieces of the lamp that had fallen to the floor, Riley blew out a rough breath. "This isn't the time to let your ego get the better of you, Kell."

"Screw this shit," Kellan muttered, shoving to his feet and heading straight for the door.

"Where do you think you're going?" Riley barked.

Kellan made a rude sound in the back of his throat. "Don't worry, *Dad*," he sneered, glaring over his shoulder. "I'm just going to take a look around the property. Make sure there's no one lingering around."

Riley was about to tell him to stop acting like a jackass, but the instant Kellan opened the door, they heard shouting coming from up at Hope and Millie's house. Sharing a look of alarm, they bolted outside and sprinted down the snaking forest path, reaching the back garden in only a handful of seconds. Riley could see Hope standing at the bay window, with Millie by her side, Hal having obviously headed home already.

And standing in the back garden, screaming a nasty stream of insults at the women, was a tall, lanky man with sunshine-colored hair. Guessing who the stranger was—and knowing a fight was going to be inevitable—Riley tested his newfound power by putting a mental hold on the back door, wanting Hope and Millie to stay inside the safety of the house.

Stepping up behind the man, Riley braced his feet in the damp lawn. "Let me guess," he rasped. "Neal Capshaw?"

The blonde spun around, his lip curling as he snarled, "And who the fuck are you?"

Riley gave him a cold, menacing smile. "I'm the man who's going to show you what happens to worthless pricks who beat up on women."

"She's the worthless one!" Capshaw sputtered, his face blotchy and red from his rage.

As Riley faced Capshaw, Hope started trying to open the back door, but he concentrated…reaching deep inside for the power to hold it closed as she struggled to wrench it open. The mother of all headaches started pounding through his skull, and as he felt a hot trickle of blood begin to stream from his nose, he gave up a silent prayer that he wasn't about to give himself an aneurysm.

"Kick his ass, Riley," Kellan suddenly shouted from where he'd propped his shoulder against a nearby tree, obviously settling in to watch the show. "The asshole deserves it."

"Riley?" Capshaw sneered, his hazel eyes darkening as he took a step closer. "You're Riley? Riley Buchanan?" The gleam of hatred in the man's eyes deepened, and Riley waited, knowing that Capshaw was about throw his first punch. And while he didn't relish the thought of violence, he couldn't wait to pound his fist into the guy's chiseled mug. He wanted to make the creep pay for everything that he'd done to Hope. For the pain he'd caused her…the terror. And for coming back into her life after all this time, trying to hurt her again.

"Well, isn't this my lucky day? You have any idea how many years I've spent wanting to take you apart?

Because of you, I never had a chance with that bitch," Capshaw shouted, pointing toward the house, where Hope was once again watching from the window, looking terrified and thoroughly pissed. "She was always hung up on you. It was goddamn pathetic!"

"My history with Hope has nothing to do with you," Riley grunted, even though he knew there was no sense in trying to reason with the man. He was obviously an asshole. One who thought the world revolved around him.

"It has everything to do with me," Capshaw screeched, jabbing his thumb toward his chest. "I'm the man she *married*."

"You're the man who lost her," Riley countered in a graveled slide of words. "And you're not getting her back."

Capshaw's face contorted with rage, a thick, guttural cry breaking from his chest as he finally made his move, hurling his rangy body straight at Riley. They hit the fog-shrouded ground hard, sliding across the soggy lawn, punches flying as they each connected with their targets. Cartilage crunched and blood sprayed, their savage, snarling grunts filling the air as Hope screamed for Riley to be careful from her place at the window. They rolled over the ground, struggling to make a clean grip as the skies unleashed a fresh deluge of rain. The hazy mist of sea-scented fog began to clear beneath the fury of the downpour, the mud only making it more difficult to maneuver as the grass gave way beneath their wrestling bodies.

"Hope owes me!" Capshaw roared, after they'd broken apart and moved back to their feet.

Riley made a thick sound of disgust as they circled one another. "Like hell she does."

"I didn't deserve what they did to me. Locking me up with the same kind of scum that I used to put away. And all because of her. Did she tell you that I lost everything because of her? Because she was screwing around?" Without waiting for Riley's answer, he sneered, "I lost it all because of that little bitch! My career. Respect. My freedom!"

Shaking his head, Riley said, "You lost the life you had because you're a worthless shit, Capshaw. One who was too stupid to appreciate what he had."

As he wiped his bleeding mouth with the back of his wrist, Capshaw's chest shook with a low, sickening rumble of laughter as he said, "You wanna know what I appreciate, Buchanan? The fact that she finally got what she deserved. And I'd do it again in a heartbeat. Hell, I doubt that baby was even mine. It didn't deserve to live."

As Capshaw's words sank in, Riley acknowledged the fact that if he hadn't left his gun back in the cabin, he'd have been tempted to shoot the bastard. As it was, he was angry enough to go for the man's blood with his bare hands. Angry enough to tear him to pieces. Capshaw must have seen the rage in his eyes, because he tried to stumble back, but Riley was too fast. One second the creep was standing his ground, and in the next, Riley delivered a swift right hook that knocked the man clear off his feet. Capshaw came up snarling, and Riley hit him again, bone crunching as he slammed his fist into the guy's nose, causing blood to spurt out over the asshole's mouth and chin, dripping onto his muddy shirt. The bastard lunged for him, and they hit the mud again, sliding a good five feet before they came to a stop. Riley was distantly aware of Kellan urging him on as he pinned Capshaw beneath him…of Hope screaming at him from inside the house, banging on the window as Millie tried to pull her away, but it all faded into white noise as the anger of the man gave way to the visceral, bloodthirsty rage of the darkness within him.

He could feel his Merrick blood rising, his fangs beginning to slip free of his gums, heavy and sharp in his mouth. Could feel the Merrick's dark, predatory desire to rip out the bastard's throat. The tips of the fingers he'd wrapped around Capshaw's throat suddenly burned, and he grunted from the sharp slice of pain as deadly talons began to pierce through his skin. Punching against his insides, the Merrick struggled to slip free, but it was too weak to fully break its way out of him. Using every ounce of strength he possessed, Riley forced the beast into submission, knowing he couldn't let it have what it wanted. Which was Capshaw's blood. His life. And while he had no problem killing as a man, if it meant protecting those he cared about, he didn't want to kill like a monster.

For a split second he turned his face to the side, away

from the temptation of Capshaw's throat as a flash of
lightning arced across the sky, and the Merrick finally
retreated, allowing Riley to finish the asshole off.
Quickly jerking Capshaw to his feet with his left hand
clamped on the guy's muddy shirt, Riley pulled back
his fist, then smashed it into the bastard's face, sending
him sprawling headfirst into the mud. Capshaw went
down hard…and stayed down.

While Riley stood there, his chest heaving as he stared
down at Capshaw's body, Kellan came over and knelt
down beside the creep, checking his pockets. Pulling
out a motel key card, he read the name on the plastic.
"Guess he's staying over at the Pacific Point Motel. I saw
it in town." Hoisting Capshaw's body over his shoulder,
Kellan moved to his feet and said, "I'll be a pal and get
this piece of shit out of here. You going to be okay?"

He nodded as he dug his battered knuckles into his
pockets, then tossed Kellan his keys. The Watchman
loaded a groaning Capshaw into the bed of the truck,
then climbed into the cab, started the engine and drove
away. Taking a deep breath, Riley finally released his
mental hold on the back door, and a second later Hope
stormed out of the house, her hair all but standing on
end in her fury, her topaz-colored eyes glittering with
rage as she marched toward him.

Pushing his wet hair back from his face, Riley jerked
his chin toward her right hand. "Put down the knife
before you hurt yourself."

She glanced down at her hands with a look of shock,

as if surprised to find herself holding the dangerous-looking weapon. Muttering under her breath, she went back and laid it on the porch banister, then turned and pointed one shaking finger toward the house, where Millie was standing in the open doorway, looking pale with strain. "Someone needs to fix that bloody door!"

Sighing, Riley said, "There's nothing wrong with the door, Hope."

"Like hell there isn't," she argued. "The damn thing wouldn't open!"

Before he'd even thought it through, he heard himself saying, "That's because I was keeping it closed."

She gave a feminine snort, as though she thought he was making some kind of joke. "And exactly how were you doing that while you were busy kicking the shit out of Neal?"

His mouth flattened to a hard, grim line as he held her stare, the lashing rain drenching them both down to the bone. Finally, he said, "Do you really want to know?"

It wasn't so much the words, but his tone that snagged her attention, and she trembled, her eyes going wide with recollection, as if she'd suddenly just remembered something important. Quietly, she said, "I do."

"Yeah, well, I think we've had enough excitement for one night," he grunted under his breath, looking away, while dread began to curl its way through his insides, sickening and cold.

He'd just started to turn away, figuring it was better just to get the hell out of there, before he said anything else that was going to raise her suspicions, when her next words stopped him in his tracks. "I saw what happened."

Shoving his hands deep in his pockets, he braced himself as he looked into her eyes. "I'm sorry you had to see the fight, Hope. But that asshole started it."

She shook her head, blinking from the rain that was pattering against her face. "I don't mean the fighting, Riley. I mean…what happened *while* you were fighting him. Just before you knocked him out. I saw your hands. Your…teeth."

Doing his best to keep his voice low and even, he said, "It's storming like crazy out here, Hope. I doubt you were able to see much of anything."

"I think you'd be surprised," she argued, and he knew she wasn't going to just let it go. Wasn't going to let him blow it off as a trick of the lightning…the torrential weather.

Hoping like hell that he could make her understand, Riley closed the distance between them, lifting one hand from his pocket with the intention of pushing her hair back from her face. But as he approached her, she took a quick step back, scrambling away from him. He flinched, as if she'd slapped him, and his hand fell, hanging loosely at his side.

Her chest was rising and falling with the force of her breathing, her mouth opening and closing twice before she finally managed to say, "I think I should go inside now."

Riley stared, while an angry rush of words that needed to be said got jammed up in his throat. Not that she gave him the chance to say anything. She simply looked into his eyes one last time, searching, seeking, then turned around and quickly made her back inside the house, shutting the door behind her.

CHAPTER TEN

Hunched within a thick hooded jacket, Gregory De-Kreznick made his way along the wooded outskirts of town, thinking over the scene he'd just witnessed from the cover of the woods, the rain masking his scent so that he could watch undetected. He didn't like the idea of anyone screwing with the Merrick's woman—unless that someone was him. The only reason she was still breathing was because he'd decided to wait for the perfect moment before having his fun with her. And until that time came, he was getting a kick out of messing with Buchanan's mind. He knew it had to be wearing ol' Riley down, waiting for Gregory to make his play for the tempting little brunette. Knew the gnawing worry had to be eating the guy raw inside, and he actually grinned a little at the thought.

Slipping through the rainy night, he made sure he wasn't being followed, same as he'd been doing since leaving Westmore's headquarters back in Colorado several weeks ago. He didn't want Westmore's goons following after him, doing their best to cover his kills. Where was the fun in that? No, he wanted the bodies

found. Wanted Buchanan to know that he was close…
and waiting. Wanted to enjoy watching him sweat, wondering when Gregory would strike out against the ones
he cared about…the ones who *meant* something to him.

And while he hungered for Buchanan's blood, he
was feeling better than he had in a long while. The
college girl on Saturday had been sweeter than he'd
expected, fighting him to the bitter, bloody end. He was
still riding high on the memory of that perfect moment
when he'd finally given her a taste of what she was in
for. When he'd allowed his fangs to slip free, and buried
them deep in one of her pale, quivering breasts. Her terrified, pain-filled scream had startled the birds from the
trees, leaving the forest around them silent and still, so
that he could hear her every whimper…every breathless
sob as he set about showing her just how foolish she'd
been to wander off with a stranger.

Smiling at the recollection, Gregory was just about to
head out of the woods, walking into the parking lot of a
local bar, when a tall, bald behemoth stepped into his
path, the man's ice-blue eyes telling him that he faced
another Casus. Though the human host was a stranger to
Gregory, it took him a moment or two to discern the
guy's true identity, same as he'd done with Pasha.

"Miles," he purred, unable to recall the bastard's last
name, but then they'd never been on speaking terms.
Miles was one of those sanctimonious assholes who
perpetually kissed Calder's sainted backside, which
meant that Gregory had always avoided him like the

plague. "I should have known you'd be coming along sooner or later. Did Calder send you here to keep an eye on us? Make sure we're all being good little soldiers?"

Shaking his head, the Casus said, "I'm here to offer some advice, Gregory. If you're smart, you'll take it."

"Let me guess," he drawled, rocking back on his heels as he pushed his hands into the pockets of his jeans. "Calder wants me to be a good boy and stop messing with his precious little plans. Am I right? Is that what you were sent here to tell me?"

"The time for warnings is over," Miles grunted. "You were already told to follow the rules. Since you refuse to obey your orders, they've made you public enemy number one. They're waging war against you, Gregory. Giving orders to kill you. You need to report in to Westmore and make amends. If we're going to win this war, we need to stand together. We can't afford to lose you."

"Actually," he murmured, "I like standing on my own. Never was any good at playing with others."

"If you don't abide by the rules and help Calder acquire the Markers," Miles argued, "there will be consequences."

He lifted his shoulders with an indolent shrug. "I have nothing, so there's nothing they can take away from me."

Miles's icy gaze narrowed. "Don't be so sure about that."

"And just what is that supposed to mean?" Gregory rasped, not liking the insinuation behind the Casus's quiet words.

"Just think about what I've told you," Miles murmured. "They're not happy with you, Gregory. Not at all."

"Aw, now you're just breaking my heart."

He expected the man to keep arguing, but Miles just
shook his head again and headed back into the shadowed forest. Gregory stood for a moment in the silvery
threads of moonlight, thinking over what the Casus had
said, then shook off his uneasiness with a muttered
growl. So what if Calder and Westmore were gunning
for him? They didn't scare him. And he sure as hell
wasn't going to head back, kissing up, promising to be
their golden boy just so that he could get back in their
good graces. Screw that. He worked for no one but
himself.

As he made his way through the town, he thought for
a minute of calling Pasha, then brushed off the idea.
They'd made their deal. If she decided to screw him
over, he would see to it that she paid for the mistake. And
for the moment, she had her uses. She was doing a
stellar job at staying close to the shifter, but then she
always had done some of her best work on her back. The
Watchman had no clue he was playing bedroom
Olympics with the enemy, and by the time he realized
his mistake, it would be too late. She would keep her
pulse on the Marker situation through the Watchman,
and once it'd been found, she would put her plan into
action. The shifter would be taken into their possession, then used to draw out the others. Knowing Pasha,
she'd probably carve off pieces of him, one by one,

tossing them out like bait, until the others came running. And once they did, she and Gregory would finally have what they wanted. Which was all three Buchanans in one place, at one time. Pasha would get the sheriff, and Gregory would not only get the pleasure of stripping the skin from that eldest son of a bitch who'd killed his brother, but also of the little sister. He'd do Ian quick, satisfying the bloodlust, and then play it slow with Saige, using her to quench his other, more interesting desires.

It was perfect, but for the Miles issue. After so many hellish years in Meridian, Gregory had grown comfortable with hatred and rage. They had become his constant companions, along with the relentless, gnawing ache for escape and revenge. Now that he was free, he was enjoying the human banquet of opportunity that surrounded him. But tonight, he needed something with meaning…and he knew just who to use. The human was a cocky bastard, which always made it more satisfying. With a soft smile on his lips, Gregory made his way to the motel he'd heard the shifter mention after the fight. A hundred-dollar bill at the front desk bought him the information he needed, as well as the assurance of privacy.

His smile broadened when he saw that the room faced toward the forest, which would make for an easy escape. Raising his hand, he knocked against the pale green wood.

"What do you want?" Capshaw sneered as he jerked open the door, a hand towel pressed beneath his bloodied nose.

"You," Gregory drawled, his fist slashing forward and connecting with the center of the man's chest. The violent blow shoved the human halfway across the room. Walking inside, Gregory locked the door behind him.

Capshaw scrambled to his feet and tried to fight back, but Gregory was too strong…too powerful. *The first bite is always the sweetest,* he thought, sinking his fangs into the human's shoulder and coming away with a warm, bloodied chunk of meat. The sound that came out of Capshaw was like something from a terrorized child, and he was forced to slice his claws across the human's throat—just enough to keep him from screaming…but *not* enough to kill. Not while he was still having so much fun.

As Capshaw tried to crawl away, Gregory tilted back his head, spread his arms wide and allowed the rest of the change to flow over him. His shredded clothes fell to the floor, and then he dropped to all fours, a low, graveled laugh surging up from his monstrous chest as he stalked toward his prey. "And now," he drawled, the graveled words distorted by the muzzled shape of his mouth, "it's time to let the games begin."

CHAPTER ELEVEN

Tuesday evening

AS THE SUN FINALLY bled into the horizon, the sky bloomed with one last violent burst of color, streams of deep ochre and crimson cutting into the heavens like a patchwork of painful wounds, while the clouds bled an endless stream of rain-colored tears. The ominous, dramatic imagery fit Riley's mood to perfection, considering they'd just endured another day of foul-weathered searching that had turned up nothing. Saige had been all apologies when she'd called that afternoon, upset that she hadn't been able to pinpoint the Marker's exact location. None of them wanted to consider the possibility that the cross might have already been found. Might already be in the hands of the enemy.

They'd searched for as long as they could, until the weather had eventually halted their efforts. Kellan had already headed into town, despite Riley's arguments, claiming that he was too frustrated to pace the cabin with him, leaving Riley to brood alone.

Though they'd visited the café for breakfast and

lunch, Riley hadn't seen Hope the entire day. He and
Kellan had talked with Millie, who assured them that
Neal Capshaw hadn't called or tried to put in another
appearance, and Riley had already made a few calls,
getting in touch with the bastard's parole officer. If
Capshaw had any sense, he'd hightail his ass back to
North Carolina and stay there, never setting foot in
Purity again.

Millie had also claimed that Hope was working in the
back office for the day, buried in paperwork, but Riley
knew when he was being avoided—not that he blamed
her. She was only doing what was smart. What was
sane. She'd wanted to use him for pleasure—to finally
scratch the itch that had been burning beneath both their
skins for far too many years. She wasn't looking to get
pulled into the middle of his nightmare. Not for the
simple sake of lust…for pleasure. And certainly not
with someone who was more monster than man. Things
might have worked out for his brother and sister, but
Riley knew he couldn't expect Hope to embrace what
he was, what he was becoming, for the simple fact that
she was *not* in love with him.

If he had half a brain, he'd be relieved that she now
knew better than to get anywhere near him. She'd keep
her distance, which would hopefully keep her safe…as
well as make things infinitely more simple for the
duration of his stay. He could find the Marker, get the
hell out of town and take the Casus with him. Find some
remote place to stand his ground, and that would be that.

And yet he couldn't deny the rush of emotion that swept through his body when he drew in a deep breath and caught her scent blowing in through the screen door. The blinding, burning spill of relief that came just from having her near. It felt so right, when everything else had gone so impossibly wrong.

Riley watched the door, waiting for her to come into sight, her warm, mouthwatering scent filling his head...his senses. Filling the places that had been hungry and empty and wanting for the past thirteen miserable years of his life. And while he couldn't deny how good it felt to see her, he dreaded what he knew was coming. What she'd come there for. Dreaded having to tell her the truth about his family and the Merrick and the Casus, knowing damn well it was going to send her running.

And maybe that wasn't all bad. Maybe it would be the thing that finally got her out of town, away from Purity, so that he could stop living in fear of her being hurt because of him.

She came up the porch steps and peered through the screen, opening it and stepping inside the instant she spotted him leaning his shoulders against the stone-faced fireplace. Her long, windblown hair was damp from the rain—her face dewy and freshly scrubbed, without any makeup to detract from the purity of her natural beauty. She wore a long, loose gray sweater that hung off one shoulder, along with jeans and her boots. Small silver hoops shone in her ears; her only other jewelry a silver ring that she wore on her right thumb.

"You know why I'm here," she said in a low voice, crossing her arms beneath her breasts as she stared straight at him with those beautiful, topaz-colored eyes, their thick lashes casting shadows against the luminous curve of her cheeks.

"After last night, I'm surprised you aren't afraid to come here alone," he drawled, and there was no mistaking the bitterness that flavored his words.

She winced, but she didn't back down. Instead, she moved farther into the spacious room, taking a seat on the foot of his bed. Rubbing her palms against her thighs, she pulled her lower lip through her teeth, then quietly said, "I'm sorry I reacted the way that I did last night, Riley. It was just too much, on top of everything else." Pressing one hand against her chest, she said, "I didn't mean to hurt you. I just… I didn't have any room inside to process it."

"And what changed?" he grunted, making sure the hem of his T-shirt was covering his fly. It was hardly the time for a hard-on, considering his mood—not to mention the circumstances—but Hope was sitting on his bed, looking so beautiful and tender and soft, there wasn't any goddamn way he could stop it from happening.

"What changed is that I finally calmed down," she said in response to his question. "To be honest, I've spent most of the day trying to find the courage to face you, Riley. Not because of what I saw. I know it doesn't make any sense. I mean, you'd think I'd be terrified, right? But…" Her voice trailed off with a nervous flutter of laughter, and she lowered her gaze as she lifted her shoulders in a baffled, what-the-hell-is-happening kind of gesture. The laughter faded, and she drew in a deep, trembling breath, staring at her hands as they fisted into tight little knots on the tops of her thighs. "I don't know. The hardest thing is facing you, after what happened with Neal. It's so embarrassing. All of it. The fact that I married such a horrible person." With another deep breath, she lifted her gaze, trapping him with its honesty…its strength. "I found the courage to come here, and now I'm hoping you can find the courage to tell me the truth. Because I think I deserve it, Riley. After everything that's happened. I think I have a right to know what you're hiding."

Guilt crept up around the backs of his ears, and he tore his gaze away, staring out the window at the darkening forest, his heart beginning to beat with a hard, heavy rhythm as he watched the fog begin to twine itself around the trunks of the trees. His throat felt tight…his face hot. "It's ugly, Hope." His voice was low…gritty, like something that'd been crushed and ground into gravel.

"And my past isn't?" she asked, giving a hard, brittle laugh.

"This isn't just my past," he grunted, scraping one hand back through his hair in a frustrated gesture. "It's my future."

She absorbed that for a moment, then simply said, "No more lies, Riley. Just tell me what's going on."

Worried about what he might accidentally "move" with his newfound power, he shoved his hands into his pockets and made his way to the window, giving her his back. "You're better off not knowing, Hope. You have no idea how badly I wish *I* didn't know."

"What?" she asked. "How bad can it be? Are you a vampire? A werewolf? Do you turn into some kind of giant green hulk?"

Despite his frustration, a ragged laugh tore from his throat at the image her words created. "No, honey. I don't go green." He blew out a rough breath, shaking his head as he forced himself just to get it out. There was no way to sugarcoat it…to make it pretty. The truth was more often than not an ugly, raw slice of reality, and he was about to dish her out an entire plateful. "But Kellan, yeah," he admitted in a low, shaky voice. "He's a…werewolf. I know how freaking insane that sounds, but it's true. Kell's brother, too. Though I think they prefer being called lycans."

He tensed, waiting for her reaction, anticipating anything from laughter to hysterics to anger, but a heavy, thoughtful silence was all that met his hoarse confession. Looking over his shoulder, he could only shake his head at how composed she looked, sitting there on the bed with her hands folded in her lap, the curious, trusting expression in her eyes saying that she was waiting for him to go on. God only knew she hadn't reacted the way most people would, but then he'd already known that Hope was unique. Special. She'd always looked at the world a little differently than everyone else, so maybe that would be his saving grace in getting her to understand the dark, sometimes terrifying, extraordinary world he'd become a part of.

Or maybe she just doesn't believe a word you've said....

Before he could dwell on that particular thought, she took a deep, shivery breath, swiped her tongue against the lush swell of her lower lip, then softly said, "And what about you? What are you, Riley?"

He turned back toward the window and hunched his shoulders, wryly aware of the fact that he couldn't look at her and say the things he had to say. Not with her sitting there watching him with that quiet intensity, taking in every nuance of his expression, every flicker of emotion in his eyes. He was too stripped down to his base elements, his face too open, revealing all the brutal, vulnerable details. He had no padding…no cushion to protect himself if it all came crashing down around him.

Bracing one arm high on the windowsill, Riley narrowed his eyes, focusing on the steady, hypnotic rhythm of the rain as he tried to sort out where to begin. He cleared his throat with a cough, then finally said, "You know my mother, Elaina, was a…a little out there."

"Just a little," she agreed, and he could hear the smile in her voice…could feel the warmth of her gaze on the back of his neck, watchful, encouraging…and waiting for him to get on with it.

Riley took a deep breath, and then the words just sort of started pouring out of him in a deep, husky rumble, the pressure in his chest growing lighter with each confession, as he began to explain everything from the beginning. He started with his mother's stories of the Merrick and the Casus, explaining about her obsession with the family bloodline. Then he told her about Ian's awakening, and the Watchmen, and the gypsy legend that spoke of the Casus one day returning to this world, causing the Merrick awakenings to begin. He told her about the victims who had been killed…about the search for the Markers, explaining that they still didn't know why the Casus and the man named Westmore wanted them so badly. He even told her about the "Buchanan gifts" and the strange power that seemed to be growing within him, enabling him to control objects with his mind, which he'd used to keep the door to her house closed during his fight with Neal.

Hope remained silent through it all, listening to his story as the rain continued to fall on the roof in a steady, comforting cadence, and before he knew it, he'd told her everything. Every detail…except for one. Though Riley knew she deserved the whole truth, he couldn't bring himself to tell her about the night he'd taken part in the "vision" ritual that had changed his life. Instead, he simply told her that once the Marker had been found, he would have to go in search of the next one, helping his family as best he could.

She didn't comment on the last part, though he could

sense that she wanted to as he turned around. Meeting her dark, curious gaze, he said, "So that's…it. Crazy, I know. But unfortunately, very, very true."

"I have a few questions," she murmured, and for the next half hour, she proceeded to grill him in detail about the things he had told her. She asked questions about the Casus, wanting to know more about Gregory and his quest for revenge. About Riley's power and how it worked, as well as the strange gifts that Ian and Saige possessed. Then she asked about Saige and the maps, and he explained how his sister had found the first Marker in Italy, and then once she had the maps, was able to use them to locate the second cross…and now hopefully the third.

She also asked about Seth McConnell, and Riley went into greater detail about how he and the Watchmen unit in Colorado had come to be allies with a man who, as an officer in the Collective Army, had once been their mortal enemy. He told her about how a troubled Seth had contacted them after learning that the Collective Generals had partnered up with a man named Westmore in a dangerous alliance, and were now allowing their greed for the information Westmore had promised them to justify his association with the Casus. He also explained why they believed, especially after Kellan's attack the previous night, that Westmore's personal unit of soldiers were anything but human.

She seemed fascinated as he told her the story of how he, Ian and the Watchmen, along with Seth and some of the soldiers who remained loyal to him, had gone into Westmore's headquarters to rescue Saige several weeks ago. That's when they'd first realized that Westmore and his men weren't human, seeing as how the bodies they'd taken down on their way into the house were no longer there on their way out. They still didn't know what species Westmore was, or if the Collective had their own suspicions about the man…or if they still believed he was as human as the Collective soldiers themselves, but McConnell was in the field, doing his best to get them answers. As an officer who was now working against the directives of his superiors, McConnell's position was a dangerous one, and they knew his life was on the line.

When he'd finally told her everything he could think of, Riley lifted one hand, rubbing at the knotted tension cramping through the back of his neck, and said, "So, I…uh, I know that you'd probably like me and Kellan to leave now, but we can't. Not until we've got that third Marker. If we go, you and Millie will still be in danger so long as it's buried on your land. But I give you my word that I'll stay away from you, keep my distance. Just…so long as you promise that you won't take any chances with your safety. Especially with the Casus out there, not to mention Gregory, who'd love to find a way to screw with my mind."

"Riley—" she began, making a move as if to stand up, but he cut her off, adding, "And it's…uh, a given that I won't try to touch you again. Hell, I didn't have any right to do it in the first place. I knew it was wrong…dangerous, especially considering the hunger that's twisting me up inside, getting more intense every day. I shouldn't have touched you the way I did in the kitchen, but I just… I had to have at least that much," he rasped, forcing the words from his tight throat as he turned, staring sightlessly out at the rain-drenched forest.

He counted the beats of his heart, until he heard the rustle of movement as she stood up. "Why do you think I'd want you to leave now?" she asked. "That I no longer want what I asked you for last night?"

A dry, gritty rumble of laughter vibrated in his chest. "You don't have to lie, Hope. I don't blame you for changing your mind. I understand."

"Actually, I don't think you understand me at all. Not if you think I don't want you."

The beats of his heart became harder…heavier, and he turned his head, slanting her a dark, questioning look over his shoulder. "What *are* you talking about?"

She pushed her hands into her pockets and lifted her shoulders, a small, kind of lopsided smile tucked into the corner of that soft, beautiful mouth that made him want to pull her into his arms and kiss some goddamn sense into her. "I trust you, Riley."

"Christ," he muttered as he turned back around, wondering what in hell he was going to do about her. "You look all grown up, Hope, but you're still as starry-eyed as ever, aren't you?"

"You know that's not true," she argued, a strange, surreal sense of calm surrounding her that made him feel shaky, off balance.

"Is it that you weren't listening, or do you just not believe me?" he demanded in a clipped, hard-edged tone that lashed out like a whip, cracking and sharp. "Honest to God, Hope. Open your damn eyes. Even if you're crazy enough not to care that I want to sink a pair of friggin' fangs in your throat, think about what I have to offer you. Nothing. That's it. A couple of hot, sweaty minutes of pleasure, and then I'll be gone. If you'd think about it, you'd realize that you don't want me coming anywhere near you. You're not that kind of woman."

Instead of storming out, as he'd fully expected, she took a step closer to him. The soft glow of the bedside lamp burned behind her, casting a deep, lustrous shine to the warm, heavy fall of her hair as it draped over her shoulders, her eyes heavy as she took her time studying his expression. His face tingled as she studied his eyes…the angle of his jaw…the grim set of his mouth. When she was finally holding his gaze again, she said, "I know this is going to come as a monumental shock to you, Ri, but I *am* all grown up now, and fully capable of knowing what I want. To be honest, a few hot, sweaty moments of pleasure would be about the best damn thing I've ever had. And you don't have the first idea about what kind of woman I am. I want to use you for some hot sex, get you out of my system, and then I'll wave goodbye when you walk back out my door."

Feeling as if he was standing on a boat in the midst of a churning, thrashing sea, Riley struggled to get his feet steady beneath him, but the entire goddamn world seemed to be shifting on him, throwing him off balance. Working for his voice, he managed to scrape out a few thick, graveled words. "That's exactly what will happen, Hope. I'll walk out, and this time, you won't ever see me again. I won't stay."

Her eyes went wide with a tender shock of surprise. "Did you really think I would expect you to?"

He stared, not a single clue what to say.

"I know you'll leave, Riley. God, even if you could stay, why would you? I'll be honest and admit that I'm a hopeless romantic. I still believe in true love and happily-ever-afters. I believe in hopes and dreams and beauty. Just…just not for all of us. Some of us, we have to take what we can get. Despite being a dreamer, I'm not a child. I'm not stupid, and I know better than to wish for things that I can never have. But I'm still greedy. I still want to enjoy you while you're here. Want to get my fill of you, while I still have the chance."

He got it then, the realization nearly knocking him back on his ass. Jesus, she honestly didn't think she was worth it. Worth the commitment and devotion and worship that she so rightly deserved. Riley would have laughed at the irony of it, if it wasn't so bloody painful. Hope Summers, the most beautiful, wonderful thing he'd ever known. The only thing that had held him together all these years. Knowing that she was out there somewhere—living, breathing, existing—it had somehow given him the strength to walk that straight-assed path he'd followed, rather than sinking down like Ian had done. And he wouldn't have had the force of will to pull himself out of the pit the way his brother had. He'd have sunk deeper…and deeper, until the end he knew was coming had no longer mattered. It would have been easier, but cowardly. And it was his memories of Hope that had kept him from taking that dive. Even knowing that she must hate his guts, he'd clung to those memories, desperate to be the kind of man she would have been proud of.

But he'd known, as a given fact, that he could never have her. It was one of those moon rising at night and shifting of the tides kinds of things. Not up for question…for debate. And as such, he could *not* get his damn head around the fact that he was standing in that room, with her smiling at him…looking so beautiful and sexy and soft that it made him tremble, offering him one last, fleeting shot at paradise, while he still had the chance to grab it.

A chance you can't take, jackass. No matter how badly you want it.

"You're not thinking clearly, Hope. Not thinking it through," he rasped, knowing he had to find a way to make her see the light. Because God only knew he couldn't mount this fight on his own. He'd never stand a chance. She'd barrel through his determination like a force of nature, and the next thing he knew, he'd have her on that bed, beneath him, with his cock buried so deep inside her, he could feel her heartbeat…the heat of her soul. "I'm not the man you think I am. Hell, I'm hardly even a man at all. Sex with me, it wouldn't be rosy and soft and nice. That's not the way I am. Even if I wanted to be, there's too much of the Merrick rising up inside me, and with each hour that goes by, its hunger is scraping me raw, wearing me down. I wouldn't be able to control myself. My fangs will come out…my hands will change, just like last night. And I haven't forgotten that look you had on your face when you saw them."

She winced, giving a small, embarrassed shake of her head. "I'm sorry. It just… It took me by surprise. I just needed some time to work it out in my head, but I…I should have known that there would be a good explanation."

"You call this good?" he barked, another bitter burst of laughter rumbling in his chest. "Christ, I'd hate to hear your idea of a bad one."

A frown settled across her brow as she said, "I've always known there was something…something different about your family, Riley. Granted, I never could have imagined it was something quite like this. But…to be honest, I shouldn't have been so surprised."

"Yeah, well, I've known about it forever," he offered in a wry, cynical drawl, "and it still shocks the hell out of me. So don't be so hard on yourself."

HOPE COULD TELL he was using sarcasm as a defense mechanism, just as she could tell that there were things he wasn't telling her. Despite the bizarre, chilling explanations he'd given her, there was something he was holding on to…hiding it behind that dark, tormented gaze. And after everything else that she'd heard, Hope was almost afraid to know what it was. At the moment, it was taking all her strength, all her courage, just to accept the things he'd told her…and to keep fighting for what she wanted. Which was Riley, for however short a time she could have him.

"I won't say that it doesn't make me a little nervous, the idea of what's inside you. But it isn't going to scare me away. I still trust you with my life," she told him, and it was true. She just didn't trust him with her heart, which was why she had to keep reminding herself that what she wanted from him was purely sexual. No promises. No emotions.

And do you really think that saying it over and over is going to make it true? It doesn't work that way, Hope. You know that.

Ignoring the quietly worded question, she took another step toward him, adding, "I meant what I said, Riley. I still want you."

He lifted his right hand with its battered knuckles and scraped his fingers through his hair, his eyes blazing with a torrent of emotion. "It's not going to happen, Hope. I won't do that to you. I *can't*. You don't deserve it."

"That's my decision to make, not yours," she argued, struggling to find a way to get through to him.

"Just…stop," he growled, holding up his hand as she tried to close the distance between them. "Please." He looked tired, the deep hollows carved into his cheeks only accentuating his haunting beauty. He was impossibly gorgeous, not to mention mouthwateringly sexy, but it was the shadow of fear…of soul-deep need that darkened his beautiful blue eyes that tore at her. Made her ache to touch him and hold him and offer him everything that she could. But he was so set on arguing…on fighting it to the bitter end.

"I don't get it," she whispered. "I could see you being afraid to touch me because you didn't want me finding out the truth. Didn't want to frighten me. But I know the truth now, so what's the problem? I won't glom on to you. Won't expect anything you aren't willing to give. Won't beg you to stay, when I know you're so set on going. If you meant all those things you said last night, then why not just do it, Riley? Why not just give me what I want? After everything that's happened, damn it, you owe it to me!"

Shoving his hands into his pockets, he held his jaw with a rigid tension as he said, "You might know the truth, Hope. Might claim you're not afraid of me. But that doesn't change anything. The Casus are still out there, waiting. Watching. Getting involved with me would just put you in deeper, deadlier danger."

A shaky, tremulous burst of laughter spilled from her

mouth, making him scowl. Holding up her hands, she said, "I'm sorry. I know this isn't funny. But think about it, Riley. I think the cat's already out of the bag on that one. You just beat the crap out of the school bully behind the bleachers for me. The gig is up."

"What the hell are you talking about?"

"It's a metaphor," she explained, wishing there was some way to smooth the hard, jagged edges of his tension, his body held in a visible clutch of strain. "If the Casus are out there, well, it's got to be common knowledge by now that we have a history. Our sleeping together isn't going to change that fact, or make it any worse. So you're going to have to do better than that."

"Damn it," he growled, his hard, lean muscles shaking with some violent, explosive force of emotion, while his sharp male energy blasted against her, burning her face. "This isn't a damned joke. If the Casus get their hands on you, you're going to wish you were never born, Hope. They get off on pain…torture, and then they'll rip you to pieces. That's a helluva thing to risk for a woman I don't love. For one I don't plan on sticking around to protect. One I'm using for sex until I find what I want and then haul my ass out of town."

His words struck with the painful force of a blow, just as he'd meant for them to. But she wasn't going to crumple so easily. With her hands clutched into damp, shaking fists, she wet her bottom lip, then carefully said, "I'm not asking you to love me, Riley. I'm not even asking you to stay. All I want is to know what it's like to be under you, with you inside me. To be a part of you, for however long you're here. And if the Casus do decide to come after me, then the closer we are, the easier it'll be for you to protect me."

He flinched, saying, "God, Hope, don't do that."

There was a tremor to his words that tugged at her heart, making her want to wrap him up in her arms and hold him, offering the comfort he so obviously needed. "What, Riley? What is it that you don't want me to do?"

"Put your faith in me," he rasped, the hoarse words shaky and rough. "I'm warning you right now. It's a bad move."

She could tell from his expression, from the haunted look in his deep blue eyes, that for whatever reason, he still saw himself as a threat to her. "What aren't you telling me, Riley?"

He stared into her eyes for a long, breathless moment, then gave a curt shake of his head. "I can't, Hope. I just…can't."

She didn't know if he meant the sex…or the confession or, hell, maybe he meant both. But she could see from the strain of his expression that he wasn't going to give in.

And when he turned his back on her, his broad, powerful shoulders hard with a gripping tension beneath the soft cotton of his shirt, Hope took it for the final rejection she knew it was meant to be.

"Watch your back," she whispered, her own shoulders heavy with the weight of disappointment. Despite how hard she'd tried, she still couldn't get through to him. "Just…don't take any chances, Riley. Millie and I are being careful, but you need to make sure that you look out for yourself."

Then she turned, walked out the door and headed back into the rain.

CHAPTER TWELVE

Wednesday morning

THE SECOND KELLAN touched his shoulder, Riley's eyes flew open, the grim look on the Watchman's face warning him that something had happened. Something bad. "What?" he croaked, jerking up into a sitting position. "What is it? Is Hope all right?"

"She's fine," Kellan told him, stepping back and sitting down on the second double bed. "It's the bastard ex."

"I'm going to kill him," Riley growled, throwing back the sheet as he surged to his feet, grabbing the jeans that he'd laid on the foot of his bed. "Where is he? If he's so much as laid a hand on her, I'm going to—"

"Riley, man, calm down," Kellan murmured, holding up his hands. "I told you that Hope's fine. But Capshaw is dead."

He froze, his fingers gripping onto handfuls of denim so hard that his knuckles were white. "What do you mean he's dead? How can he be dead?"

"They found his body in his motel room," Kellan explained. "He'd been torn up...bitten. Hell, you know the routine. They think it happened late Monday night, and the cops don't have a clue what's going on. I feel sorry for the bastards. No matter how hard they try, they're going to have a heck of a time getting to the bottom of this one."

"His fingers?" Riley grunted, trying to wrap his head around it. The noise in his brain was deafening—a jumbled, crashing blend of his pulse and too many angry, condemning voices all shouting at once.

"His fingers were missing, same as the girl up in Wellsford," Kellan said with a tired sigh. "Which means Gregory's body count is stacking up. He's still hanging around, but God only knows what he's waiting for. I'm starting to find it hard to believe he's still just biding his time, waiting for us to find that bloody Marker."

"I don't like it," he muttered, buttoning his fly and pulling on a T-shirt, then reaching for the shoulder holster and gun that he'd left on the bedside table. "You're right. He wouldn't be this patient, unless he had a reason."

"And why go after the ex?" Kellan asked as he leaned forward, bracing his elbows on his spread knees, his hands clasped loosely together between his legs. "Gregory must know that no one's going to be upset over that asshole's loss. Least of all you."

Checking to make sure he had a full clip in the Beretta, Riley snapped the gun into the holster. "How did you hear?" he asked, dreading having to face Hope after this…and wondering just how she was taking it.

"Millie told me when I went up to the house for some coffee."

Clearing his throat, Riley glanced through the window at the pouring rain that would make it impossible to dig before it let up, and said, "What was Hope doing? How's she taking it?"

"I didn't see her, but Millie said she was holding together. Thinks she's more shocked than anything else right now. She was working in the kitchen when I left, keeping busy."

Riley wanted to go to the café and check on her, but couldn't get past the idea that she might slap his face when she saw him. Couldn't get past the fear that she might finally look at him and with hatred and revulsion for the chaos he was wreaking on her life.

Picking up his phone, he stared down at the keypad, thinking he could call her first…try to get a read on her that way. She might scream at him, but he could take it. He just needed to hear her voice, damn it. To know that she was okay.

Punching in the number, he lifted the phone to his ear. She picked up on the first ring, saying, "Riley, thank God. I was just getting ready to call you."

He could tell by the tone of her voice that something was wrong. Something more immediate than Neal Capshaw's murder. "What's going on? Are you okay?"

"I'm fine," she answered in swift reply, though he could hear a tremor that sounded suspiciously like fear in her words. Before he could question her, she said, "But there's someone in the café. He hasn't done anything. Just ordered some coffee and took a table over in the far corner of the room. But there's a really weird vibe about him. I don't know. I mean, I feel crazy for bothering you, but after Neal—"

"What's he look like?" he asked, cutting her off as he started pulling on his boots.

"Attractive. Muscled and tall, like you and Kellan. Chin-length, golden-brown hair." She paused, then lowered her voice as she said, "But his eyes are what's strange. I swear they're the same pale, icy blue you told me the Casus have, even when they're in human form."

"Stay the hell away from him," he ordered, his heart racing as he snatched up a flannel shirt to cover his gun. He jerked his chin toward Kellan, who'd already moved to his feet, signaling that they needed to go. "And don't go anywhere by yourself," he was saying as they went through the door. "In fact, make Millie stay in the front with you, behind the counter. We're on our way."

Filling Kellan in while they ran like hell for the house, Riley knew that no more than thirty seconds had passed by before they reached the café. He spotted the human-looking Casus the second he ripped open the front door, the blast of warm air doing little to ease the cold burn of fear twisting through his insides. Not for his own life, but for those of the people around him. Hope, Millie, Kellan. The innocent customers enjoying breakfast on a rainy Wednesday morning.

The Casus was sitting at one of the back tables in the far corner of the café, just as Hope had said. He was wearing a black T-shirt and a cocky smile, his muscular arms crossed on the tabletop. A cup of coffee sat before him, and as he watched Kellan move to Riley's side, their bodies held hard and tight with predatory aggression, he lifted the mug to his smiling lips for a drink, acting as though he didn't have a care in the world.

Riley had known, the instant he set eyes on him, that it was Gregory.

Casting a swift glance at Hope and Millie to make sure they were behind the counter, Riley stalked toward the table. "You have a lot of nerve coming here," he rasped, careful to keep his voice low. "What do you want?"

"You know what I want," the monster drawled, leaning back in his chair. He lifted one sun-darkened hand and scratched lazily at his chest. "But for now, I just wanted to gloat a little. Maybe even hear a thank-you for ridding you of that worthless worm of a human. God, you should have seen him. It was pathetic, how he refused to give in. And the harder he fought—" he paused as his smile widened, looking somehow grotesque as it spread across his face "—the longer I made it last."

Riley heard the breathless sound that Hope made, and flinched, knowing he'd brought this on her…that he'd dragged it into her world. This violence and evil and danger. He might not have killed Capshaw, but he was the reason the man had been targeted. The reason he was dead.

And that means this asshole knows about Hope. Knows your dark, dangerous little secret.

Shaking off the terrifying thought, Riley focused on keeping the fear out of his eyes as he listened to Gregory say, "I realize I was doing you a favor, which…let's face it…just isn't my thing. But I couldn't have ol' Capshaw getting to her first, damaging what I plan to hurt. Where's the fun in that?"

"You wanna have some fun?" he snarled, the vicious, guttural rasp of his voice no longer something that was entirely human, the Merrick seething beneath his skin, outraged at the fact that it couldn't break its way out of him and tear into the murderous monster. "Let's take this someplace private, Gregory, and I'll give you all the fun you can handle."

Shaking his head, the Casus lifted one hand to push a sun-streaked lock of brown hair from his brow, a mocking note of humor in his deep voice as he said, "What's that expression? The one about writing checks that your ass can't cash? That would be you, Buchanan. Or have you forgotten that your search hasn't turned up that precious little cross you're looking for?"

Bracing his hands on the table, Riley leaned forward, knowing the Casus could see the gun resting beneath his open flannel shirt. "You never know, Gregory. Maybe I'm simply planning to put a bullet in your head, sending your ugly ass straight back to Meridian. After all the trouble you've caused, I doubt they'll be letting you out any time soon."

Gregory tilted back his head and gave a rich, husky

rumble of laughter. "Oh, God, that would be priceless, just to see the look on Calder's face."

Riley was about to ask who this Calder was, knowing that Gregory had mentioned him before to Saige, but Kellan cut in to the conversation, saying, "Where are your buddies, Gregory?"

"I'm afraid I'm playing for my own team now," the Casus drawled.

"I guess that means you have some pretty stiff competition for me then," Riley remarked in a gritty slide of words. "Worried someone is going to get to me first, Gregory? Steal your chance for revenge? I know there's at least one Casus who you're poaching on. I doubt they're going to be very happy with you."

"You mean the one who jump-started you?" The corner of the Casus's mouth kicked up in a knowing smile. "Don't worry, Merrick. I have things under control." Sniffing the air, he added, "And at any rate, you're still not ripe enough yet. They're all just going to bide their time, which leaves the playing field wide-open for me." Leaning forward, he lowered his voice to a soft, husky whisper as he said, "And who do you think I'm going to play with next? Any guesses?"

One second the Casus was sitting there wearing a shit-ass grin, and in the next Riley had his hands fisted in the fabric of Gregory's shirt, ripping him to his feet and slamming him against the back wall of the café. Behind them, there was a mad scrambling of bodies as customers moved to put distance between themselves and what they probably thought was going to turn into a fight. Thankfully, there was no one sitting at the nearby tables, but they still had the attention of every person in the room.

"Riley!" Hope called out, and he watched her move closer from the corner of his eye, stepping from behind the counter.

Gregory gave another low, wicked rumble of laughter, something cold and evil burning in the depths of his pale, chilling gaze. "I'm going to enjoy taking you apart, Merrick. But—" he nodded his head toward Hope "—not as much as I enjoy her. For her, I'm going to do everything I can to make it last. To make it count."

It wasn't easy, but Riley refused to let Gregory get any more of a rise out of him than he already had. Choking back his fear for Hope's safety, he forced a sarcastic sound from his throat, and shook his head. "You guys need some new lines. Ian told me your brother made the same pathetic threats about his woman, and look what happened to him." Enjoying the flare of rage in the Casus's eyes, Riley leaned closer, getting right in the bastard's face as he said, "Tell me, Gregory. Will you run when I face you down with the cross? I heard you did before. Quinn and Saige told us all about how you left your buddy Royce behind to die, and ran to save your own pathetic ass."

"I was smart enough to choose my fights, Buchanan.

Going up against a Raptor with a Marker is a lot different than going up against you. And you don't have your pretty little cross yet, do you?"

"You're right, I don't," he admitted, giving a sharp smile as he lifted his brows. "So just what are you holding out for, Gregory? Why not have a go at me right now? Is it my awakening you're waiting for?" He narrowed his eyes, searching for the answers in Gregory's icy gaze. "Or is it something else?"

"I'm afraid you'll just have to wait and see," Gregory drawled, obviously not going to tell them anything more. "I hate to give away the ending."

Just wanting the son of a bitch to get the hell out of there, Riley finally released his hold on Gregory's shirt and took a step back, wishing like crazy that he had the means to go ahead and fry the asshole now. The Casus straightened his shirt, then walked to the table and tossed a wad of bills beside the empty cup of coffee. Casting a meaningful look toward Hope, he said, "Till later, sweetheart." And then he walked across the floor…and out the front door.

Riley had no more than a second to reach out and grab hold of Kellan's arm before the Watchman rushed past him. "Where do you think you're going?" he grunted, spinning the younger man back around.

Kellan shot him a look as if to say *are you crazy?* "What do you mean where am I going?" he forced out through his gritted teeth. "I'm going to follow him."

"And do what?" Riley demanded, distantly aware of

Millie doing her best to calm the other customers, assuring them that everything was fine.

"I'm going to give the son of a bitch exactly what he deserves."

"Not without a Marker you aren't," he argued, understanding only too well how Kellan felt, but knowing he couldn't just let the Watchman rush off to his death. "You might have gotten away from those Casus the other night, but Gregory isn't going to just lie down and let you rip into him, Kell. I'm not going to let you take that risk."

Vibrating with a sharp, explosive rage, Kellan said, "You don't have the authority to tell me what to do, Ri."

"But I do have a gun," he snapped.

The Watchman gave a low, sarcastic laugh. "What? Are you going to shoot me now?"

"I will if I have to. If it's going to keep you from doing something stupid."

"I'm outta here," Kellan muttered, pulling out of his hold and heading for the door.

"Damn it," he snarled, following the Watchman outside. A light, drizzling mist of rain floated on the salty wind, the crashing of the waves against the cliffs accompanied by the distant rumble of another storm brewing out over the churning gray waters of the Pacific.

"Let it go," Kellan called out over his shoulder. "He's long gone by now and there isn't a chance I could track him through this rain."

Riley braced his hands on his hips. "Then where are you going?"

"To blow off some steam. We can't dig in this weather. It's nothing but muddy slop out there right now."

Following Kellan down the cobbled path that led to the road, he asked, "And exactly who are you going to be blowing off steam with?"

"None of your damn business," Kellan grunted, turning suddenly and facing him, the dark auburn strands of his hair whipping around his pissed-off expression. "What the hell, Ri? You planning on following me all the way to town like a mother hen?"

He knew he didn't have any right telling the other man what to do, but it drove him crazy, the thought of Kellan getting killed because of him. "Just be careful. And take the truck," he told him, pulling the keys from his pocket and tossing them over.

Arching one brow, Kellan said, "Gee, thanks, Pops. Do I get an allowance now as well?"

Shaking his head, Riley muttered, "Just try not to get yourself killed. Your brother will have my ass if you do."

"I'll try," Kellan snorted, heading toward the side parking lot, where Riley's truck was parked.

Turning back toward the gray-shingled house, Riley swiped the beads of water from his face, then took out a cigarette, cupping his hands as he lit it to shelter the fragile flame from the wind and the rain. Taking a deep drag, he welcomed the burn of the smoke in his lungs, focusing on the sharp sensation as he struggled to ground himself. To find a level of calm through the rage still pounding through his blood. He wanted to go back into the house and assure himself that Hope was okay, but held back, worried. Second-guessing. Unsure of how she felt about things. Her ex's murder…him…Gregory. He didn't suppose she would be shedding any tears over Capshaw's death, but she must be frightened. And then to have Gregory showing up in the café. Christ, was she blaming him?

What kind of jackass question is that?

He grunted under his breath as he headed toward the white picket fencing that followed the cliffs, knowing only too well that he was to blame for bringing this shit down on her head. He knew he should stay away, but who gave a damn? He was tired of doing what he should. Of being the bloody Boy Scout.

"Screw it," he muttered, taking another drag on the cigarette as he headed back toward the café. Dropping the cigarette into the damp grass, he ground it out with his boot and headed inside, unsurprised to see that Hope and Millie had left two employees to deal with the front counter. Ignoring the curious, startled looks thrown his way, he headed through the kitchen, into the living room of the house. Millie was sitting on the sofa, looking tired as she sipped a cup of tea. She sent him a small smile, but he noticed the way her hand shook as she placed the cup atop the coaster on the coffee table. Hope was nowhere to be seen, and he pushed his damp hair back from his face as he said, "Is she okay?"

Millie nodded, pulling her sweater tighter around

her shoulders. "I sent her upstairs to take a hot bath. Hopefully it will help calm her down."

For a moment he wondered if Hope was soaking in a steaming tub of water, doing her best to wash away the stain he'd made on her life, but then he threw off the melodramatic idea with a scowl. Scraping his palm over his bristled jaw, he said, "She must be pretty pissed at me."

"She isn't angry," Millie corrected him, her gray gaze following him as he walked to the bay window, staring out at the back lawn. "She's worried, Riley. Terrified that something's going to happen to you."

The words hit his chest like a physical blow, stealing his breath. His throat worked as he threw a stunned look over his shoulder, and then he finally managed to say, "She's worried about *me?*"

Millie looked as if she wanted to smile. "Don't sound so surprised. You're not an idiot. You must know how she feels about you."

Turning to face her, he said, "I take it that she hasn't told you about our…uh, talk."

"No, she did," Millie corrected him again, taking another sip of her tea.

Riley went hot around his ears. "And you're still okay with me being here?" he asked. "You don't want us to leave?"

Setting down the fragile teacup, Millie said, "I'm not going to blame you for the circumstances, Riley. I'm trying to have an open mind about things, and I trust

Hope's judgment. If that cross is buried on our land, then all this would have come crashing down on us sooner or later. But Hope… I'm not sure how to explain it." She paused, her troubled gaze sliding away for a moment, before she looked him in the eye again. "She's been more alive these past few days than she has been in years. Since things went wrong between the two of you. There's a fire in her again. A spark. So, no, I don't want you to leave, Riley. I do, however, want your promise that you're going to do everything in your power to keep her safe."

"You know I will. But aren't you going to warn me not to hurt her?"

"Do I need to?" Millie asked, pinning him with a matronly gaze that would have made most men think twice about crossing her.

Cutting his gaze to the nearby wall, Riley shook his head and gave her the honest truth. "I don't know, Millie. It's the last thing in the world I want to do. But…"

"But you think it's inevitable?" she supplied, finishing his unspoken statement as he swung his gaze back to hers. "Hope knows you aren't staying. And however different I wish things could be, I guess I'd like to think that she could have at least a little happiness, for however short a time, instead of none at all. And you're the thing that makes her happy, Riley. It isn't fair, but then life rarely is. If Hope were to ask my advice, I'd tell her to hold on to it for however long she can, and enjoy the moments that she has with you."

"Yeah," he breathed out, unable to get anything else past the choking knot of emotion that had lodged in his throat. Feeling as if the floor were falling out from beneath him, he tried hard to mutter something that he hoped sounded like a halfway decent goodbye and headed out the back door. With his hands shoved deep in his pockets, he trudged across the back lawn and into the soggy forest, heading toward the perimeter markings that he and Kellan had set up around the search area. He couldn't go and chill out in the cabin, and he couldn't sit and make small talk with Millie. He needed to keep moving…going…until maybe he'd worked out some of this seething frustration that wouldn't leave him in peace.

But he was sliding, skidding into a dark, dangerous unknown, and the only one who could save him was Hope. She was his only lifeline. The shining beacon of light that could guide him through the blackened, toxic waste of his soul.

Suddenly, he stopped walking, looking down to see that he had looped his way through the woods and was once again standing in the middle of the path that snaked its way through the trees, leading up to the cabins. Every muscle in his body was coiled hard and tight, and he knew what he was going to do. It was wrong, in more ways than he could name, but he was still going to do it. He *had* to.

The rain had soaked him to the bone, but he wasn't cold. No, he was burning, so hot he was surprised steam wasn't rising from his clothes. Lightning crackled overhead, ripping through the dark gray sky like a blade, the echoing thunder vibrating up through his boots.

He was just about to turn, heading back toward the house, when he felt it. Felt *her*.

Turning, Riley could only stare, unable to believe she was there. That she was real. She was everything he'd ever wanted…ever needed…so vibrant and beautiful that it almost hurt just to look at her. He didn't understand how she did it. How someone who'd gone through what she had could stand there and look at him as if she was seeing something worth believing in. Trusting. Saving.

He wanted so badly to take her in his arms, but fear swelled up, crashing over him, and he heard himself say, "You need to go home, Hope."

CHAPTER THIRTEEN

The instant the graveled words fell from his mouth, Riley wanted to strangle himself. Why in God's name was he sending her home?

Gritting his teeth, he watched as Hope came closer, until she stood no more than a few feet away from him. Her mouth trembled, and though she didn't say anything—just stood there wrapped up in jeans and a white button-up shirt, clutching a dark gray sweater around her shoulders—he could read the question in her eyes. The unspoken *why?*

Swallowing past the knot of emotion in his throat, Riley fisted his hands at his sides to keep himself from reaching out and grabbing her. He stared at the way the raindrops glistened on her long eyelashes...at the lush swell of her soft, pink mouth, and struggled to put his tormented emotions into words. "I don't want to be the thing that hurts you."

Shaking her head, she said, "I'm afraid we passed that point a long time ago, Ri. When you walked away from me, I should have been able to blow it off. Cry for a few weeks and get on with my life. But it never left…never faded. That raw, wrenching pain, like something important had been ripped out of me, and I had to go on living without it. It hurt worse than you could ever imagine."

"I left you a virgin," he argued, as if that could somehow make it better. Make him less of an ass, when he knew damn well that it couldn't.

She made a hoarse sound that was too painful to be a laugh, and flattened one hand against her heart. "You may not have claimed my body, but what you did to me in here. God, Riley. I don't know how to explain it. It's like you marked me. Cursed me. And it's never gone away."

"Christ, Hope. What do you want from me?" he growled, hating how the rain looked like tears slipping across her skin. But her eyes were dry, and he suddenly realized that no matter how upset he'd seen her get, she never cried. The realization jarred him, as if it was a sign of some deep, emotional scar that had never healed. That was shutting her down…closing her off. "If I could undo the past, I would."

"Yeah, well, you can't," she breathed out on a shaky whisper. "And you owe me for that."

"Hope," he said in a warning tone.

"I want what I missed, Ri. After what happened to Neal…and then that monster coming into the café, threatening both of us, I'm worried and I'm scared, but I'm not going to just hide up in my room, shaking with fear. I've been wrenched around on an emotional roller coaster since the moment you walked back into my life, and I'm tired of it. Enough already. You told me you wanted me, though God only knows why. Still, I'm not so stupid as to argue when the man I've always longed for says he wants me, too. I'm ready for you to make good on those words."

"Damn it, it isn't that simple," he argued.

"Because you're leaving, right? You don't love me? You won't stay?"

"I can't," he said for what felt like the hundredth time, the sound of his voice fractured and raw, as if something inside him had broken…shattered. He felt like an idiot bleating the same things over and over again, but he couldn't stop. What if he touched her and started making excuses not to go through with his plan? It was too dangerous for him to want things for himself—to want more time with her. The temptation could lead him to thinking of ways to put off the inevitable, and he'd end up making a crucial mistake that could be costly. "Why do you insist on making this so goddamn difficult?" he growled, the harsh, hard-edged words torn up from the depths of his soul. "You're asking for something that I can't give you, Hope."

Stepping closer, she tilted her head back as she stared up at him. "I just want you to be close to me, Ri. I'm not asking you to give me anything other than that."

"Bullshit. You want to go back to where we were," he roared, his words lashing with frustration, "and I can't do that."

"No, I'm not asking you for that," she whispered. "I just want you now. For however long it lasts."

Staring down into her upturned face, Riley tried to hold firm in his conviction, but he could feel it slipping away, like grains of sand sliding through his fingers. He'd wanted her…had hungered for her for so long, but Hope was no longer the girl he'd known. He'd lost his hold on that girl a long time ago, and couldn't get her back. But the hell of it was, he wanted the woman standing before him even more, because the woman affected him in ways the memory of the girl never had.

The need was so much that it hurt, down in his blood…in his bones. All the passion and aggression and wrenching, gnawing years of wanting…craving, and not being able to have. And now that the Merrick's hungers were blending with his own, he felt crushed beneath its force.

"It's going to happen soon. The fight…the end." His voice was low…breathless. "I can feel it, Hope. And then I'll leave you. Even if I want to stay, I'll go, and I'll never come back."

"I know that," she breathed out, her voice so soft, it was like a cloud…an ethereal stream of smoke. Something magical and filled with mystery.

Lifting his hands, he held her face in his palms. "Then tell me to turn around and get the hell away from you."

She blinked, the tiny movement sending a cascade of water droplets running down her cheeks as she told him, "No."

His breath jerked from his lungs, his body hard and shaking. "Don't do this, Hope."

She wrapped her fingers around his wrists. "I know it will kill me when you leave, but if I don't do this, then I'm already dead inside. I need you, Ri. I need to know, at least once in my life, what it's like to have you covering me, inside me. I need to be a part of you, no matter how much it's going to hurt. No matter how this all comes to an end."

Damn it, he didn't need to wonder…to guess. He already knew exactly how it was going to end. With Hope getting hurt. Because of him. And he had no one to blame but himself.

"You hurt me before, and you'll no doubt hurt me again, Riley. It hurts just having you here. Seeing you. Breathing you in. I might as well get some pleasure out of it, to soften the blow." He could feel the way her words chipped away at the tattered remnants of his control, the way it cracked and gave way beneath the gentle pressure, and then she said, "I'm so scared, Ri. Not of you…but of everything. I'm cold inside, and you're the only one who can make me warm. I just need… I need to feel the heat of your body to remind me what it feels like to be alive."

As the last soft, halting word left her lips, he finally broke. One moment he was standing there, trapped in hell. And in the next…he was in heaven as he kissed his way into her mouth, tasting every sweet, delicious part of her. It was paradise. One that he knew he would never get more than a glimpse of. A forbidden taste, like Eve sinking her teeth into the apple. The consequences were going to be disastrous, but the flavor… Christ, it was unreal.

Powerful. Darkly sensual. Wild and seeking and hungry. The kiss was nothing short of hard, explosive aggression, both of them going at each other as if they wanted to devour…conquer…dominate. She matched him every step of the way, blowing his mind, making him harder than he'd ever been in his life. Every movement, every moment, was sucking him in deeper, pulling his head under the water, until he was caught. Trapped. He couldn't get out. Like sinking into quicksand, he just kept going under…and under.

And if he'd taken one bite of that exquisite, forbidden fruit, Riley figured he might as well eat the whole damn thing.

Pulling her against his chest, he carried her into the cabin as she eagerly wrapped her legs around his waist, her arms thrown around his shoulders, stroking his hair with her fingertips…the back of his neck, each touch sending a shiver of sensation racing through his system. He had no idea how long Kellan would be gone, but he wasn't taking any chances. Without breaking the kiss, Riley carried her into the small space that connected the cabin's massive bedroom to the bathroom that lay beyond the closed door on their right. With only a small vanity counter and mirror, the room was really only good for giving a woman a place to do her hair and makeup. Riley had thought it was a complete waste of the cabin's floor space, until now. He didn't want their first time to be in the goddamn bathroom, and yet he wasn't about to risk Kellan walking in on them in the bedroom.

Kicking the door shut behind him, he set Hope on her feet as he ripped off his flannel shirt and shoulder holster, tossing them onto the floor. Then, with his breath jerking from his lungs in hard, sharp bursts, Riley pressed her back over the counter, the sweater falling from her shoulders as he kissed his way over her chin, down the delicate line of her throat, while his hands attacked the buttons on her shirt. He'd only worked his way through the top half when he lifted his head, staring down with hot, burning eyes as he ripped the half-opened shirt off her shoulders, leaving it to bunch at her elbows. With shaking fingers, he pulled down the satiny cups of her bra, and bared the pale, exquisite perfection of her breasts to his gaze for the first time ever.

Swearing softly under his breath, Riley beat down the snarling, vicious demands of his body, and simply gave himself a moment to soak in her beauty. She panted beneath him, her chest rising and falling with short, shallow breaths, while her soft fingertips stroked the burning heat in his neck, in his face, and then he couldn't hold back anymore. He made a thick sound of lust that vibrated through his entire body, and lowered his head. Closing his eyes, he opened his mouth over one soft, swollen nipple…and then the other, intoxicated by their texture, their taste. The way they fit against his tongue. Reaching between their bodies, he started to wrench open his jeans with his right hand, still working one plump, velvety-soft nipple against the roof of his mouth, when he looked up at her from beneath his lashes, and his breath caught at how beautiful she was. He was mesmerized by the way her head tilted back at that perfect angle. By her long, dark hair as it flowed across her bare shoulders, gleaming against the paleness of her skin. By the smooth, tender line of her throat that called to the savage, visceral darkness within him.

As if she felt the primal heat of his stare, she lowered her head, staring straight into his eyes while he held her nipple against his tongue.

And then she smiled. Beautiful, sweet, perfect.

The wrenching intimacy of the moment swept through Riley like a hot, blistering wind—the inherent purity of her trust…her shining, shimmering goodness a stark contrast against the dark, midnight pitch of his soul—and he suddenly felt like a criminal. Like something dirty and corrupt, soiling her with his filth.

"Stop," she whispered, cupping his hot face within the coolness of her palm. "Wherever you were going in your head, Ri. Don't go there."

He blinked, drowning in the luminous depths of her eyes, while his own felt gritty and raw. She should have hated him for what he'd done to her life, in the past and now. God, she should have been trying to kill him—but not Hope. No, instead of raging at him, she was *worried* about him. Wanted to give him the gift of her body…to seduce him with tenderness…with her light and her heat. It made him vibrate with some strange, inexplicable energy. Lust. Need. Hunger. Adoration.

He moved his hands down her sides, over the womanly curve of her hips, and caught the flare of uneasiness in her eyes, before she quickly snuffed it out, her chin lifting to a proud angle.

"What?" he asked, his voice little more than a guttural rasp.

"I know I'm not a scrawny little wisp," she whispered, wetting her kiss-swollen lips, her eyes heavy-lidded and smoldering with need. "I know that I'm scarred and plump and not at all like the women you usually do this with, but I don't care. It's not going to stop me. I'll do whatever you want, Ri. Give you whatever you need."

She blazed, vibrating with desire, the sexual frequency so high and vivid and sharp that he felt burned…scorched, as if he'd touched his hand to a flame. And he could have wrung her precious little neck for saying those things about herself.

Working to find his voice through the raging storm of emotion blasting through him, Riley finally managed to say, "You're beautiful, Hope. The most beautiful woman I've ever known. Every part of you. Every inch."

She shook her head, a small, chastising smile curling the corner of her mouth. "You don't have to lie to me, Riley. It's enough just knowing that I'm the one you want right now."

"Damn it," he growled, his control slipping as he suddenly leaned over her, fisting one hand in the soft hair at her nape to hold her in place. He pressed between her parted thighs, his unbuttoned jeans slipping off his hips, a pair of black cotton boxers the only thing that kept him contained. "Don't give me that shit about wanting you *right now,* as if it's some kind of goddamn miracle," he growled, grinding his cock against her mound, wishing that the layers of clothing weren't separating them so that he could shove himself deep inside, proving just how much he wanted her. "Christ, Hope, I want you *all* the time," he practically roared, going nose-to-nose with her, her sweet breath pelting against his face. Her eyes widened with surprise at the way he was holding her…at the barely leashed violence of his tone and hard, shaking body, and it tore a low, bitter laugh from his throat. "I tried to warn you," he rasped. "You're playing with fire, being here with me…offering yourself up like a tender little sacrifice. I'm not the man you think I am. I'm not the boy from your past. And if you don't stop this now, before it goes any further, you're going to find yourself getting fucked by someone you don't even know."

She narrowed her eyes, bristling with challenge. "Do you know what I think, Ri? I think you're the one who's scared…who doesn't recognize himself. I think you're hiding. Behind anger. Behind your fear. I think you're terrified of letting yourself feel anything that isn't angry and hard, anything that makes you feel vulnerable. But I'm not asking you to feel anything you can't handle, that you don't want to. I'm not asking you to be anything other than what you are. I'll take whatever I can get from you. Hard. Angry. Violent and out of control. Take me on the floor, right now. Up against the wall. I don't care. Just stop running, because we both know it's going to happen!"

He pulled in a deep, shuddering breath. Held it, then slowly let it out, and tried one last time to make her come to her senses. To push her away, when all he really wanted was for her to stay. Forever. "I could walk out of this room, right out that front door. Head to one of the bars and find someone. Bet you wouldn't want anything to do with me after that. Would you, Hope?"

"Go ahead, then," she told him, the vibrant gleam in her dark eyes telling him that she wasn't buying it. That she was onto him. Knew exactly what he was trying to do. "You want me out of your hair? Fine. Go pick up some nameless woman and take her to bed. Problem solved with nothing more than a quick exchange of bodily fluids. Go on, Riley. I dare you."

He glared…shaking…shuddering, every muscle in his body coiled hard and tight with fury, with tension, his angry refusal to follow through on the asinine threat carved into the harsh lines of his expression. He wanted to just throw off the asshole spiel and sink into the moment, wallow in it…surrender to its power…its beauty. But he could *not* make it happen. Even after coming this far, he couldn't let go of the fear…the bitterness that *this* was all he could have. These stolen moments in this tiny room, while guilt coiled heavily around his throat, painful and tight.

"This isn't a game," he finally choked out, the words gritty enough to scratch against the tenderness of her skin. But she didn't flinch. Didn't pull away.

As if she could see all the torment and frustration roiling through him, ripping him apart like so many knives, she softened, and her gaze slid away for a moment, past his shoulder, before pulling itself back to his. She blew out a shaky, trembling breath, and said, "I'm not playing games, Riley. I wouldn't even know how to play your kind of games if I wanted to. They're too confusing, and my head's already messed up enough as it is."

"Goddamn it." His expression and his tone were bitterly grim, but she didn't seem to mind as the last remnants of control were torn from his grasp. He started in on her jeans, ripping them open. "This doesn't change anything," he warned, crazed with need...with hunger, and hoping like hell that he was going to be able to force the starved, ravenous Merrick part of his soul into submission. "Nothing will change. No matter how good it is. No matter how perfect. I won't stay."

"I didn't ask you to," she gasped, helping him to shove the denim over her hips. "I'm a big girl, Ri. I don't need you to sugarcoat the truth for me. I can swallow it down just fine. I might not like the taste, but I can take it."

With her jeans around her soft white thighs, he shoved his shaking hand into the front of a tiny pair of black cotton panties, seeking out that warm, liquid heat that he knew was going to melt him down. Burn him to ashes. A fine sheen of sweat covered his body, the fabric of his clothes sticking to his fever-hot skin, but he couldn't take the time to rip them off. He stared into her face, his gaze hard, wanting to believe her, but he couldn't. Her eyes still gave her away, letting him see beneath the brittle shell of her anger and pride, down to the taffy-soft emotions that dwelled beneath. But it wasn't going to stop him. Thrusting two big fingers up inside her, he rubbed against the walls of her sex, twisting and pressing deeper, his body shuddering at the tight, cushiony hold. She was so wet that his hand made slick, slippery sounds as he slowly slid his fingers inside her.

"Why are you waiting?" she moaned as he added a third, the fit so tight, Riley knew it was almost too much, but he didn't want to hurt her when he finally drove himself into her.

"You're small and I'm not," he groaned, knowing it was going to kill him when all that tight, drenched silk was surrounding his cock. "I need to get you close. Need to get you ready."

"DAMN IT," HOPE SOBBED, pulsing around his fingers. "I'm ready for you now."

With her breath seized in her lungs, she struggled to keep breathing past her excitement as Riley quickly turned her around, bending her over the counter so that she faced the mirror, her damp, flushed face staring right back at her, looking like someone she didn't even recognize with that wild bloom of hunger burning beneath her skin. She sank her teeth into her lower lip to keep from screaming for him to hurry as he ripped her panties down, his hot, callused hands rubbing over her bottom, between her thighs, a low, sexy sound of pleasure vibrating in his chest, as if he enjoyed what he saw…what he touched. He pushed down his boxers as far as his thighs, and she choked back a sob as she felt the hot, damp weight of his cock against her backside. He fumbled for the back pocket of his jeans for a moment, pulling out his wallet, and then he reached down to roll on a condom. The instant he was sheathed within the thin latex, he fitted himself against her, pushing his thick, massive head inside the tight, slippery entrance.

Hope cried out from the intense pressure, his body stretching the fragile flesh to the absolute limit, and he paused. He stared at her in the mirror with a dark, searching expression, the raw desire in his eyes burning with a sharp, primal, predatory intensity. She couldn't take her eyes off him, thinking he was the most gorgeous man in the entire world. His dark hair was spiky and windblown from the rain, the hard, rugged angle of his jaw locked tight, as if he'd clenched his teeth, while those seductive Buchanan blue eyes glowed with an otherworldly light, as if there were a flame inside his head, burning behind them. She wished he'd taken the time to pull off his T-shirt so that she could drool over the mouthwatering muscles detailed beneath the damp cotton of his shirt.

The hard, male power of his big, beautiful body en-
thralled her, making her want to lay him down for hours
while she took her time exploring…touching…tasting.

But they didn't have hours. All they had was this
stolen moment in time, and she was going to devour
every vibrant, stunning second of it, holding on to the
memories for the rest of her life, unwilling to forget a
single breathtaking detail.

She tried to breathe her way through the pressure, but
it was too intense…too everywhere. He was massive,
the size and heat and power of him as overwhelming as
it was incredible. She felt bruised from the force of
emotion surging through her—from the sheer, powerful
depth of her need. With a rough, husky groan, he worked
himself in deeper, filling her…stretching her…pushing
her into that place that was a crazy blend of pleasure and
pain. And then he stopped, held, watching her face in
the mirror. She saw her own wild gaze, trembling
mouth. Took in the hard, rugged cast of his expression.

There was a hot, quivering tightness in her chest as
he pulsed inside her, pressing an inch deeper, and
asked, "More?"

She nodded, searched for the air to breathe out a
throaty "All of you."

He shoved then, putting his strength behind it, his
fingers digging into her hips hard enough to bruise as
he worked those last, thick inches in, and then his head
fell back on his shoulders and he groaned, the rough,
guttural sound the sexiest thing she'd ever heard.

She wanted to scream from the pleasure. From the thrust and drag of his heavy, vein-ridden cock as it moved inside her, each powerful thrust digging deeper…forcing her to open…to accept. The decadent, breathtaking rhythm was hard and fast, stunning her with the savagery of emotion she could feel in each heavy, hungry push of his body into hers. Every touch revealed a desperate aggression, a clawing need to get as close to her as he could. And when his head lifted, his dark eyes finding hers in the mirror, she could see the beast…the darkness rising up within him.

He tore his hands from her hips, flattening them against the countertop on either side of her, and she knew his talons were breaking through the skin at the tips of his fingers. His eyes blazed with a hunger…with a craving so intense, she couldn't help but want to give him what he so desperately needed. To be the thing that nourished him, like some lush, primal earth goddess, and her body swelled with the provocative thought, drawing him deeper…bathing him in moisture and heat. He shuddered, slamming into her so hard that she had to brace herself against the mirror, her palms damp against the cool, reflective surface, and then she slowly tilted her head to the side, exposing the curve of her throat. His lips pulled back over his teeth, the Merrick's fangs startlingly white within the dark beauty of his face.

"Go ahead," she told him, the words soft and thick on her tongue. "It's okay, Ri. Take what you need."

He shook his head, a deep, guttural "I can't" scraping past his lips.

"Don't you ever get tired of saying that?" she snapped, glaring at him in the mirror. "If your brother can feed from his woman, then why can't you take what you need from me? What's the damn difference?"

"They're in love, which changes everything. He'll be there to protect her…to keep her safe. Allowing me to take your blood is a helluva thing to sacrifice for an affair, Hope. And that's all I can offer you."

"I wasn't asking you to give me anything. I was simply offering you something that you obviously want."

"I can't," he growled again, looking as if he would explode with fury…with frustration.

BUT HE WANTED TO. God, did he ever. Riley could feel the Merrick punching against his insides, demanding its freedom. Insisting that he take what it needed, but he fought it back, choking down the pain, refusing to give in. He would not sink his fangs into her throat and drag her any deeper into this nightmare than he already had.

And he wasn't willing to risk where he knew the raw, primal intimacy of the act would take him. It was too dangerous…too possessive.

Closing his eyes, he forced the hunger into submission as he felt her body tighten, on the verge of a powerful climax, and gave himself over to the pleasure as well, to the jaw-grinding sensation that was quickly turning him inside out. Stripping him down. Bracing himself against the counter, he went at her hard, his head flung back, lost in the hot, silken perfection of her body, while the dark, raging intensity of the experience burned through him, scorching his veins. The pleasure built up from the soles of his feet, rolling through his body in a huge, voluptuous wave, crashing through him with gaining speed…mounting violence. And then a savage, animallike sound roared from his chest, the visceral release tearing through him just as Hope began to cry out with her own stunning climax. It was explosive…shocking…incendiary. He felt blistered and scorched, as if a naked flame had swept through his body, making him burn until he had to clench his teeth against the devastating pleasure. It was unlike anything he'd ever experienced before, the breathtaking sensations going on…and on, blowing his goddamn mind.

The encounter had been hard and fast. Gritty and primal. Exactly what they needed to burn away their anger and fears. But as the haze of mind-shattering pleasure faded, reality crept back in, and so, too, did the cold…even worse than before.

The shivery, lost sensation started in the pit of Riley's stomach, and spread outward, shaking in his chest…his throat, until that cold, icy burn spilled into his eyes. Fighting his way out of the sweet, silken hold of her body, he gave her his back as he got rid of the condom and pulled up his jeans, the Merrick's talons having already receded. Pressing his damp forehead against the wall, he did everything he could to hold it together. To keep from falling apart.

You're a tough one all right, a snide voice drawled in his head. Just another one of the many assholes who seemed to keep him company these days.

He could hear Hope moving behind him, soft whispers of sound as she set her clothes back to rights. She was going to say something, and that would be it. The last thing that pushed him over the edge.

She whispered his name, and he lifted one hand, signaling for her to stay back.

"Go home, Hope," he said in a husky, halting voice, unable to stop himself from looking at her over his shoulder.

Finishing with the last button on her shirt, she lifted her chin and stared into his burning eyes. "Are you serious? That's it? Just 'Go home, Hope'?"

His gaze slid away, unable to meet the shocked disappointment in her eyes, the rosy glow of pleasure fading beneath his casual dismissal, leaving her trembling and pale. And no doubt pissed as hell. Snatching up his shirt and holster, he opened the door, relieved to find they were still alone as he pulled on the items in his hands and headed for the open doorway, silently cursing himself when he realized he'd left the door unlocked.

"Keep your phone on you," he grunted as he pushed open the screen. "If anything happens, call me. Don't be stubborn about it. Just…pick up the phone and call."

And then he headed out into the rain. Tilting back his

head, Riley let the coolness of the shower absorb the heat in his eyes…in his face. He could feel Hope behind him, standing in the doorway, watching…waiting to see what he would do.

Without looking back, Riley shoved his hands into the pockets of his jeans and set off into the forest, hoping like hell he could find a way to forget.

CHAPTER FOURTEEN

Wednesday night

BY THE TIME Riley had returned to the cabin, Hope was gone. Not that he'd expected her to stick around and wait for him. Knowing he couldn't leave her alone with Gregory out there somewhere…not to mention the rest of the Casus…he'd stayed close by, keeping an eye on the cabin as he smoked his way through enough cigarettes that his throat now felt raw. When she'd finally grown tired of waiting for him to return and walked back to the house, he'd headed over to the search area, pacing around, doing God only knew what. Trying to…to sense the Marker, as ridiculous as that sounded. He'd even tried excavating another patch of land, but the weather had finally sent him back inside the shelter of the cabin, and after he'd taken a shower, he'd passed the time staring at the television screen, listening to the endless warnings about the severity of the coming weather system.

The worst storm to hit that area in over a century was surging toward the shore, set to wreak complete havoc once it hit. Thrashing waves, tropical storm force winds, and enough rain to flood the inland areas. It was the last bloody thing that they needed, considering it was going to make their search for the Marker all but impossible. But it was more than just the crappy working conditions that had him on edge. Riley couldn't shake the eerie feeling that the end was rolling in along with the foul weather, as if the monsters were being carried in on the waves…dropping from the clouds like acid rain.

He'd called to check in with Kellan earlier, just to make sure the guy was okay. After the strange attack on Monday night by one of Westmore's men, as well as the mysterious blue-eyed stranger who'd warned Kellan of the coming danger, Riley didn't like the idea of the Watchman being in town on his own. He only hoped Kell wasn't taking any chances. With so many enemies roaming around, the last thing the Watchman needed to do was make himself an easy target.

Rolling his shoulder, Riley moved to his feet and began pacing from one side of the warm, rustic room to the other, trying to convince himself that he was just on edge because of the run-in with Gregory that morning…his worry over Kellan. But he knew there was more to it.

And why don't you stop hiding from the real issue? a tired voice drawled in his head. *You're doing everything you can to keep from thinking about her. About what happened. Pointless, really, when you know it's going to haunt your every waking moment, as well as*

*your dreams. Might as well suck it up and face it
head-on, like a man.*

Stopping in the middle of the floor, Riley braced his
hands on his hips and closed his eyes, concentrating on
keeping his breathing even and slow, while his pulse
kept gaining speed…rushing faster and faster. God,
what was the point of denying it? Whatever smart-ass
part of his psyche had delivered the lecture, it was right.
He couldn't avoid thinking about what had happened
that morning, because it was all he could hear, see,
smell. The lush, exquisite clutch of her body as she'd
taken him deep, holding him tighter than any woman
he'd ever known. The mouthwatering scent of her skin.
The addictive taste of her mouth.

It'd been madness to think that he could have her
once and ease a measure of his craving. Instead, it'd
only geared his hunger—the clawing, insatiable need—
up to the point that he could all but feel his reason
slipping away. The desire was a thousand times greater
now that he knew just how incredible it was to make
love to her. There'd been a level of intensity to it that
he'd never even known he was capable of experiencing.
His style had always been aggressive, but nothing that
could have prepared him for what had happened with
Hope. He'd been crazed. Out of control. And the connection between them had been mind-blowing, looping
the pleasure back again and again, magnifying every
moan…every gasp.

Knowing he couldn't keep pacing the floorboards…reliving those moments again and again, driving himself out of his mind…he walked to his bed and grabbed the jacket he'd laid across it earlier, pulling it on over his white linen shirt and shoulder holster. Since Kellan had yet to return, he figured he'd brave the weather and spend some time searching the grounds again, making sure nothing was out there that shouldn't be. He couldn't shake the thick cloud of uneasiness hanging over him, scraping against his nerves, as if something else were about to happen.

He'd only just reached the door, when his phone began ringing on his hip. Glancing at the screen, his muscles clenched as he saw that it was Hope's number. After the way that he'd treated her that morning, Riley couldn't imagine she'd be calling him unless there was a problem, and he went ahead and started making his way down the path as he talked to her.

"What's going on?" he asked, the strange prickle at the back of his neck growing worse, creeping him out.

"I'm sorry to bother you," she burst out, the husky words tumbling over themselves in her rush. "But I need you to come up to the house, Ri. Please. As soon as you can."

"I'm already on my way," he told her, hating the ragged edge of fear he could hear in her voice. "Are you okay?"

"I'm fine, but…just hurry. I'll tell you everything when you get here."

Seconds later, the house came into view, and he

could see that Hope was waiting for him on the back porch. The instant she saw him, she started running, launching herself into his arms. Riley caught her against his chest, shaken by the feeling of how right she felt there as she clutched onto him, burying her face against his shoulder. He could feel her shuddering, though there were no tears on her cold cheeks. Her breath was coming in short, painful gasps, and he steeled himself as he said, "What is it, honey? What happened?"

Shivering, she shifted in his hold until she could look into his face, her luminous eyes shadowed by worry. "He went after Hal," she said unsteadily. "His niece just came by to pick up Millie on her way to the hospital up in Wellsford. He's in emergency surgery. They're saying that it was some kind of…of animal attack. He would have been killed, but some kids who were walking past his house heard him screaming and called the police. I guess he's lost so much blood, they don't even know if he's going to make it."

Cursing under his breath, Riley ran his hands down her back, over her shoulders, stroking the thick, silken weight of her hair, just to assure himself that she was safe and unharmed. He knew it had to have been Gregory who made the attack, just as he knew that the Casus had purposefully picked Hal Erickson because of his association with Hope's family.

"I want to go up and see Millie at the hospital," she said, staring up at him. For the moment, the endless rain had eased up and the stars had burned their way back into the early autumn skies, the tiny shimmering lights reflected in the burnished depths of her eyes. "Will you go with me, Riley?"

"God, Hope. Of course I will," he replied in a heavy voice, pulling out his phone to call Kellan, asking him to meet them there. After Hope gave the Watchman directions, she ran inside to get her car keys, since Kellan still had Riley's truck. They left immediately for the hospital, and made the trip in good time, the respite from the rain making it easier to navigate the highways. Hoping to avoid Millie's wrath, Riley waited out in the hall, talking with Kellan, who arrived not long after them, while Hope went in to see her aunt. Hal's niece had apparently known, like Hope, that there was more than just a friendship brewing between Millie and her uncle, and had arranged for Millie to be allowed into the private family waiting room.

Standing beneath the harsh fluorescent lights that ran the length of the ceiling, Riley got Kellan to agree to stay and keep an eye on things at the hospital until Millie was ready to leave, so that he could go ahead and get Hope back home. She finally came back out a half hour later, looking tense with worry, and thanked Kellan for staying to look after her aunt. Hal, she said, had come out of surgery okay, but was expected to be in recovery for a while. Riley shared a meaningful look with Kellan, and he knew they were both wondering what Erickson would remember from his attack, and what he would be willing to admit to the police.

Just as they were leaving, Millie caught up with them near the exit, running up and grabbing hold of his arm. Expecting her to slap him—or worse—Riley tensed, ready for the blow. But she simply stared up at him, her gray eyes red-rimmed and swollen as she pulled him away from Hope, obviously wanting to speak to him privately. "I don't blame you," she said in a low voice. "So you just get that gutted look off your face, young man. I saw that monster for myself and I know there's no explanation for evil like that. I should have warned Hal, but I...I just didn't think. Didn't realize..." She cleared her throat, then firmly said, "I want you to do something for me, Riley."

He nodded, expecting her to tell him that she wanted revenge. Gregory's blood. The bastard's head on a stick, which he would have been only too willing to give her. But she asked for none of those things. Instead, she said, "Take care of yourself. I know you'll take care of Hope, so I won't even ask. But it will kill her if anything happens to you. She's already lost too much in this world. So you just make sure that you watch out for yourself."

She turned and walked away then, and Riley made his way back to Hope, heading out with her to the car, while running his mind over everything that had happened. He offered to drive again, and after they were both settled in the car, he reached out, pushing her hair back from her face, studying her with a worried frown.

Riley knew that no matter how he looked at it, the

truth couldn't be denied. He was a curse creeping over this family. These lives. He was already wreaking destruction, and the true nightmare hadn't even started. This was just the preshow, giving them all a taste of what was to come. And he would end up bringing them all down with him.

There were so many things he needed to say to her, but all that would come out was a gruff, quiet "I'm sorry."

Heat flared in her eyes, burning away the fear that had shadowed her gaze since walking out of the waiting room. "Don't you dare apologize. It's not your fault that Marker is buried on our land. You didn't put it there. And you're not the one who hurt Hal."

"But it's my fault that bastard's fixated on you," he argued. "Our past…the present. Maybe you should be thankful this happened now, before you let this thing between us go any further."

She stared back at him in disbelief. "So because of what happened to Hal, I'm supposed to be glad that you've only had sex with me once? What does *that* mean, Riley?"

He would have smiled at her spark of temper, if he wasn't so wound up inside, sick with worry. "It means that if you're smart, you'll cut your losses while you still can and get the hell out of here, Hope."

"Well, I won't," she snapped, bristling with anger and frustration. "I'm not running. I'm not going to let that monster scare me away from my home."

Wondering what the hell he had to do to get through

to her, Riley tore his gaze from hers and stared out the front windshield. "Gregory's only going to keep at it," he said in a low voice, bracing his left elbow on the door as he rubbed his fingers against the pulsing pain in his forehead, the mother of all headaches knocking around in his skull. "And eventually the others will make their moves. The Collective. Westmore. The danger is only going to get worse, Hope. I just…" He blew out a rough breath, struggling for the words. "I just wish I hadn't brought all this shit down on you. That I'd never even started looking for that goddamn Marker."

"Instead of blaming yourself," she said softly, "have you ever considered the fact that maybe you were meant to come back into my life, Ri?"

He snorted, shaking his head. "To do what? Screw it up?"

"No. To save me. Think about it. Even if you toss the issue of the Marker aside, what would Neal have done if you weren't here? How far would he have gone?"

He cut her a dark look, not knowing what to say.

"In a way, you've been like my knight in shining armor," she told him with a small, teasing smile. "So stop blaming yourself already."

"I only do it because I *am* the one to blame," he persisted. "You need to get that through your head, Hope. I should have known, after Capshaw, that Gregory might try something like this. Should have had Millie warn Hal, but my goddamn head isn't working. I'm not even thinking straight anymore."

"Well, if it makes you feel better, we can keep arguing about who's to blame later," she said with a tired sigh, pulling on her seat belt. "Right now, I'd just like to get back home."

They made the drive back to Purity in silence, the sound of the windshield wipers and the light rain that had started to fall the only sounds within the cozy confines of the car. As they pulled into the parking lot on the side of the house, Riley turned off the engine, while Hope's words kept playing through his mind, pushing him...tempting him to do the unforgivable. To actually believe that there was something positive in his being there. Was it possible that she was right? That in some weird, mystical way, he'd been meant to come back into her life? How else did you explain it? The way they'd been pulled back together? There was no logical explanation. No sound reason. There were forces at work that he didn't understand. Ones you couldn't see or touch or feel. Ones you simply had to accept, and take the miracle when it was offered.

And as corny as it sounded to his bitter psyche, that was what she was. His miracle. His glimpse of heaven before he slipped into hell. He was so tired of fighting it. He just... He couldn't keep waging the battle. It had worn him down...left him too wanting, too needy. Hope wanted him, though God only knew why, and as they sat there in the quiet car, Riley finally accepted the fact that he was going to play the bastard and take her. For one night, he was going to shut out the rest of the world and take everything that he'd ever wanted from her. And then he'd suck it up and do what was right. Do whatever was necessary to give Hope her life back. One without danger and evil and fear.

Which meant that he needed that bloody Marker. Tomorrow, he would tear up the entire goddamn forest if he had to, rain or no rain, and find the cross. No more putting it off…no more waiting. And then, even if he didn't find it, he'd face Gregory…and make sure that Kellan got Hope out of town, whether she wanted to go or not. He hated doing that to her, but until they knew for sure that the Marker wasn't on her property, he couldn't take the chance of leaving her behind to deal with the monsters on her own. The Casus and Westmore and the Collective. Everyone who wanted to get their hands on the prize…and who would make her life a living hell because of it.

Clearing his throat, Riley finally broke the breath-filled silence. "It's too dangerous for you to stay by yourself, Hope. If it's okay with you, I'd like to move my things into the house."

She turned her head to look at him in the shadowed darkness, a teasing light glittering in her eyes as she smiled and said, "In that case, I might as well go ahead and warn you now, Ri. You stay, I expect you to put out."

A harsh, gritty laugh jerked out of his chest, scraping his throat. "Is that right?" he asked, the corner of his mouth almost twitching into a full-fledged grin. The first one in what felt like forever—and it was as if that easy gesture unlocked something inside him. Some hidden, secret place that he hadn't had access to for so long, he'd forgotten what it was like. It allowed a tiny spark of happiness to shine through. One that he was going to hold on to through the long hours of the night, until tomorrow came, and he had to snuff it out.

Her cheeks were warm with an endearing flush of color, but she didn't back down as she held his stare. "I mean it, Riley."

He knew he was tempting fate, but he was too damn tired to care anymore. After everything that had happened that day, he just wanted to be with her someplace where they could tune out the world, the chaos, for a night. Just one goddamn bloody night, and have it all to themselves.

"If I'm gonna put out," he drawled, "then I want you upstairs this time. In your bed."

"You'll get no arguments from me," she quickly replied, the excitement in those breathless words melting him down, making him want to hold her…cherish her. Shower her with the things that she'd always deserved, but had never been given.

His grin faded and he reached across the space between them, cupping her jaw as he rubbed his thumb into the corner of her mouth. "I barely held myself together this morning," he admitted in a husky rasp, fascinated by the lush, petallike softness of her lips. "I won't be able to control it this time."

Her mouth moved beneath his touch, curving into a

sensual smile. "I'm not asking you to control anything, Ri. Whatever you're willing to give me, I'll take."

"Hope, about this morning…"

She rushed to cut him off, whispering, "You don't have to say any—"

"I shouldn't have just walked out on you," he grunted. "It was a dickhead thing to do and I'm sorry."

"You can make it up to me when we get upstairs," she said over her shoulder, already climbing out of the car.

Following behind her, Riley kept his silence until she'd unlocked the back door, and they were standing in the shadowed living room, the rain pattering softly against the windows. He drew in a deep breath of her warm, mouthwatering scent, and then moved up behind her as she hung her jacket over the banister of the staircase. Curving his hands around her shoulders, he leaned down and pressed a tender kiss to the corner of her jaw, loving the soft, whispery sigh that she made. He didn't want to pop the bubble that surrounded them…the easy camaraderie they'd shared in the car after the chaos of the day, but he had to be honest with her…at least about this. Had to make sure that she understood exactly what was going to happen.

"I'll take your blood this time," he warned her, putting the dark, graveled words into the curve of her throat. He touched his tongue to the sensitive flesh, and she gave a soft, trembling moan, as if the thought excited her as much as it did him. "I won't be able to stop it. To fight it back."

"I KNOW." HOPE'S VOICE was soft...thick. "I don't want you to fight anything."

He released his hold on her then, following behind her as she made her way up the stairs. It felt like a ceremonial rite, leading him to her bedroom in the heavy, breath-filled silence, as if the moment were rich with meaning. One that Hope realized had been such a long time coming, after years of hunger and pain and grief. Of longing and aching.

When they reached her bedroom, he locked the door behind him, resetting the sensors that Kellan had installed while she made her way to the side of the four-poster bed, flicking the lamp onto its lowest setting. Only a soft, hazy glow of light spilled across the snowy expanse of linens, not even reaching into the shadowed corners. It was a sensual, seductive setting, and she could hardly control the tremors of excitement prickling beneath her skin, wanting nothing more than to launch herself at him, taking him to the floor.

He stared at her from across the room, his eyes dark...intense, as if he were imprinting the moment on his brain, and then he came toward her, moving with a purely male, predatory purpose. When he reached her, he took her face in his rough, callused hands, and then he kissed her. Covered her lips with the rich, delicious heat of his mouth, and she melted...shivering, wanting so much, so badly, it felt as if the need was going to shatter her into a million pieces. Burst out of her in a bright, blinding light of pleasure. Pulling his soft linen shirt from his jeans, Hope attacked the endless row of buttons, undoing them with shaky, trembling fingers while he threaded his hands through her hair, holding her still for the hot, devastating demands of his mouth. When she finished with the last button, he broke the kiss and stepped back, pulling off the jacket and holster, placing them on the antique chest that sat against the wall.

"Oh, God, wait," she whispered, holding up her hands for him to stop when he started to move toward her again. "Don't move, okay? Just stand there for a minute and let me look at you."

A low, embarrassed rumble of laughter vibrated in his chest, but he stood still, hands hanging loose at his sides, and let her look her fill. She pulled her bottom lip through her teeth, thinking he was just too freaking good to be real. The pose could have been made into a poster that sold millions, it was so gorgeous and rugged and male. She loved the way that the snowy white shirt hung open over his mouthwatering chest. Like a purely masculine work of art, it was sculpted with hard, flat muscles, his nipples small and dark against the golden beauty of his skin. And those abs. God, the man was nothing but stark lines and raw, harnessed power just waiting to be unleashed. Tall and broad and perfectly proportioned. She loved the dark, silky trail of hair that arrowed down from his navel, into the low-hanging jeans. Loved the hard, heavy bulge of his cock beneath the worn denim. Loved the way his hands clenched into fists at his sides, the veins beneath his golden skin snaking up the strong muscle and sinew of forearms revealed by the rolled-up cuffs on his sleeves.

Unable to wait any longer, wanting to see all of that hard body in the raw, Hope moved forward and pushed the shirt off his broad shoulders, her breath catching in her throat at the sight of the black, swirling tattoos that covered his left bicep and shoulder. "They're beautiful," she whispered, touching the intricate pattern with her fingertips, before lifting her gaze, falling into the searing heat of his stare. "You're beautiful."

He groaned, the low, graveled sound somehow tortured, and then he was against her, all over her, pulling off the sweater she wore over a champagne-colored camisole, opening her jeans…pushing them down her legs so that she could kick them away.

"Do you want this off?" she asked, plucking at the clingy camisole, unable to ignore the niggling thread of suspicion that told her he'd left her in that particle item of clothing on purpose.

He shook his head, his dark gaze sliding away, and her stomach cramped. Though there were several pale, jagged lines on her arms and legs, the worst of her scars were the ones on her torso. The ones he'd left covered. "I get that I'm not perfect," she whispered, hating the tremor of insecurity in the soft words, knowing he could hear it, too. "If you want, we can just turn out the light."

"CHRIST, IT'S NOT THAT," Riley breathed out, catching her face in his hands as he stared into the glistening depths of her eyes. Other than that one time in the kitchen when he'd touched her stomach, he'd purposefully avoided her scars, knowing that they would fire his rage…his fury, the powerful emotions simply channeling back to the Merrick, when he'd been trying so hard to keep it under control. Even now, he couldn't bring himself to touch the jagged scars in the ways that he wanted. Pressing his lips to them. Trying to heal them with his…

No, damn it. Don't go there. You can't.

Shying away from the dangerous territory of that particular thought, he said, "You have to know how beautiful I think you are. Every part of you, Hope. I wouldn't change a single thing, except to take those scars away. To erase their existence. Not because of how they look, but because of what they represent. Because of what you went through. The pain. The loss."

She blinked, trying to smile, but he could still see the shadow of doubt darkening her gaze. Knowing he needed to make her understand, he leaned closer, wanting her to see the truth burning in his eyes as he said, "I want you, Hope. Every part of you. In ways I've never wanted anyone or anything. But the idea of you hurt. Bleeding. Of what that bastard did to you. It's going to push me somewhere you don't want me to go. Not when you're here with me. Alone."

And just like that, he could see her doubts give way

beneath a wave of indignation. "I'm not afraid of you, Riley."

"You should be," he whispered, pressing his forehead to hers. "Christ, even I'm afraid of what's inside me, baby."

"Well, I'm not," she snapped, the disgruntled words bringing the grin back to his face, managing to soften his fear.

"In that case," he rasped, pressing a kiss to the corner of her mouth, "you'd better get your sweet ass on that bed before I have at you right here."

Breathing deeply, Riley couldn't take his eyes off her as she hurried to do as he'd said, settling on her knees in the center of all that innocent-looking linen and lace, her long hair streaming over her pale shoulders, his fantasy woman come to life. Pulling off his shoes and jeans, he took out a condom and laid it on the antique bedside table, then jerked his chin toward her, his voice nothing more than a husky scrape of sound as he said, "Lose the panties. Then lie back and spread your legs for me."

Heat burned in her face, but she didn't hesitate… didn't balk. Riley could see her excitement…her own sharp, urgent desire in the racing of her pulse at the base of her delicate throat. Hear it in the rushing cadence of her breath. Feel it shimmering from her in warm, incandescent waves that blasted against him as she pulled down the small panties, throwing them over the side of the bed. The heat of her burned through his guard, his masks, until there was nothing but the raging, desperate need to be a part of her storming through his body, pounding through his veins.

Stepping out of his boxers, he heard her breath catch as she got her first look at him…at the dark, thick, brutal-looking evidence of just how badly he wanted her. It sounded as if there was a smile in her soft voice as she said, "Good God, Riley," but he couldn't take his eyes off the breathtaking perfection between her thighs long enough to look at her face. The instant she'd spread her legs for him, revealing her damp, glistening, candy-pink center, he'd been caught…unable to look away. She was…perfect. Swollen and wet and unbearably pretty. Tender and smooth and delicate. The most exquisite thing he'd ever seen, and he couldn't wait to get his mouth on her.

Crawling up on the bed, Riley moved between her shyly parted thighs and grasped her behind her knees. Her breath caught, as he forced her knees out wider… higher, opening her all the way up, so that he could see every slippery, intimate pink detail. He made a thick sound of lust, unable to wait a second more.

"Keep them right there," he growled, using his thumbs to separate her plump folds as he bent down and took a hot, hungry lick with his tongue. She arched beneath him as if a jolt of electricity had shot through her body, a sharp, shocked sound breaking out of her chest while he lost himself in her, his pulse roaring in his ears like the crashing surf. Greedy for every part of her, Riley swirled his tongue over her…inside her,

dipping into the honeyed sweetness, her taste so perfect…so addictive, it was as if she'd been made for him.
He couldn't get enough as he thrust his tongue deep,
then lapped…licking…rubbing it against her small,
tightly knotted clit. He could have lingered there in that
drenched, silken paradise forever if he'd had the time,
but the urgent throbbing in his cock was too demanding, insisting that he bury himself inside her, as soon as
humanly possible. But he couldn't stop until he'd tasted
her pleasure. Until he'd felt that intense, gushing rush
of energy pouring through her, spilling into his mouth.

"God, Riley, I can't take it," she moaned, trembling
beneath him. "It's too much. Too…good."

"Just remember to breathe," he told her, his voice a
husky, graveled rasp. "If you pass out, then you're going
to miss what comes next. And it's the best part."

"Oh." She shivered…her body arching…drawing
closer…closer. "In that case, I wouldn't dream of it."

"That's my girl," he murmured with a low, wicked
rumble of laughter, and as he thrust his tongue back
inside, rubbing one thumb against her softly pulsing clit,
she broke, surrendering to the ecstasy…giving him everything that he wanted.

HOPE HAD TRIED not to get lost beneath the stunning,
crashing waves of pleasure, but in the end, she'd lost her
hold…and had seen stars glittering across the endless
midnight stretch of her mind. When she came floating
back to the world and could focus, she lifted her heavy

lashes to find Riley right there, pushing her hair back from her damp brow, a boyish, wondering smile at the corner of his mouth that made him look endearingly young... fresh. Untouched. As if this moment were taking them back in time, all the pain and torment and stress of the years since they'd last been together forgotten, wiped clean from the board, leading to a shiny, sparkling future that was just waiting for them. Only...it wasn't.

Before she had time to dwell on that bitter dose of reality, he asked, "Are you on the pill?"

She licked her bottom lip as she shook her head. "Didn't see the point. Sex isn't really my thing. Or at least...it wasn't." A smile tipped the corner of her mouth as she stared up into the devastating beauty of his face. "But I'm thinking now that maybe I need to reevaluate my priorities."

Riley would have laughed, but he was too raw inside. Too tense. Desire was pulling him tight. Hunger breaking him down. And jealousy slithered like a serpent through his veins, taunting him with the knowledge that there would be men who came after him. All he could offer her was this moment...this night. And when he was gone, some other lucky bastard was going to come along and sweep her off her feet. The only reason it hadn't happened so far was because she'd been closed down. Locked up. Hiding away. But she was open now. In bloom. Flushed. She'd draw the eye of every man who came into the café, and he'd turn into a memory, forgotten...lost.

It made him want to howl. Made him want to imprint himself on her so deeply that the mark could never fade.

He wanted nothing more than to take her skin-on-skin, but couldn't take that risk. Not when he'd be leaving her here alone to raise his child. Locking his jaw, he reached for the condom he'd left on the bedside table, ripped open the packet and rolled it on. And then he gathered her beneath him, fit himself against her, and drove deep into the melting, softly pulsing depths of her body. A harsh, guttural groan filled his mouth, and he buried his head in the curve of her shoulder, closing his eyes, soaking in the mind-shattering details as he began to move, not wanting to miss a single sensation. Their skin turned slick with heat, bodies sliding against one another, warmed by lust and hunger and need. A dark, devastating desire that had been smoldering for so many years.

Pushing up on his arms, he said, "I want you to come before me this time." Then he dipped his head, nipping her lower lip, before thrusting his tongue into the sweet, moist well of her mouth, unable to get enough of her taste, the pansy-soft texture of her lips. The sweet suction of the kiss was intoxicating, the touch of her hands fluttering down the length of his spine making him groan.

Breaking the kiss, Riley straightened his arms and stared down at the place where his body penetrated hers, watching the heavy thrust of his cock as he pushed into her. She was so tender and silken and pink around his dark, vein-ridden shaft. He was built too big for her, and yet she took everything he had to give, yielding and soft and infinitely sweet.

"God, that's so sexy," he groaned, his voice deep…breathless. Pulling his gaze up the graceful, feminine line of her body, he bent his elbows, using his teeth to pull the edge of the camisole over her right breast. He took the plump, swollen nipple into his mouth, loving the way that she cried out, arching against him. Releasing the tight, tender bud, he stared down into her eyes, his own savage expression reflected back at him in the luminous depths of her gaze. Changing the angle of his thrusts, Riley watched her eyes goes wide as he ground his body against her clit, pushing her into the orgasm, taking in every subtle nuance of her expression as she crashed over the edge.

"Beautiful," he groaned, loving the way she surrendered to the pleasure, her body thrashing beneath him as she arched her neck and gave a throaty, provocative cry that made him pulse deep inside her, his own release bearing down on him. And with it came the rise of the Merrick, its fangs slipping free of his gums, heavy and sharp in his mouth, its talons slicing through his fingertips.

"Hope," he growled, knowing it was time. "Oh, God, baby. I don't want to hurt you."

"You won't," she whispered with a soft, womanly smile, as if she instinctively knew things that his male mind could never understand. As if she saw the universe in a way that would forever be closed to him.

"I'm ready," she gasped, pulling the heavy weight of her hair to the side, exposing the pale curve of her throat.

He growled again, lowering his head...touching his mouth to her silken flesh, and then he drove his fangs deep into her shoulder, holding nothing back. Her taste spilled through his senses, making him shudder, his body slamming into her as the ecstasy of the feeding exploded through him with a savage, visceral intensity. He came with his talons embedded in the mattress...his fangs still buried deep, the rich, succulent heat of her blood heavy on his tongue, driving him wild. When he finally pulled them free, he lapped his tongue against the small, angry wounds until they no longer bled, coveting every drop... the power of the feeding filling him with indescribable warmth, as if a strange, exotic fire burned in every cell of his body.

Collapsing at her side, he waited for his fangs and talons to recede, before he rolled to his back as he took care of the condom, leaning over the edge of the mattress to toss it into the wastebasket beneath the bedside table. Then Riley rolled back and pulled her onto his chest, his hands smoothing over the silken length of her hair...her back, her damp cheek pressed to the violent beating of his heart.

Lifting her hand, Hope circled her fingertip around the dark nipple before her eyes, and with a wry drawl to her words, she said, "You might live like a saint, Riley, but you don't make love like one."

His body went tense beneath her, and as she lifted up to look at his face, she watched as shadows darkened the unearthly glow in his eyes, like thick, suffocating clouds choking off the warmth of the sun.

"I'm sorry if I hurt you." His words were hoarse, more scraped out than spoken, his tension so thick, she could feel it vibrating through his muscles. "I didn't mean to lose control like that."

The corner of her mouth curved with a smile. "There's no need to be sorry. A woman likes to know that she's capable of making a man go over the edge." He didn't respond as he stared into her eyes, the moment stretching out between them, and then she said, "Now that you've fed...you'll fully awaken. The Casus...they'll know, won't they?"

"Yeah," he whispered. "They'll know."

"I know you needed to do it," she told him, pressing her palm against the heavy beating of his heart, "and I'm selfish enough to be glad that I'm the woman who gave you what you needed. But...I can't help feeling that we've just sped up the clock."

His gaze slid away from hers, focusing on the ceiling as he said, "You can't look at it like that, Hope. I can't just hang around here digging forever, while they have their sick fun with the town. At least now they'll go ahead and come after me...make their move, and that will be the end of it."

Shivering at the thought, she sat up on the edge of the bed. She could feel the intensity of his stare on her back as she touched her fingers to the pulsing wound in her shoulder. "I thought you would bite my throat."

"I'd love to," he rasped, "but I didn't want to put you in an uncomfortable situation with Millie when she gets home."

Looking at him over her shoulder, Hope started to say, "She'll know sooner or…" But her voice trailed off, and she read the question in his eyes. "Sorry," she murmured, looking away and moving to her feet. She grabbed the thin robe draped across the foot of the bed and made her way to the window. Cracking the blinds, she stared out at the stormy view of the sea, the churning waves mirroring the twisting and turning of her own emotions. "I was going to say that she would have to know sooner or later, but then I remembered that we don't really have a later. So, I guess it's not really an issue."

He cursed something foul under his breath, and she turned in time to see him roll up off the bed in a powerful ripple of muscle that made her heart skip. "Really, Ri. I'm the one who's been telling you that this was what I wanted," she said quietly, watching with wide eyes as he advanced on her, the look on his rugged face one of hot, predatory intent. "Just some time with you. Stolen hours of pleasure. And I'm fine with that, okay?"

"No," he grunted, herding her back toward the four-poster bed. "Nothing about this is okay, and I'm nowhere near done with you tonight, so stop talking and get back in the damn bed."

She studied the smoldering look in his eyes for a moment, then slipped out of the robe and climbed back onto the sex-rumpled bedding, lying on her back. A sharp, wicked smile curled his mouth as he shook his head. "Not like that," he told her.

"How then?" she asked, her voice thick with excitement.

He sheathed himself in another condom, then climbed onto the bed with her, forcing her onto her knees with her face against the sheet, and Hope braced with a deep breath for the thick, heavy push that she knew was coming. But he shocked her with the soft, lapping thrust of his tongue instead. His hands settled onto her bottom, thumbs holding her open as his mouth covered her with a hot, ravenous urgency. His deep, fractured groan vibrated against screamingly sensitive flesh, making her claw at the bedding. His low chuckle followed, breath hot against her folds, and he pushed his tongue into her, moving it slowly, hungrily, as if she were the most delicious thing he'd ever tasted. The instant she started to come apart, to shatter and pulse, he buried the long, heavy weight of his cock inside her, taking her hard and fast, until the violent, scorching waves of pleasure overtook them. They collapsed together against the soft bedding, panting and breathless. Then he pulled her into his arms again, holding her possessively against the heavy pounding of his heart as they both drifted into a deep, exhausted sleep.

CHAPTER FIFTEEN

Thursday morning

As Riley opened his eyes to the watery stream of early morning sunlight spilling in through the window, he found Hope sitting beside him on the bed, the sight of her softly glowing face making something warm settle in the center of his chest. She had the same thin, silky robe that she'd worn last night pulled around her shoulders, the soft fabric draping her body like a sensual second skin. Guilt should have been eating him alive, and though he could feel it lingering at the edges of his consciousness, he refused to let it take hold just yet. There'd be plenty of time for self-recriminations later, when he had to leave this room…and Hope, heading out to the forest to find the Marker. Instead, he focused on the hot, primal burn of lust that stirred his blood. Reaching out with his hand, he stroked the pale, feminine length of thigh revealed in the robe's parting, and with his voice still scratchy from sleep, he asked, "How long have you been up?"

"Not long," she murmured. "Rhonda, our manager

in training, was already scheduled to handle the café this morning, but I wanted to check on Millie. I caught up with her in the hallway just before she headed out again this morning. She'd grabbed a few hours of sleep after Kellan brought her home at two-thirty, and was on her way downstairs to meet Hal's niece. They're driving back to the hospital to spend the day with him. He's stable, but still hasn't regained consciousness."

"Did Kellan go with her?"

She shook her head, looking down at the hand he'd placed on her thigh while she traced the dark veins beneath his skin with her finger. "She told Kellan to stay here. Said she didn't want him to be bored out of his mind at the hospital. She promised not to go anywhere on her own, so she should be okay, don't you think?"

"Yeah," he rumbled huskily, beginning to slide his hand farther up her sweetly rounded thigh, when the sound of his name being shouted from the bottom of the stairs made them both jump. "Shit," he muttered, jerking up into a sitting position, the white sheet tangled around his hips.

Hope's eyes went wide with surprise. "That didn't sound like Kellan."

"That's because it's my brother," he grunted, throwing back the sheet as he climbed from the bed.

"Ian?" she gasped, moving to her feet. "What's he doing here?"

"I don't know," he grunted, quickly pulling on the jeans he'd left lying in a pile on the floor. "But whatever the reason, it isn't going to be good. I'll go see what's going on while you throw on some clothes."

She was already moving to get dressed while he disabled the sensor that she'd reset and walked out the door, a heavy feeling in his gut as he wondered what had brought his brother all the way to Washington. Making his way down the stairs, he found everyone waiting for him in the living room. His brother, Watchman Aiden Shrader and Kellan were spread out over the sofa and love seat, mugs of steaming coffee sitting on the mahogany table that was centered between them. The rich scent of cinnamon rolls drifting in from the kitchen made his stomach growl, but from the look on his brother's face, Riley knew food was going to have to wait.

Though his brother and Shrader were both tall, with hard, muscular builds, Ian had Riley's same dark hair, only shorter, and blue eyes, while Shrader had hazel eyes and thick, caramel-colored hair that fell to just above his shoulders, as well as a wealth of tattoos on his arms and hands.

"What are you two doing here?" he asked, glancing between the two of them.

It was Kellan who answered the question. "They said they needed to talk to you."

Riley arched a brow as he stopped in the middle of the room. Crossing his arms over his bare chest, he threw Ian a sharp look of frustration. "And you couldn't have called? You know damn well that with Malcolm dead, it's too dangerous for you to be out wandering around right now. You're a free meal to any Casus that has the balls to come after you. What the hell were you thinking?"

"We told him that, but he was determined to do this in person," Aiden drawled, nodding his tawny head toward Ian, who sat with his left elbow braced against the high arm of the leather sofa, his left hand rubbing over his chin as he studied Riley's face through dark, shadowed eyes. Angry tension poured from his big, powerful frame like heat coming off a towering blaze, filling the room with a sharp, electric presence.

Whatever was going on, Riley knew he wasn't going to like it. He started to tell Ian to go ahead and spit it out, when Hope came down the stairs behind him in jeans and a T-shirt, instantly snagging the attention of every male eye. Her mouth was kiss-swollen, cheeks flushed, hair falling around her shoulders in wild, sexy disarray, as if she'd only taken the time to run her fingers through it and not a brush. Ian arched his brows at the obvious fact that she looked as if she'd been thoroughly ravaged, while Kellan and Shrader both snuffled warm, appreciative rumbles of male laughter under their breaths.

She murmured a quiet "Good morning" as she took the vacant spot on the love seat beside Kellan, her hands clasped nervously between her knees. Though he hadn't spoken to Ian since getting to town, Riley knew that Saige had told him about Hope…and no doubt filled him in on their history. And while he didn't think that Ian had ever known her very well, odds were he remembered her from school or around town. His brother took a moment to study her face, as though looking for remnants of the girl he'd known back in Laurente all those years ago, then slid his hawklike gaze back toward Riley. Narrowing his eyes, he drew in a deep, searching breath. "You've fed," he announced in a low voice, the husky words making everyone freeze. Hope's face turned bright red, her eyes going round with one of those deer-in-the-headlights kind of looks.

Riley responded with a curt nod, warning his brother with his eyes to drop the subject before he embarrassed her any more than he already had, but the guy apparently didn't give a damn. "Shit," Ian muttered, and Riley's own eyes narrowed with suspicion.

"What do you mean by 'shit'? I thought satisfying our hunger was a good thing. Isn't that what you've all been nagging me to do? Now that I've finally done it, I can face Gregory as a Merrick and take him to pieces."

Kellan looked from him to Hope, then back again, the corner of his mouth twitching with a grin as he gave a low whistle. "Oh, yeah," he murmured. "You're blasting out Merrick vibes like a beacon. They'll be tripping over themselves to get to you now, whether you've found the Marker or not. The Casus will probably be swarming around this place by tonight."

"Good," he grunted. "I'm ready to end this."

"Goddamn it," Ian snarled, leaning forward and

smacking his fist down on the surface of the table so hard that everyone's mugs jumped a good inch...as well as Hope.

"What the hell is your problem?" Riley snapped. But his brother just sat there, looking ready to explode with some violent emotion, while the tension in the room cranked up another uncomfortable degree.

"I don't suppose you guys brought the first Marker with you?" Kellan injected into the heavy silence, looking between the two men who sat across the table from him and Hope.

Shrader shook his head, saying, "Riley won't be needing it, so we left it at Ravenswing, rather than risk losing it. Especially now that Westmore has his hands on the one that Saige found down in Brazil."

Kellan arched his brows. "Why won't he be needing it? What do you guys know that we don't?"

Shrader leaned back into the corner of the leather sofa and glanced at Ian. "I think it's time you go ahead and tell the big guy why we're here," he said.

With his elbows braced on his spread knees, Ian scrubbed his hands down his face, then cut his dark gaze up at Riley, and the uneasy feeling in his gut flared with warnings of something bad...something ugly.

His brother just kept staring, and Shrader sighed, saying, "Ian had a dream."

Kellan snickered. "I thought that was Martin Luther King Junior."

"Shut up, smart-ass," Ian growled, glaring the younger Watchman into silence, while Riley absorbed the telling words. Though they still didn't understand everything about Ian's "gift," it seemed that his dreams could sometimes be a form of precognition, enabling him to see things before they actually happened.

"So you came all this way because of some damn premonition," he said in a low, raw-edged voice. "Why in God's name didn't the others stop you? What are they all doing?"

"Quinn tried, but he was no more successful than I was," Shrader explained. "He's back at Ravenswing with Molly and Saige. All three of them are working on the maps now, which I'm sure Saige has already told you. And Kierland has been called to Austria to stand before a special meeting of the Consortium. He's on the plane as we speak."

Riley knew that the Consortium was a sort of paranormal United Nations, comprised of elected officials from each of the remaining ancient clans. The Watchmen reported directly to the organization, acting as the Consortium's eyes and ears around the globe. The shifters were forbidden to interfere in problems that arose among the clans, unless given special permission by the Consortium. Kierland and the others in the Colorado unit had broken that rule by stepping out of the shadows and making contact with Ian when his awakening had begun, which was probably why Kierland had been called forward. Riley assumed the opinionated Watchman would use the opportunity to go ahead and argue his position that the other clans could no longer stand by and allow the Casus's return to go unchecked. He also knew that Kierland was trying to work out a way of sharing the Marker between the different Watchmen units, so that more Casus could be taken down. Though his plan made sense, especially as Saige continued to work her way through the maps and more of the crosses were found, no one had much hope that the Consortium would agree, knowing the issue would be argued and debated for so long, it would probably be a moot point by the time they came to any sort of decision.

He was ready to ask again what Ian had dreamed, when his brother finally moved to his feet. Standing in front of the sofa, his tall body vibrating with violent emotion, Ian said, "I thought I knew you." The words were soft…bitter. "I mean, I know we've never been close. And I get that it's my fault. I bailed. Left you behind to deal with everything back at home. But I thought we at least had respect between us, Ri."

His stomach churned, but he managed to rasp, "We do."

"Like hell we do," Ian growled, suddenly taking a step toward him, his hands fisted at his sides. "Brothers don't lie to each other. They don't keep each other in the dark, especially not when it counts."

The dread coiled tighter, like something constricting around his neck. "What do you want from me?"

"I want the truth!" Ian shouted, his dark features twisted in a grimace of fury. "Is that so goddamn much to ask?"

He didn't respond. Instead, Riley uncrossed his arms and headed for the back door. But leaving the room meant turning his back on Ian, which was never a smart move. One second he was walking away, not wanting to have this conversation in front of Hope, and in the next Ian was gripping his shoulder, jerking him back around, getting right in his face. "Don't you dare walk away from me!"

"I don't need this right now."

"If not now, then when?"

"There's crap going on here that you don't know about!" he roared.

"Because you won't tell me!" Ian fired right back, shoving at his shoulders hard enough to send Riley slamming back against the door.

He sagged there for a moment, letting the door support his back, clueless as to what he should say…how to explain. It amazed him that the floor was still holding him up, when everything else around him seemed to be dissolving into a pile of shit. "Christ, Ian. I don't want you to have to be a part of this."

"I already am." His brother lifted one hand, ran it back through the midnight strands of his hair, then slowly shook his head. "I know what you have planned. What you're going to ask Kellan to do."

Riley locked his jaw and stared into Ian's glittering eyes, a vein beginning to throb in his temple.

"What?" Kellan asked. "What's he going to ask me to do?"

Ignoring the Watchman's question, he said, "It has to be done," in a low, emotionless tone that seemed to infuriate Ian even more.

"Like hell it does. What are you thinking?"

His mouth twisted with a bitter smile as he said, "I'm assuming that in your little dream, you didn't hear the explanation I give him when I make my…request?"

"What request?" Kellan burst out with impatience. "Would someone tell me what's going on?"

"I don't give a rat's ass what kind of reason you have," Ian growled. "Nothing could make me believe that your idiotic plan is the only answer. It isn't going to happen."

"If Kellan doesn't do it, I'll find someone else who will."

His brother sneered. "Yeah, well, they're going to have to get through me first."

He stared into his brother's eyes, doing everything he could to avoid looking at the others. To avoid looking at Hope. "Stay out of this, Ian. It has nothing to do with you."

"It has everything to do with me. You're my goddamn brother, and after everything we've been through, I'm not about to lose you like this. I want an answer, and I want one now."

A choked laugh grated against Riley's throat, and he swallowed, trying to breathe down the shivering heat that was rising up inside him. Lowering his gaze to the floor, he could feel each heavy, hammering beat of his heart as he said, "You left."

"Left? Left what, damn it?"

He pulled in a deep breath. Slowly let it out. "Home."

Silence…and then Ian said, "I asked you to come with me."

"And I couldn't," he rasped, rubbing his damp palms into his thighs, the wood grain of the floorboards blurring as his eyes went hot. "You knew that. And Elaina, her obsession with the Merrick never stopped. She just became more desperate to know what was coming…to see a glimpse of our futures." Lifting his head, he held his brother's bleak stare as he said, "And what you didn't let them do to you, our mother begged me to let them do to me, hoping she could get her answers."

Ian flinched, his expression pulled tight with dread. "Please tell me you told her no," he said hoarsely.

Riley rolled his shoulder, cutting his gaze to the floor again, aware of the others staring at him…the weight of their gazes burning against his skin. "At first, yeah. But then I just got tired of fighting her on it. And I was afraid that she'd try to use Saige, who was still so young. So I finally let her hold the 'vision' ritual with that group of quacks she hung out with, just to shut her up."

"What happened?" Ian asked. "Did they hurt you?"

"Naw, nothing like that. And it worked, which totally blew my mind, since I'd thought they were out of their freaking skulls. But they held their little ceremony, and I saw…"

"What?"

"I saw the future," he said in a low voice. "I saw what I would become."

"Christ, Riley. Just spit it out."

"It wasn't pretty. Hell, it was…" He took another breath, finally forced it out. "I become a killer."

"Of things that deserve to be killed," Ian grunted. "That's what we're all becoming."

"I wish." He laughed, the sound painful and stark. "But it's worse than that. I can't control it when I change. Not like you and Saige. The rage, the aggression, it gets the better of me. Takes me over. And I become as bloodthirsty as the things we're fighting."

Breath-filled silence, and then Ian whispered, "I don't believe you."

"It's true," he breathed out, doing his best to control the tremor in his throat. "I saw it with my own eyes. You and Saige, you're able to handle it. But when I'm forced to face the Casus, I… Hell, I don't know. It's like my rage overwhelms me and I just lose it. I saw myself killing. Brutal, bloodthirsty, and they weren't all monsters. I think… Christ, I think they were just people." He lifted his gaze, forcing himself to hold his brother's furious, tormented stare. "If you care about me at all, Ian, you won't let me turn into that. You won't let it happen. You'll do the decent thing and kill me before you let me hurt anyone."

He was painfully aware of Hope making a thick sound of surprise…of Kellan and Shrader cursing to themselves, but he couldn't look their way, not wanting to face their expressions. Not wanting to see the disgust he knew Hope must be feeling now that she knew she'd given herself to a monster…a killer.

"There's got to be another way," Ian argued.

"There isn't. I had already realized it was time to suck it up and deal with it, when I learned you'd headed back to South Carolina to face Malcolm. When the Watchmen showed up and told me what was happening, I knew the time had come. I'd do the damn thing myself, but I don't know if I'll be able to once I've lost my control. And the only reason I haven't done it before now and eaten a bullet is because I'm a stubborn bastard and want to take as many of the Casus out with me as I can, before I go. I know it's a hell of a thing to ask of you, but I need your promise. If it… If it happens, I need you to make sure that I'm put down."

"Nothing's going to happen," Ian growled. "God, Riley, you're the most righteous man I've ever known. The idea of you turning…" He shook his head, his voice a gritty, graveled rasp as he said, "It's impossible. Whatever you saw in that goddamn ritual, it *isn't* going to be like that."

"But if it *does* happen," he said through clenched teeth.

His brother vibrated with a gripping tension, then finally gave a jerky nod, relenting for the moment, and Riley leaned back against the door, feeling as if a weight had been lifted off his chest. Ian might not be happy about it, but he trusted him to make sure that the right choices were made.

"So if we end up not having to off ya," Shrader drawled with his typical pain-in-the-ass sarcasm, "are you gonna bring Hope here back to Ravenswing?"

The leaden weight that had begun lifting from Riley's shoulders suddenly crashed back down, nearly bringing him to his knees. His gaze gravitated to Hope against his will, the expression on her beautiful face making him feel like the biggest bastard alive. A stark, wrenching blend of fear and anger and betrayal. Her mouth trembled, her skin too pale, as if everything had just drained right out of her. Already, she was closing down. Locking up.

Swallowing against the knot of emotion in his throat, he said, "She isn't coming back."

Ian took a step forward, demanding his attention, and he dragged his gaze away from Hope to refocus on his brother. "Once the Marker is found, you need to come home, Riley. Until the war is over, it's too dangerous for you to stay here with Hope. The Casus will just keep coming for you, one after another. You guys need to be somewhere safe. Somewhere you're not having to look over your shoulder every hour of the day and night."

"I won't be going anywhere," he rasped, holding up his hand when Ian started to argue. "And even if I was, Hope still wouldn't be going with me." Not that he wouldn't have wanted her to. He just knew what his future held, and didn't want her anywhere near it. If a miracle happened, and he faced the Casus that night without losing control…that didn't mean he was in the clear. Didn't mean that it wouldn't happen the next time…or the next. Sooner or later, that damn vision was going to be a reality, and Riley had no doubt it would be that night. Somehow, he just…knew.

His brother glanced at Hope for a moment, a dark expression of disbelief carved into his features as he looked back toward Riley. "What the fuck were you thinking?" he muttered. "How could you involve her in this—*feeding from her*—if the thing you two have got going isn't permanent?"

He opened his mouth, ready to tell his brother to mind his own business, when Hope suddenly headed for the stairs, saying, "I think…I think I should go now."

With his heart all but pounding its way out of his chest, Riley watched her quickly climb the stairs, feeling as if she was taking a part of him with her. The good part. The worthy one. Throughout the night, he'd kept waiting for the moment when she was going to open her eyes and come to her senses. Tell him to get lost. That she wanted nothing more to do with him. He'd tried to brace himself for it—only, the wrenching moment never came. Instead, she just kept giving of herself, so freely, so sweetly, accepting every part of him, no matter how dark or hard or aggressive.

He wanted to go after her so badly, the need was like a physical thing raging inside his body, but knew there was nothing he could say to make things right. No rosy spin that was going to erase that gutted, devastated look on her face. Instead, he just stood there, leaning against the door with his gaze glued to the empty stairs.

The silence was eventually broken when Kellan cleared his throat, saying, "So I'd be willing to bet my right arm that we'll be facing those bastards tonight. When the Casus get a whiff of you, they're going to rain down on this place like a swarm of locusts. And having Ian here is only going to sweeten the temptation. So we need to be prepared."

"Yeah." Raking one hand back through his hair, Riley finally pulled his gaze away from the stairs and looked back at his brother. "And just so you know, I don't plan on leaving her here to fend for herself. If something happens to me, I expect you guys to see that she has protection until that damn Marker is found and off her property. Then there won't be any reason for those bastards to hang around Purity, and Hope will be able to get on with her life."

Ian nodded, and Riley went on to say, "What exactly did Shrader mean earlier, when he said I wouldn't be needing the Marker you've got back at Ravenswing?"

His brother shoved his hands in his pockets. "In the dream I had, you were wearing the cross you'd found here in Purity."

"Then in that case," Riley grunted, pushing away from the door, "I guess we'd better get off our asses and go and find the damn thing."

CHAPTER SIXTEEN

AFTER HOURS OF digging throughout the long day, the Dark Marker still hadn't been found. There'd been some decent weather that morning, but then the rain had started again in the afternoon, the predicted storm front finally starting to roll its way toward shore. Their efforts had been a waste of time at that point, but they'd kept going, until finally calling it quits a half hour ago. The rain was coming down so hard now that visibility was nil, which had made the search impossible. Riley had been positive they would find it that day, after what Ian had seen in his dream, and yet they were still no closer to having possession of the ancient cross. Disappointment sat heavily in his gut, his hands blistered and sore from the hours he'd spent slamming that damn shovel into the ground, but the pain in his body didn't come close to the one in his head…and his chest.

He hadn't spoken to Hope since that morning. Before he could get upstairs, she'd already come back down, ignoring him as she headed past everyone on her way into the kitchen. Thinking she'd finally call when she was ready to talk, Riley had gone up to finish dressing, then joined up with the others, and hadn't been back to the house since. And though he'd tried to stop himself, he kept remembering the look that had been on her face after she'd learned the truth about him, about his future, and couldn't help but feel that she'd been avoiding him on purpose. It was no less than he expected, but it still sucked.

Leaving the others to get showered and changed back at the cabin, he'd made his way up to the house with his bag, determined to make her talk to him before he sent her away. Everyone agreed that the Casus would make their move that night, which meant that Hope couldn't stay there. Riley fully expected her to argue, but even if he had to drag her out of there kicking and screaming, she was going to go.

Letting himself into her room, he pulled off his rain-soaked jacket and tossed it on the floor, along with his holster, not wanting to ruin any of her antiques with water damage. Standing before the window, he stared out at the violent fury of the storm as it raged over the ocean, the dark clouds streaked with crackling bolts of lightning, the deafening waves of thunder rolling in hard and fast. It was almost as if nature knew what was coming…and had felt the need to provide the appropriate imagery.

He'd just pulled off his T-shirt, thinking he'd try to warm himself in a hot shower before heading down to the café to find Hope, when she came into the room, shutting the door behind her. Bracing himself, Riley stood with his back to the window as he waited to hear what she would say.

She crossed her arms over her chest, staying near the door, her eyes somber and shadowed as she stared at him across the room. "I just ran into the others down in the café," she said in a quiet voice. "They told me about your day. If all of you really believe that they're coming tonight, why can't you just run? It's madness to face the Casus without a Marker, Riley."

Shoving his hands deep in his pockets, he shook his head. "If they still believe the Marker is buried here on your land, we can't just take off. No way in hell would I do that to you and Millie. And now that I've awakened, they're going to come on strong. It's best to go ahead and face it. I'm tired of wondering what they're up to, worrying about what they have planned. It's better just to get it over with." Lifting one hand to rub the tense muscles in the back of his neck, he stared at her from beneath his lashes as he asked, "Did Kellan tell you the plan?"

She nodded, a fine tremor visible in the hold of her arms…in her shoulders. "He isn't happy about it. And neither am I. But I've already called Millie and told her to wait at the hospital until she hears from us that it's okay to come back home."

"Kellan might not be happy about missing the battle," he rasped, "but he'll protect you with his life, Hope. He won't let anything happen to you."

"I KNOW," HOPE WHISPERED unsteadily. She paused, a deep breath lifting her chest, before she managed to say, "When you said that you would leave…I thought you meant here. Purity. *Me.* I never could have imagined that you were talking about the end of your life."

His expression revealed raw, tormented agony. "I should have told you, but I…I couldn't. I didn't want you to know. God, Hope. I'd have given anything to keep you out of this." He shook his head again, a bitter laugh falling from his sensual lips. "Damn it, I *did* give. I sacrificed and sucked it up, just to keep you out of it, and for what? Here you are, stuck right in the middle."

She swallowed, understanding exactly what he meant. "So that ceremony that Elaina begged you to take part in. That's why you broke up with me, isn't it? Why you twisted a knife through my heart when you slept with Amee, who'd always hated me? Did you pick her specifically, Riley? Just so it would hurt me more?"

"Yes," he admitted, the single word painfully gruff… hoarse, as if it'd been ripped out of him. "I needed to destroy the connection between us. If there'd been any chance of getting back with you—if you'd have still wanted to have anything to do with me—I wouldn't have been able to resist. I had to make you hate me, Hope. I had…I had to make it stick."

"To protect me?" she whispered, torn between wanting to slap him for hurting her so badly, and throwing herself at him because of the heartbreaking reasons he'd done it.

He nodded in answer to her question, his throat

working, every hard, beautiful muscle in his broad chest and powerful arms rigid with a brutal, gripping strain.

"And look what happened." She snuffled her own burst of bitter, jagged laughter under her breath, the heat in her chest climbing, spreading into her throat, her face, tingling beneath her skin. "God, sometimes life is so screwed up. It amazes me we all don't just say to hell with it when things get like this."

"You don't mean that," he challenged in a low, hard voice. "You're too bloody brave to mean that, Hope. Too strong. No matter what life has thrown at you, you somehow find the strength to keep going."

"Don't I? Look at you, Riley. You're the bravest man I've ever known, and yet you're going to give up. Run."

"From myself," he argued, the words biting and grim. "From what I'll become."

"Says who?" she snapped, lowering her arms as she took an angry step toward him, her hands fisting at her sides. The future could be theirs, damn it, if he was only willing to fight for it. To find the faith in himself that would bring him back to her after he faced his demons. But instead of fighting, he was willing to just throw it away. To leave her, when she'd only just found him again. Only just remembered what it was like to be alive. "God, Riley, the future is never set in stone. Never a given!"

"Mine *is*," he shot back, his jaw clenched so hard that it looked painful. "And because of that, my entire life has been a joke. Some kind of stupid bid to keep this from happening, always doing the right thing, and look where it's gotten me. I'm still standing here, with this shit bearing down on me, same as I've always known I would be. It *is* going to happen, Hope. No matter what I do, I saw what's coming."

"Life is all interpretation," she whispered. "Point of view. Perspective. Maybe…maybe you misunder-stood."

He snorted, rolling his tattooed shoulder in an angry gesture. "There's only so many ways you can *interpret* ripping someone's body apart with your bare hands."

"Damn it," she cursed, the sound brittle with impa-tience. "You don't know it will happen!"

He pressed his right hand against his chest. "But I *feel* it. In here." His hand moved lower, pressing against his stomach. "And here. No matter how much I wish it could be different, I know that it can't."

"Because that's what you were shown?" she practi-cally shouted, wanting to scream. To pick something up and hurl it against the wall in a childish outburst of temper. "Because it's what you were told? God, Riley, you can't let that control you! You have to fight for what you want. It all comes down to will, and I've never known a man with a stronger force of will than you. Look at what you were willing to give up when we were young, because you were afraid of hurting me. You're strong enough to fight this. I know you are."

"It's not that simple," he growled, his blue eyes glowing with a wild, unearthly light, as if his Merrick was rising within him, climbing toward the surface. But she wasn't afraid. No matter what Riley believed, Hope knew in her heart that he wasn't a killer. She only wished she could find some way to make him believe in himself the way she did. She was going to lose him if he didn't, and it was going to kill her. Smash her down into tiny pieces, until there was nothing but a pile of broken fragments that could never be put back together again.

Struggling to control her quivering jaw, she said, "I never should have let you take my blood, but I was greedy. Selfish. I wanted to be the one who gave you what you needed, and now…now I'm going to lose you because of it."

"This isn't your fault!" he burst out, the graveled words biting and sharp with frustration. "It's mine. *I'm* the bastard. The one who should have stayed away from you, but couldn't. The one who's been risking your life every time I've touched you. God, Hope, look at what happened last night. I took you, here, alone, with this…this evil inside me. It scares the shit out of me, knowing what I'm capable of…what I can be pushed to. Who knows what it's really going to take to unleash what's buried somewhere in here?" he seethed, jerking his thumb toward his dark chest. "That's why I can't touch your scars. Even though Capshaw's gone, the hatred I feel for that son of a bitch is so powerful, I don't trust myself. Don't trust where it might take me. What might take me over if I give it so much as an inch. If that happened and I... If I hurt you..." His throat worked, and he shook his head. "I *never* should have touched you, but I wanted it bad enough to take the risk. You should hate me for that."

"To use your favorite line, Ri, *I can't.* I can't hate someone who I—"

"DON'T," RILEY BARKED, knowing it was going to kill him if he heard her say it. "Christ, whatever you do, don't say that, Hope." But the words were in her eyes, written all over her beautiful, precious face, and he couldn't take it. Knowing that he had to get the hell out of there, Riley turned and headed for the door that connected to her private bath. "I'm cold," he muttered, painfully aware of her gaze tracking him across the room. "I'm going to take a shower."

Moving in a daze, he closed the door behind him, stripped off his boots and the rest of his clothes, set the water on hot and climbed into the shower. He'd been standing with his head under the scalding stream for a few minutes, waiting for the heat to finally seep beneath his skin, melting the cold knots of fear twisting him up inside, when he heard the bathroom door open. A moment later, Hope pulled back the curtain and stepped into the back of the tub, the heavy weight of her lashes making it difficult to read the expression in her eyes. She wore only a thin tank top, the erotic sight of her nipples pressing against the soft cotton and the dark, glossy curls nestled at the juncture of her thighs sending his blood rushing south. His cock went granite hard…thickening with need, his heart hammering in his chest so hard that it hurt.

"What are you doing?" he rasped, feeling as if he'd slipped into a fantasy…a dream.

"You said you were cold," she murmured, slipping to her knees in front of him. Flicking him a smoldering look from beneath her lashes, she reached up and curled both of her soft, sweet hands around his throbbing shaft, squeezing…testing his size…his broad width. "I thought I'd do my best to warm you up."

"You don't have to do this," he somehow managed to say as he stared down at her, thinking she was the sexiest, most beautiful woman he'd ever set eyes on.

"I know I don't," she whispered, brushing her lush, velvety lips against the taut, slick head of his cock, the provocative touch of her mouth making his goddamn legs almost give out beneath him. "But I want to, Riley. I've *always* wanted to."

"Damn it," he groaned, threading his shaking fingers into the soft, heavy silk of her hair. "I don't know if I can take it."

Hope smiled as she ran her tongue across the swollen, plum-size tip, loving the way it made his breath hiss through his teeth, a violent shudder rolling through his long, powerful frame. "Just remember to breathe," she whispered, giving him back the seductive words that he'd said to her the night before, while her fingers milked his incredible length, marveling at his raw power and strength, like sensuous satin over thick, rigid steel.

Unable to wait any longer, she opened her mouth over him, her hands wrapped around the wide base, holding him…stroking, his low growl filling the air, visceral and deep and wonderfully male. He was heavy against her tongue, swollen to bursting. Throbbing and hot and impossibly hard. His taste was mouthwatering…delicious, like something sweet and ripe that she wanted to savor for hours on end. Hope lost herself in the intimate, intoxicating details, the primal burn of pleasure magnified by the way he gripped her head, staring down into her eyes, with no secrets between them, no lies, as if she could finally see beneath his anger and shields, to the truths that lay within. She could feel his fear, his desperation, and it made her want to scream. To fight for him. But she knew he'd never allow her to be involved in the battle. He would give her this moment, and then shove her away, like he did all those years ago. Not to be cruel or to hurt her, but because he would do everything that he could to protect her.

Again, his breath hissed through his teeth, his body shaking as he locked his knees. "No more," he growled, pushing her away. "I *can't* take it."

Before she could argue, Riley pulled her to her feet, pressing her spine against the cold tiles of the shower. She gasped as he lifted her up with his hands gripping onto her sweetly rounded ass, and shoved himself into her. "I won't come in you," he growled, nearly dying at the intensity of sensation from sinking into her without a condom, the hot, cushiony depths of her body making him tremble, it was so jaw-grindingly good. She was liquid and tight and soft, pulsing around him, gripping his naked shaft like a greedy mouth, taking him deeper and deeper as he kept working himself in, until he'd buried every inch inside her. He nailed her to the shower wall with a violent, explosive hunger, needing to imprint himself on her soul, on her heart, even though he knew he had no claim to them. The slick, suctioning friction broke him down, peeling back the layers until he was nothing more than a creature of pure, primal instinct. Until he felt like an animal, feral and out of control. And yet the way she looked at him made him feel like a god, invincible and strong, as if there was a sliver of light glowing inside him, after all. One that she'd started. One that would die without her there to feed the flame.

Steam rose, surrounding them in a thick, sensual mist as she ran her small hands over his wet shoulders, down the bulging power of his biceps. "I love your body," she told him, her voice husky and soft with passion. "I love its power. Its strength. But it's not these incredible muscles that are going to save you, Ri." Pressing her hand over his heart, she said, "It's what's in here that will keep you whole. Keep you true to who you are."

He shuddered, his throat dry. "I wish you were

right. You have no idea how badly I wish that could be true, Hope."

"It *is* true. I know it is."

"And what am I meant to do?"

"You're meant to find faith in something that will help you through this, so that you can come out whole on the other side." Her mouth trembled into a shaky smile, her eyes glassy and bright as she cupped his damp face in her hands. "You have to have hope, Ri. Please. Promise me that you'll at least try."

"I'll try," he groaned, wanting to give her the words that she deserved, but he couldn't force them past the knot in his throat. So he showed her with his body instead. There were no words to express what he was feeling, anyway. And though the Merrick wanted to take her blood again, Riley forced it down, knowing that it was too soon, after all that he'd taken from her last night. Instead, he found her lips and lost himself in the exquisite taste of her mouth, rubbing his tongue against hers, swallowing her breathless, husky cries. And then he broke the kiss, staying close, wanting to watch the fire in her eyes when the scorching, white-hot burn of pleasure overtook her, nearly ripping him over the edge. Gritting his teeth, Riley wrenched himself free at the last second, erupting onto her pale thigh in hard, violent surges, his own graveled cry filling the air.

He collapsed against her afterward, his mouth buried in the curve of her shoulder, his heart hammering against her breast. Eventually, he set her back on her feet, turned and stepped beneath the steaming spray of water, letting the shower rain down over his bent head. Hope lifted her hand, trailing her fingers over the beautiful tattoo that whorled over the top of his shoulder. Her hand moved farther down his back, mapping out the firm, compact muscles…the long line of his spine.

She whispered his name, and he flinched, as if she'd struck him. Without a word, he stepped out of the shower and grabbed a towel. Hope turned off the water and followed him out of the bathroom, watching as he pulled boxers, jeans and a shirt out of his duffel bag. He began to dress, each article of clothing that covered his muscular, breathtakingly beautiful body like a sheet of armor that cut him off from her. A series of locks that she couldn't break through. That kept him imprisoned in a place she couldn't reach.

The pain ripping her open inside was suffocating and dark, like being stabbed. She rolled her lips inward, blinking rapidly, but it was no use. The flood of emotion came pouring out in a deep, violent torrent, and a dry, choked cry jammed up in her throat, her vision blurring as hot tears ran down her face. Walking to her closet, she pulled off the damp tank top and dressed with her back to him, then made her way to the window, staring out at the violence of the coming storm that seemed to be swallowing the horizon like some angry, gaping black maw.

He quietly said her name, and she forced herself to turn and face him, swiping her fingers beneath her wet eyes, the tears falling in an endless, burning rush that she couldn't stop…couldn't control.

"Please don't cry," Riley groaned, the husky words cracking with emotion, the sight of her tears making something inside him clench with pain.

"I can't help it," she sobbed. "I haven't cried in years. Not since I lost my baby. And now I'm losing you. I can't… I just—"

"Christ, Hope. I'm sorry. For everything," he said in a ragged, gritty burst of words. "I never…I never meant for this to happen. I knew I didn't have any right to touch you. I just… I couldn't stay away. But I didn't mean to hurt you. Not again. You're the last person in the world I would ever want to hurt."

"Riley…I—"

He shook his head, knowing that whatever she was going to say would destroy him. "You need to get going," he told her, cutting her off, the gruff edge of his words making her flinch, as if they could physically bruise her. "Do you know how to shoot a gun?" he asked, taking the Beretta from his holster.

She nodded, and he walked to where she stood, handing her the weapon. "I want you to keep the gun with you, Hope. Whatever you do, keep it close. There's no telling how this is all going to play out, and I don't want you taking any chances."

She stared down at the gun with a puzzled frown. "Will it do any good against them?"

"The human host they inhabit can be killed, though

not quite as easily when they're in Casus form. But if you put a bullet in the head or the heart, it should do the trick and send the bastard's shade back to where it came from."

She slipped the gun into the canvas bag she'd slung across her body, and he glanced at the clock on her bedside table, checking the time. "Kellan should already be downstairs waiting for you."

She nodded, and he could see the gut-wrenching truth in her eyes. The bright, shimmering, fragile emotion that burned deep inside her. It set her alight. Made her glow. Made him want to grab hold of her, and never let her go.

Her glistening gaze moved over his face, as if she was memorizing every feature, and then she drew in a shuddering breath and turned away from him, walking toward the door. She opened it, her small hand gripping the handle, and then suddenly said, "Whatever happens, don't forget your promise." Then she walked out of the room, pulling the door shut behind her.

Feeling hollow, as if his heart had just been scraped out of his chest, Riley stalked from the room, down the hallway, to the narrow window that looked out over the rainy parking lot. Moments later Hope walked outside with Kellan, and they climbed into his truck. She kept her head down, swiping her fingers under her eyes, and he knew she was still crying. It left a raw feeling in his gut, the painful sensation keeping company with the jagged wound that had been carved inside his chest.

Holding his breath, he watched as they drove away, unable to move until the taillights finally faded away beneath the falling rain. Then he turned and made his way back to her bedroom, shutting the door. Walking to the bed, he crawled over the snow-white linens and grabbed her pillow, burying his face in the soft, Hope-scented cotton. And as the lashing rain continued to fall against the window, he let it soak in the hot, rushing burn of his tears.

CHAPTER SEVENTEEN

Thursday night

WAITING FOR THE END of the world. When measured against good ways to spend your time, Riley didn't rank it particularly high on the list. It came in right around the bottom, along with having your heart torn out and sticking a red-hot poker in your eye. The café had been closed down for a few hours now, and Ian and Shrader were grabbing some food in the kitchen, while he stood with his shoulder braced against the wall, staring through the living room's bay window. He kept his attention on the stormy woods, doing his best to keep focused on the coming battle. He wondered where Gregory was, and what he was doing. Not to mention all the other psychotic players who would no doubt make an entrance before the night was over. The Collective. Westmore's men. The other Casus who had attacked Kellan. And where the hell was the one whose escape from Meridian had awakened him? It didn't make any sense that they were waiting. All of them. Everyone. Something had to be going down, and he didn't like it. It made Riley's skin crawl, his insides churn.

He heard the door push open, and a moment later his brother was standing at his side, offering him an ice-cold longneck. "So she's the one, isn't she?" Ian asked, bracing his shoulder against the opposite side of the alcove.

Taking a long drink of the icy beer, Riley wiped the back of his wrist over his mouth, wincing from the cold in his throat as he said, "The one what?"

Ian stared down at the beer in his hand, watching the icy vapor dance as he swirled the liquid around inside the bottle. "I've always wondered why such an upstanding guy like you never had a steady, when you were such a rock in everything else. Why you didn't have the whole wife and kids and white-picket-fence thing going on. Now I get it. You've been holding out, wanting someone you thought you couldn't have."

Riley shook his head, a dry, sarcastic sound jerking in his chest. "Would you listen to you? You don't even sound like my brother. What the hell did you do with him?"

Ian took a drink of his beer and smiled, his dark blue eyes glittering with a wry edge of humor. "Blame it on my soon-to-be Mrs. She's helped me get in touch with my softer side. It's like looking at the world through new eyes, and I see things now that I never would have before. Like the fact that you're head over heels for Hope Summers."

Riley looked back through the window, his mouth

pulling tight with a crooked, bitter smile. "Even if I am, it doesn't matter." His voice was low…gruff.

"Yeah?" his brother asked. "And why's that?"

"I already told you," he muttered. "No matter what happens, she's not coming back to Ravenswing."

"Seems it would be a simple matter of asking her," Ian offered in a low rumble, taking another deep swallow of beer.

Scraping one hand against his bristled jaw, Riley kept his gaze focused on the stormy night, hoping to avoid another argument about what would happen at the end of the evening. "I guess we'll just have to wait and see."

Ian gave a low grunt of frustration. "I know what's going through your head and it's madness. I'm telling you, Ri, you're *not* going to cross over," he growled. "It's just not possible."

Before he could argue, Shrader came in from the kitchen, making his way toward them as he drawled, "So if ol' Riley isn't interested in Hope enough to keep her around, does that mean she's free game?"

One second the cocky ass was walking across the room, and in the next Riley made a quick motion with his right hand, ripping the Oriental runner beneath Shrader's feet out from under him and the Watchman's back hit the floor. Hard.

"Uh, Riley?" his brother murmured, staring at him with wide, wondering eyes. "Did you just do that?"

"Kellan didn't tell you?" he asked, pushing his hand into his pocket.

Ian shook his head. "Tell me what?"

"I, uh, found what I can do," he said, his tone flat, devoid of emotion. "The Buchanan 'gift' thing."

"I'll say you did," Shrader grunted, moving to his feet. Rolling his head over his thick shoulders, the Watchman muttered, "So what else can you do, Mr. Sunshine?"

Riley curled his lip. "I can wipe up the floor with your ass if you don't shut up."

Wearing a shit-eating grin, Shrader braced his feet and spread his arms wide. "Wanna give it a shot?"

"Damn it," Ian grunted. "Don't let him rile you. And you," he barked, pointing a finger at Shrader. "Stop causing trouble."

Rolling his shoulder, Riley turned back toward the window and lifted the bottle in his hand, finishing off his beer. He answered a few of Ian's questions, explaining about his strange, newfound ability to control physical objects, telling him about the lamp and Thermos, as well as the way he'd been able to keep Hope locked inside the house while he'd fought Capshaw.

"So…I, uh, talked to Saige a little while ago," Ian murmured, changing the subject as he rested his back against the wall. "She thinks they might be close to finishing the next map."

"I don't see what the rush is," Riley commented. "We haven't even found the third Marker yet."

"We'll find it," Ian said with a hard note of determination. "And then we'll go after the next one."

"Yeah, we'll be like the Energizer bunnies," Shrader

snorted as he sprawled into a corner of the sofa. "We'll just keep going and going."

Riley started to ask if Saige had any idea where the fourth Marker would be, when the lamp sitting on the end table beside Shrader suddenly went out, casting the room into shadowed darkness.

"There goes the power," Ian grunted, turning to peer out the window. "And it looks like we've got company on the way."

Staring out at the distant woods, Riley searched for whatever had caught Ian's eye and spotted the flashes of movement through the swaying trees. "I guess we were right about them coming tonight," he muttered, a strange sense of finality falling over him.

Opening the back door, Shrader stared through the violent, lashing rain, a slow smile curling his mouth as he said, "This is going to be fun."

"Did anyone ever tell you that you're one crazy son of a bitch?" Ian asked with a low rumble of laughter.

"All the good men are," Shrader drawled, his smile widening. "That's what makes us so good."

They stepped out onto the porch, and Riley pulled the door shut behind him. "Remember, we're looking to take down the Casus any way that we can," he rasped, taking the gun that Shrader had loaned him out of his holster. It was a gleaming 9 mm Glock, and although he wished that Ian had one as well, he knew his brother would refuse. Since the night he'd seen their father hold a gun to their mother's head during an argument, Ian had never set hands on a gun, choosing instead to fight with the knife he always carried on him, or in the powerful form of his Merrick, which Riley knew he would be using during the coming battle. "At this point it's better to send them back to the pit and get out of here alive. We'll worry about sending them to hell next time around."

"Sounds like a plan," Shrader replied. "I'll unload as many rounds into them as I can, then make the shift."

He nodded, knowing he was going to have to do the same, allowing the darkness within him to fully break free, transforming his body into Merrick form for the first time. As a tiger shifter, Shrader would most likely allow his claws and fangs to release, while keeping the human shape of his body, instead of slipping fully into the shape of his beast.

Just before they headed down the porch steps, Riley reached out, grabbing hold of Ian's hard shoulder. When his brother turned his head to look back at him, he said, "The minute you see that I've slipped away, you do it."

Ian's dark eyes narrowed with anger. "I'll do it only if it has to be done, Ri. And not a second sooner."

He started to call out something to Shrader, and Ian cut him off, snarling, "Don't even bother. Aiden knows I'll gut him if he even tries it."

He tried again, saying, "Damn it, you can't—" when his brother cut him off for a second time.

"Trust me, Riley. If I see...if I see it isn't you

inside," Ian muttered, his deep voice tortured and low, "I'll make it right."

He saw the truth glittering in Ian's deep blue eyes and nodded. Looking toward the woods, he said, "Okay, then. Let's get this over with."

As they quickly made their way across the slick lawn, the fury of the storm crashed down over their heads, drenching them from head to toe, providing the cover they needed to reach the woods. Ian made the change as they moved, his body fluidly shifting into the powerful shape of his Merrick. Deadly talons slipped through the tips of his fingers, his body expanding, bulging with muscle, while the bones in his face cracked and shifted, his nose flattening against his face, the Merrick's fangs slipping from his gums. Riley and Shrader held their guns aimed at the trees as they moved, making their way into the cover of the forest. Shrader signaled that he'd go west, coming up behind whoever was out there, while Riley and Ian kept moving forward, separating as they traveled deeper into the woods. The seconds stretched out, ticking away…one by one, and then Riley caught a flash of blond hair from the corner of his eye, and in the next instant, a man was rushing toward him. Riley fired off a shot, but the bastard just kept coming, slamming him into the rough trunk of a tree, pinning his forearms against the bark.

No way in hell is this thing human, he thought, struggling to break free of the man's powerful hold, when the blonde threw back his head, revealing a long, lethal set of fangs.

"Ian! Shrader!" he called out, lifting his knee and nailing his assailant between the legs. Riley could feel his own fangs stinging within his gums, the power of the Merrick's fury pumping through his system, building…drawing closer…closer…urging him to rip the bastard's throat out. He could smell the heat of the man's body…of his blood. Could feel the beat of his heart. The rhythm of his pulse.

"No," he growled, his eyes burning from the sting of the wind and rain as he bashed his forehead into the guy's hawklike nose. The blow whipped the man's head back, but he released Riley's left arm and countered with a sharp right that damn near broke his jaw.

"Get down!" Shrader's guttural voice suddenly shouted, and Riley threw himself to the side just before the Watchman unloaded a round of ammo into the man's back. The blonde spun and fell to the ground, his body jerking as though he'd been electrocuted, his muscles contorting with violent spasms.

"He isn't human," Riley panted, using his free hand to push his wet hair back from his face, while Shrader kept his gun trained on the man lying face-first in the mud. "He had fangs."

"Do you think he's one of Westmore's—" Shrader began, when the man stirred, pushing sluggishly up onto his arms. Shrader made a move, as if to fire again, but Riley held up his hand, catching sight of the healing wound in the man's throat as the blonde straightened his upper body and gave them a cold smile.

"You didn't get those pearly whites out for Kellan the other night," Riley called out over the distant boom of thunder.

"He didn't give me enough time," the man replied, wiping his bloodied face on his arm.

"And before, when we fought your kind at West-more's headquarters?" Riley asked, wondering what the hell this guy was. They'd known that Westmore's men weren't human, but he was no closer to identifying their species now than he'd been before.

"We can only release our fangs at night," the man explained, his thin eyes beginning to glow a strange, demonic red. "Plus, Westmore didn't want us flaunting our abilities. The fewer who know what we really are, the better. But these are special circumstances tonight."

"Oh, yeah?" he asked, wondering where Ian was, and hoping like hell that he was okay. "And why's that?"

"We've been given orders to do whatever it takes to bring you in before Gregory gets his teeth into you."

Riley's mouth tightened. "And why do you want me?"

"If he decides not to let your Casus have you, Westmore thinks he might be able to trade you for the code to the maps," the blonde told him, his words cut with cocky arrogance, as if he enjoyed bragging about their plans. "But really, I think he just likes the idea of screwing Gregory over, since he knows how badly that bastard wants you."

"And is that why you were trying to get your hands on Kellan? Does Westmore think he'll make a good trade as well?"

The jackass smiled. "It would be fun to see just how easy it would be to break the two of you. We're pretty creative when we want to be. Just think of the things we could do to any one of you. How long do you think your friends and family would hold out before giving us exactly what we want?"

Ignoring the asshole's taunting question, Shrader growled, "So where are your Collective buddies? We've heard they're in town as well."

"Following Gregory," the man said, pulling himself up to his feet. "They've finally been given the order to take him down. Calder had hoped one of you would manage to fry his ass so that he didn't have to deal with him back in Meridian, but you were taking too long."

Riley was about to demand an explanation of just *what* Westmore and his men were, when Ian showed up, his lethal talons pressed against the throat of the man he steered before him. Looking at Riley, he said, "I don't know who this prick is, but he claims you'll vouch for him."

Riley took in the stranger's short black hair and pale, ice-blue eyes. "You're the one who warned Kellan the other night, aren't you?"

The corner of the man's mouth kicked up with a wry grin, his rugged, arrogant face showing not a trace of fear. "I'd nod," he drawled, "but I rather like my throat in one piece. But, yeah, that was me."

"And just who the hell *are* you?" Riley asked, slipping the Glock back into his holster.

"Call off your brother," the stranger murmured, "and I'll be happy to tell you everything, including what I know."

Riley nodded at Ian, and his brother snarled as he lowered his hand, shoving the guy away from him.

"Now, first things first," the man said. "Right now, there are about fifteen more of Westmore's men closing in on you."

As if in response to his words, several figures rushed from the shadowed forest and surrounded them, the pouring rain having made it impossible to scent their approach. Though the men didn't carry any weapons, every last one of them was fanged, their eyes burning with the now familiar flickering glow of red.

Facing their attackers, the four men backed into a tight circle, while Riley slanted a dark look toward the blue-eyed stranger who stood on his left. "If you know how to kill these bastards," he snarled, "now might be a good time to share it."

"Only wood can kill them," the man said in a low voice.

"Wood?" he grunted. "Are you friggin' serious?"

The stranger nodded. "Sounds bizarre, I know. But the only way to take them down is to stake them through the heart with solid wood."

Shrader made a rude sound in the back of his throat, reaching behind him to slip his gun into the waistband of his jeans. "Are we seriously going to listen to this prick?" he grunted, releasing the deadly claws and fangs of his beast, his eyes glowing a bright, glittering amber in the stormy darkness.

"We can argue later," the man said. "Right now, I suggest we pick up any branches we can find and start taking them down."

"I have a better idea," Riley muttered, cutting his gaze up toward the windblown branches of the trees, the storm-tossed limbs reminding him of raised arms swaying to some violent, primal rhythm. "When I give the word, you guys hit the ground. I'm talking flat out."

"What the hell are you going to do?" Shrader snarled, while Westmore's men started moving in, their red eyes flickering like demonic bursts of light in the rain-drenched darkness.

"Just do it!" Riley shouted, taking a deep breath as he closed his eyes, focusing on what he wanted... creating the image in his mind with sharp, specific detail. "Now!" he suddenly roared, clenching his teeth as he opened his eyes and blasted out the mental command. The power surged through him, a sharp, piercing pain radiating through his head, and he bent forward, a warm spill of blood pouring from his nose, same as it had when he'd used the gift to keep Hope's door closed during the fight. But this time it was stronger...the pain ripping through him like a knife as he lifted his gaze, watching the trees shake, almost as though a violent earthquake was vibrating up from the ground beneath them. A deep, guttural roar tore from his throat, the pressure in his head excruciating, and then the trees exploded into movement, the gnarled, heavy branches slashing toward the ground and spearing through Westmore's men. Bloodcurdling shouts of agony filled the air as the branches drove through their backs, piercing straight into their hearts, then bursting from their chests with bright, gruesome sprays of blood.

Riley held it for as long as he could, until the pressure became too great and he released his hold on the power, the branches instantly whipping back up into the air, taking the bodies of Westmore's men with them. A great, crushing wave of relief swept through him, and his legs gave way, his knees hitting the muddy ground, sinking into the wet earth, his lungs working so hard it felt like they'd explode. He heard someone mutter, "Holy mother of God," and Riley lowered his head, not wanting to see the horrific results of what he'd done.

"Are they all dead?" he gasped, working to draw in a deep breath.

"Most of them got staked and the rest are running," Shrader told him, his deep voice cut with a note of awe, as if he couldn't believe what he'd just seen. "I gotta tell you, man, that was some pretty serious—"

"Are you okay?" Ian grunted, cutting the Watchman off, and Riley could tell by the tone of his brother's voice that he was once again in his human shape.

"Yeah, I'm okay. Just have a helluva headache." Riley glanced up at the blue-eyed stranger, who was standing to his left, the man's expression one of curiosity and caution. "Thanks for the tip," he muttered, pushing his wet hair back from his face.

The guy nodded, and Shrader approached him, a belligerent expression pulling the Watchman's face into a hard scowl, his fangs and claws withdrawn back into his body for the time being. "My, what blue eyes you have, Grandma," he sneered in a warped rendition of the classic line from *Little Red Riding Hood*. "You wanna tell us what you're doing helping out the ones your kind is trying to kill?"

"I might be one of the unlucky few in my family to inherit the Casus's baby blues, but I'm not a bad guy," the stranger murmured. "At least, not yet.

"And if you're smart, you'll listen to me. From what I can tell, Westmore's men were the first wave of tonight's attack. The second wave should be coming along any second now."

"Until then," Riley gasped, pushing himself to his feet, "why don't you go ahead and tell us who you are."

"Better yet, *what* are you?" Ian demanded, while Riley made his way to one of the nearby trees, resting his back against the rough bark, his body still drained from the effort of using his power.

"My name's Noah Winston, and I'm someone whose family bloodline is pulling me into the middle of the coming war, just like it's done to the Buchanans." A wry smile tipped at the corner of his mouth. "We're just not intended to fight for the same side."

Shrader gave a low, rough laugh. "Winston? I get it

now. You belong to one of the Casus bloodlines. I've heard the name before." Looking toward Ian and Riley, he said, "The Winstons have been under Watchmen surveillance as long as the Buchanans. They're one of the strongest Casus bloodlines known to exist. Descendants of human women who were raped by those Casus bastards, and somehow managed to survive."

Catching Noah's icy gaze, Riley said, "If your bloodline's so powerful, why haven't the Casus shades used you as hosts yet?"

"Rumor has it that they're saving us for when the big names come across. Personally, I'd rather remain standing in my own skin, and so would the rest of my family. Like the Buchanans," Noah explained, "we've had our own students of the paranormal. Family members who devoted their entire lives to discovering what they could about the return of the Casus. Along the way, they've uncovered pieces of the puzzle that I believe can help you. For instance, what do you know about Westmore and his men?"

"We know they're not human," Riley admitted. "But that's about it."

Noah nodded, saying, "We figured you weren't aware of their species. To be honest, outside the Deschanel—or vampires, as they're more commonly called—there are few who even know of their existence. But they're called the Kraven, the unfortunate byproduct of a Casus and a vamp. Like the human females who bore children after Casus attacks, there were even a greater number of vampires who gave birth after being raped by those monsters. The Deschanel clan looks on the Kraven as an embarrassment—an abomination—which is why their existence is such a closely guarded secret. One that few of the Consortium even know about. The Kraven can pass for humans, and it's believed that while they have incredibly long life spans, sometimes living for hundreds of years, they also go through long periods of hibernation. They're not as strong as a pure-blooded vamp, and their fangs only come out at night. For the most part, the Kraven live in the shadow of the Deschanel, treated little better than slaves."

"That would explain how Westmore was able to give the Collective the location of the vampire nesting grounds," Shrader muttered.

Noah nodded. "They're considered somewhat unstable, but not stupid. For Westmore to betray the Deschanel, he must have a good source of protection in line."

"Which might explain why he wants to bring back the Casus," Ian murmured.

"Possibly," Noah replied. "Though he's an idiot if he thinks he can make a deal with the devil and survive. But to be honest, we don't know a hell of a lot about his motivations or what he's after. And, at this point, we don't understand his obsession with the Markers any more than you guys do."

Scrubbing his hands down his wet face, Shrader

muttered, "Christ, this thing is like a fucking onion. The deeper we peel it, the shittier the smell." Glaring at Noah, he said, "And how is it that no one knows you're here? Where's your surveillance?"

Noah's mouth curved in an arrogant smile. "I slipped them back in San Francisco."

Shrader grunted in response, muttering something about the Watchmen unit assigned to the Winstons. Though Riley tried to focus on what the Watchman was saying, it was becoming harder to concentrate, his heart pounding…his body burning with heat, despite the frigid chill of the rain. He hadn't experienced the full change yet, but it was coming.

Narrowing his gaze on Noah's rugged face, he suddenly said, "If you've been hanging around town watching everyone, do you know where Gregory is?"

"He's most likely with the female," Noah murmured. "I imagine they'll be coming along anytime now."

"Female?" Ian grunted, his body going rigid with the same jolt of surprise that had just slammed through all three of them. "What female?"

Noah looked around at their shocked expressions, then slowly shook his head. "You didn't think the Casus would all be males, did you?" he asked with a low laugh. "Immortality didn't come until puberty, and from what I've heard, very few of the women made it that far. But there *are* females. Pretty vicious ones, too. Not the kind of bitches you want to go messing around with. Your redheaded friend must have some serious balls to try to screw this one for information." Frowning, he said, "How is it that he knows about her but you guys don't?"

"What the hell are you talking about?" Riley growled, his heart beating so hard it damn near burst its way out of his chest, as he straightened away from the tree.

"The little green-eyed bitch," Noah grunted. "She's one of them."

"A Kraven?" he asked, while a cold, deadly fear began to creep through him, sickening and rank, making him feel ill.

"No, a *Casus*," Noah told him, an uneasy look spilling over the man's face.

"But she has *green* eyes," Riley growled, fisting his hands at his sides. "And the Casus's eyes are blue, damn it."

Noah shook his head again. "*Not* the females' eyes. Those are always green."

"Oh, Jesus," he gasped, reaching out with one hand to steady himself against the tree as his head began to swim.

"What?" Ian asked, the single word thick with frustration. "What's going on?"

"Kellan," he growled. "It's all been some kind of setup!"

"What has?" Shrader grunted, sounding thoroughly confused.

"Kellan has been seeing some woman in town since we got here. Picked her up at some bar. Christ, he told

me he was going to call her and have her come to the
motel to wait with him and Hope tonight. He was
worried about her being alone during the storm."

Shrader and Ian were both stunned into silence, their
grim expressions mirroring their dread.

Taking an aggressive step toward Noah, Riley
snarled, "Why didn't you warn him?"

"I thought he knew!" Noah shot back. "That he was
using her to try to get information. It never occurred to
me that he didn't know she was one of them!"

Shaking with fear, Riley pulled out his cell phone,
but there was no service. Cursing under his breath, he
took off running, thinking that if he could just reach the
house before the second wave of the attack arrived,
then he could grab Hope's keys and use her car to get
to town. He could feel his control slipping, the Merrick's rage struggling to break free, but he did his best
to beat it down. Whatever happened, he couldn't lose
it.

Not yet, damn it. Not yet.

Pushing his body as fast as it would go, he raced
through the forest, knowing only that he had to do whatever he could to reach her...before it was too late.

STANDING AT THE motel-room window, Kellan watched
as the storm seemed to swell with rage, a series of
jagged lightning strikes illuminating the drenched night
in violent splashes of brilliance. He cast a quick look
down at his watch again, wondering where Pasha was.

He'd called her on his way into town with Hope, and they'd agreed to meet at this motel, since it was closer to Millie's than the one where she was staying. But now he wished he'd just gone ahead and picked her up. She should have been there by now, and the worry was only adding to his sharp, seething frustration. He didn't mind protecting Hope—knew that Riley would never have let her go with him if he didn't trust Kellan to keep her alive, which was a hell of an honor. But it still chafed that he was missing out on the battle.

Choking back a growl, he wondered when they were going to stop treating him like a kid, then immediately found himself shaking his head. Hell, they were probably just waiting for him to stop acting like a screwup. Waiting for him to grow up and stop letting his dick get him into trouble.

"Do you think he's going to be okay?" Hope asked from the chair she'd been sitting in for the past half hour, her soft voice pulling him from his internal grumblings.

Sending her a crooked grin, Kellan did his best to ease her tension, noticing the way her hands were twisted together in her lap, her face pale…eyes shadowed by fear. "Yeah. Riley's a tough son of a bitch, and he's got Ian and Shrader with him. That should be enough to scare the shit out of anything or anyone who tries to mess with them."

"I tried to call his cell phone," she murmured, "but the storm's knocked out my reception."

"Yeah, mine, too. But they'll come into town and meet us here just as soon as they can." Trying to get her mind onto something other than her worry, he said, "Hey, did Riley ever tell you about those tattoos on his shoulder? About what they mean?"

She shook her head, giving him a curious look. "No. I thought they were just designs."

With an easy smile tipping the corner of his mouth, Kellan explained how Riley's tattoos were actually a blend of different symbols and words, ranging from Celtic to Asian to Egyptian, all of them with one basic theme. *Hope.* According to Riley, the design had started with one small symbol, and then he just kept adding from there, until the dark tattoo had eventually grown into the swirling pattern that it was today. She absorbed the story with a soft look of wonder on her face, obviously making the same connection that he had between her name and that symbolic badge of "hope" that Riley wore on his body.

Checking his watch again, Kellan cursed a soft string of swearwords under his breath, and she said, "Do you think something's happened to your friend?"

"I hope to hell not," he rasped, hating the sickening slide of guilt that was beginning to creep through his insides. He'd told Pasha several times not to tell anyone that she knew him, and he'd always been vigilant in making sure that no one followed him when he met her in town. He'd been careful, damn it. But he still couldn't get the weird feeling out of his gut. The one telling him that things were going south…and fast.

When headlights suddenly flashed across the window, he blew out a rough breath of relief, and immediately went to the door, yanking it open. Though he hadn't gone into detail, Kellan had told her that his friends were expecting some trouble out at Millie's tonight, explaining that he was bringing Hope into town to keep her out of any possible danger. She probably thought he was crazy, but he didn't give a damn. All that mattered was keeping the women safe until this thing had played itself out. She parked next to Riley's truck, and he watched as she climbed out of her car, holding her coat over her head as she made her way through the heavy rain, the wind whipping her long hair across her face.

"Has something already happened?" she asked, taking in his and Hope's tense expressions as she rushed into the room. "You both look pale."

"Not yet," he muttered, shutting the door behind her. "But I've been worried about you. What took you so long?"

"Sorry," she told him, tossing her coat onto the foot of the bed as she sent Hope a friendly smile, "but the weather's awful. Most people are leaving town until the worst of it's over, and I got caught in the traffic."

Kellan made the introductions, and then went back to his place by the window, too restless to sit down. He half listened as Pasha made idle chitchat with Hope, talking about the town, the café, while his thoughts centered on his friends back at Millie's. He'd just checked his phone for the umpteenth time, shoving it back into the case clipped on his belt, when Pasha came up behind him, her cold hands massaging his tense shoulders. "Don't worry," she murmured, pressing her voluptuous body against his back, her fingers dancing their way up the strained cords in his neck. "I'm sure the Buchanan boys will handle themselves just fine tonight."

Before her words could sink in, there was a sharp sting on the side of his throat, and he lifted his fingers to the burning skin, jerking around to face her. Wondering what in God's name was going on, he winced from the pain in his neck and said, "How did you know that, Pash?"

"How did I know what?" she asked, taking a step back, her expression one of confused innocence.

Sweat was covering his skin now, his mouth dry, the fire in his neck spreading…climbing into his face. Sinking into his chest. "I didn't say anything about Riley's brother being in town," he growled. "So how did you know that he's here? How do you even know who the Buchanans are?"

She lifted her shoulders in a shrug. "You must have mentioned them to me when you called."

From the corner of his eye, Kellan caught Hope's quick shake of her head, assuring him that he hadn't mentioned Ian when he'd called Pasha on their way into town. She'd been in the truck with him and would have heard every word of the brief conversation.

"Yeah, I guess you're right," he grunted, going along

with her story to buy himself time, while struggling to wrap his mind around what was happening. He didn't understand how Pasha was involved, but he knew he'd screwed up. Again. And this time, his friends were going to be the ones who paid.

He took a sluggish step forward, his body uncoordinated and heavy, positive now that Pasha had injected something into his bloodstream. The burning spot on his neck was swelling, pulsing with fiery heat, and he sent a narrow look toward her hands. When he spotted the heavy silver ring on her right index finger, he knew that she'd somehow used the ring to drug him.

Lifting his blurry gaze to her face, Kellan tried to focus as she suddenly gave him a slow, knowing smile. "Oops," she whispered, a soft, husky chuckle slipping from her lips. "Looks like my little game is over now, shifter boy. But don't worry about the drug. It won't kill you. It's just going to put you down for a while."

He tried to shout at Hope, telling her to run, but his throat wouldn't work. Pasha quickly reached behind her back and pulled a gun from the waistband of her tight jeans, pointing the barrel straight at Hope, who had already jerked to her feet. "Stay right there, beautiful, and keep those hands up where I can see them," Pasha purred, motioning for Hope to sit back down. Then she looked back at Kellan. "Thanks to the little deal I made with Westmore this afternoon, I'm back in his good graces. Even scored myself this nifty little ring from that gorgeous red-haired assassin he's working with now.

Clever, isn't it? You've heard of Spark, no? I have a feeling the two of you are going to become pretty well acquainted once Westmore comes to collect you. I hear she has quite a thing for redheads."

"Bitch," he slurred, wishing he could get his mind to work long enough that he could figure out just what was happening.

She pushed out her lower lip in a dramatic pout, making a tsking sound under her breath. "Now, don't be that way. I could have just gutted you, and been done with it. But you've had your uses. I'd been planning on taking you, once Buchanan had found the Marker and was fully awakened, then using you to draw out that brother and sister of his for Gregory. But then things changed. Still, you've proven useful, after all. Seems ol' Westmore was pretty eager to get his hands on one of the Ravenswing Watchmen. They're looking forward to finding out just what your pals will be willing to trade for you. And in return for handing you over, they're going to make sure that Gregory doesn't get his claws into *my* Merrick."

He finally got it then. Pasha was a Casus. One of the monsters. And the one who'd caused Riley to awaken. Disgusted with himself for being such a colossal screwup, Kellan fell to his knees, using all his strength to force out a thick "Fuck you."

"Been there, done that," she drawled, blowing him a kiss. "And though it shocks me to say it, you were pretty incredible. Not my usual taste, but enough to make me come back for more."

Slumping to the side, Kellan hit the floor, sprawling sideways across the orange and yellow carpet. Pasha stepped forward, the gun still aimed straight at Hope's chest while she used the pointed toe of her boot to push him to his back. Her beautiful face swam into focus, her bright green eyes staring down at him with a chilling, terrifying look of triumph, and as she smiled, he glimpsed the glittering point of a fang just beneath the curve of her upper lip.

Kellan blinked, the acidic burn of guilt stripping his insides raw at the thought of what Hope would suffer for his stupidity.

And then everything went black.

CHAPTER EIGHTEEN

As RILEY RAN THROUGH the lashing rain, his heart pounding with fear for Hope's safety, the forest around him filled with the stark, chilling sound of Casus howls. But he didn't care. He'd let the bastards rip him to shreds, so long as he could get to Hope in time to save her. He'd almost reached the edge of the trees, when a hard, powerful body tackled him from behind, taking him to the ground. His brother's voice roared with rage as they rolled across the muddy floor of the forest, crashing into the gnarled roots of a massive oak tree.

"Goddamn it," he growled, trying to break free from Ian's brutal grip. "Let me go! I have to get to her!"

"Not like this," Ian argued, twisting with a grappling move that pegged Riley beneath the heavy weight of his body, his forearms trapped against the ground. "I'm not letting you run off to get yourself killed! Didn't you hear what's coming? We're going to be surrounded any second now!"

"Hope is with one of them!" he snarled, the sound of his voice too guttural to be human, his Merrick clawing its way to the surface, seething with fury, preparing to break free.

"Which is why you need to calm down," Ian growled. "You'll never save her if you get killed before you even get there. We have to face these things together, and then we'll track down that green-eyed bitch and rescue Hope."

He wanted to keep fighting, damn it, but as Ian's words sank in, Riley knew his brother was right. "Okay," he panted. "I get it. But promise me that if something happens to me, you'll do everything you can to find her, Ian. Promise me!"

"You have my word," Ian told him. "No matter what happens, I'll get her back."

Moving to his feet, Ian offered Riley a hand, pulling him up from the muddy ground just as Shrader and Noah joined them. The Casus howls were getting closer, the beastly sounds punctuated by the deafening blasts of thunder that seemed to be growing in intensity. The rain and wind whipped violently around their bodies, making it impossible to see into the moonlit darkness…while obliterating their ability to scent the enemy.

Glancing at Noah, Riley struggled to force down his fear for the moment and focus his mind on the coming battle. "Looks like you were right about the second wave."

"And we can't see shit in this weather," Ian snarled.

"Could be worse," Shrader drawled, threading his fingers together and cracking his tattooed knuckles, the aggressive vibes that poured off his massive body saying that he was more than ready for the coming fight.

Riley cut the Watchman a sharp, incredulous look. "How the hell could it be worse?"

Shrader lifted his shoulders. "We could already be dead."

"Do you have a blade?" Ian asked Noah, who nodded, before reaching down and pulling a long, sinister-looking knife from the sheath attached to his right calf. As the only human in their little group, the guy was going to need all the help he could get when they faced the coming Casus.

"If you see Gregory," Riley grunted, pulling the Glock from his holster as he looked around at the men, "find me. That bastard's mine."

Before anyone could comment, a group of eight men came into view through the pouring rain, about five yards away. They stood with six massive, fully shifted Casus, the monsters' leathery gray skin slick with rain, sinister fangs gleaming within their deadly jaws.

"Now those are the real deal," Shrader muttered, his lip curling with disgust as he drew his gun. "Collective soldiers, and they're fully armed. But luckily, bullets actually work on these assholes."

One of the soldiers stepped forward, flanked by two of the towering Casus. "Stand down!" the human shouted. "We're not here for you."

"That's not what Westmore's men said," Ian called out.

"Westmore's the one who wants the sheriff. All we want is the Casus named Gregory. We followed him here, so we know he's nearby."

"Sorry," Shrader shot back, "but we don't trust anyone who plays footsies with the monsters. And let me just tell you. Those are some ugly-ass guard dogs you've got there. You ought to shoot the damn things and put them out of their misery."

The Casus snarled, their black lips pulling back over the jagged rows of teeth that filled their muzzled mouths, until the man motioned for them to be silent with his hand. "You don't want to fight us," he said in a graveled warning.

"And why's that?" Shrader asked, his gun aimed right at the soldier's chest.

The man's mouth tipped with a cocky smirk. "For one thing, we've got more firepower than you."

"Not for long," Riley muttered, realizing that this was at least one problem he could remedy. Narrowing his eyes, he stretched out his left arm, splayed his fingers and focused his power. As he closed his fingers into a hard fist and pulled back his arm, the soldiers' guns were torn from their hands. The heavy weapons flew through the air, before landing with a splash against the wet ground near Shrader's feet.

"Oh, man," the Watchman drawled, giving a low whistle. "I *so* wish I could do that."

"Noah, grab a gun," Riley grunted, reaching down and picking up a weapon for his empty left hand, while Shrader did the same.

The Collective soldiers fell back, their expressions ranging from disbelief to fury, while the Casus moved forward. The tallest one looked almost as though he was smiling as he said, "Looks like we'll be handling the situation now." He turned his icy gaze on Riley and his smile widened. "And would you look at what we have here. Town's been buzzing all day with the news that you'd finally ripened up, sheriff. I wonder if you have any idea how many eyes have been on you lately. Watching. Waiting."

"Two Buchanan Merrick," a second Casus growled, stepping forward to join the first. "Yum yum."

"Must be our lucky day," sneered a third as he cut an eager look toward Ian, who had just shifted back into his Merrick form. "Now that Malcolm's gone, you're fair game, Merrick."

"Give it your best shot," Ian growled, the guttural words followed by a violent crack of lightning that struck the ground no more than twenty feet away. The earth shook from the force of the strike, and then everything erupted into chaos as the two sides suddenly charged one another. The cracking blasts of gunfire battled the jarring roar of the thunder, accompanied by the gritty, bestial snarls of the Casus as they slashed with their claws and snapped with their deadly jaws. When he ran out of bullets, Riley stopped fighting the burning heat at the tips of his fingers and allowed the Merrick's talons to finally slip free. As he tore his talons across the leathery gut of one Casus and sent it writhing to the ground, he watched from the corner of his eye as Noah tossed his empty guns away, using his knife to slice through another Casus's thick, corded throat. But the wound was too shallow, and instead of going down, the monster charged the human, who continued to fight with the kind of skill that only came from years of training, making Riley wonder just what the mysterious Winston did for a living.

He looked for Ian and Shrader in the driving rain, and spotted his brother backing toward him through the downpour, his drenched T-shirt splattered with crimson splashes of blood. "I think some more Casus have shown up," Ian shouted over his shoulder, his gaze whipping cautiously around. "It's time for you to make the complete change, Riley. Stop putting it off."

He nodded, forcing himself to let go of the fear, knowing he had to do everything he could to make it out of there alive, so that he could rescue Hope. He couldn't let himself think about what might be happening to her…what she might be suffering.

Pulling in a deep breath of the storm-scented air, Riley finally stopped fighting it, and allowed the dark, predatory blood of his ancestors to rise up within him. A hoarse, guttural cry broke from his chest, his arms shooting wide as the primal Merrick broke free for the first time, its power at full strength after the feeding that Hope had given him. His muscles and bones expanded, straining the seams of his jeans and T-shirt, while heavy fangs burst into his mouth, his face reshaping itself into something that was *more* than human. Something that felt at home there in the midst of the bloodthirsty battle against its mortal enemy.

With his Merrick in full possession, Riley began to fight his way through the monsters, and it soon became clear that all the hours he'd spent training with the Watchmen in recent weeks had been worth it. He'd just downed a Casus with a vicious swipe of his talons, when he turned to find one watching him from the shadowed darkness, its powerful body partly concealed by a massive, swaying maple. Certain that this Casus was a newcomer to the fight, Riley stalked toward him with a purposeful stride. Watching his approach, the creature stepped out from behind the tree, the rain drenching its body, slipping over the beast's huge shoulders and muzzled, wolflike head. And when it smiled at him, there was something about the curve of the cruel mouth that told him it was Gregory.

"It's about time you showed up, you son of a bitch! Where are they?" he roared, wanting nothing more than to take the Casus apart with his bare hands. Sink his fangs into the bastard's leathery throat. "Where is Hope? Does the female have her?"

"Your little Hope's already dead," Gregory sneered with a cold, cruel smile. Riley had been moving with increasing speed, driven by the urge to take the Casus down—but those five words brought him to a jarring, staggering stop.

He stared, his mouth working, wanting to shout that Gregory was a liar. That it wasn't true. But nothing would come out. And though he tried to keep it to-gether…to hold tight to the reins of his control, he could feel them slipping away as a niggling thread of doubt wormed its way into his mind. It coiled itself around his fear with devastating, destructive skill, tearing him down, crushing him beneath the pain of her death…and Riley knew, in that moment, that this was the end. The one he'd always known was coming.

"Get back, Merrick!" one of the Collective soldiers suddenly shouted over the heavy sound of the wind and the rain, moving in from Riley's right, while three of the man's comrades approached from the left, each of them gripping a long, silver blade. "This one is ours."

"Like hell he is," Riley snarled, ready to launch himself at Gregory, when another powerful crack of lightning struck the tree at the Casus's back, sending shards of wood showering over the area. A hazy veil of smoke filled the air, destroying what little visibility there'd been, just as Riley felt himself begin to go under.

So this is it, he thought, numbly aware of something black and wretched and foul climbing up from the darkest depths of his being, spilling like a toxin through his veins as he threw back his head and let out a chilling, bloodcurdling cry of fury and grief. There was a distant corner of his mind watching on in horror as Riley and the soldiers rushed forward at the same time, racing to get their hands on Gregory. Screams filled the air as he began tearing his way through the human soldiers, a red, visceral haze washing over his vision as he slashed out and ripped into their muscled bodies.

It's just like the vision, he thought, picking up one

human soldier and hurling him through the air, before reaching out for another. He could hear Ian and Shrader shouting his name—but he couldn't respond. The rage was too savage...too strong, Gregory's words slicing through his brain like a blade, scalding and sharp. Riley fully expected Ian to order one of the others to put a bullet through his head at any second, and he closed his eyes, trying to pull Hope's memory around him in his final moments.

Needing to make his brother understand, wanting him to know why he'd lost the battle against the raging darkness, Riley used every last ounce of his strength to shout, "She's dead, Ian! Gregory said she's already dead!"

"Goddamn it!" his brother roared, the furious, terrified sound of his voice reaching deep and fighting its way through that violent, red-tinged haze of hatred and pain. "He could be lying, Riley! Are you going to let that son of a bitch win, without even fighting for her? What if she's out there? Alive? What if she needs you?"

He shuddered, lifting the man in his arms above his head, his talons digging into the soldier's arm and leg as the man screamed, fighting to break free. The maddened, primitive rage of the Merrick seethed inside Riley's mind, demanding blood...vengeance, telling him to tear the bastard into pieces.

But it was the soft, husky words in his heart that made him pause, his body gripped by a powerful, heaving tension as he struggled to listen to her words.

"Are you just going to give up on me, when you don't even know for sure?" Hope's beautiful voice whispered through his mind. *"When you don't even know if he's lying?"*

She was right, damn it! She'd made him promise to have hope, and Riley knew that he couldn't let himself slip into the writhing mass of visceral, primitive rage without doing everything he could to fulfill that promise. He couldn't give up, not when there was still a chance that she was out there, needing him. Within the darkness of his mind, he glimpsed that tiny spark of *light* in his soul, that same one that he'd seen before, and he grabbed on to it. Reaching out with his mind, he cupped that shimmering flame within his hands, and instead of burning his skin, it spread its life-giving heat throughout his body, pouring into him, the shocking, incandescent burst of light blasting through the cold burn of madness and fury. And with it came the strength to fight his way back to the surface.

Throwing the soldier to the ground, Riley hunched forward, bracing his talon-tipped hands on his bent knees, working to breathe through the painful, clawing emotion still ripping through him. Lifting his head, he glared at the injured Collective soldiers as they pulled themselves to their feet. "Get the hell out of here," he forced through his clenched teeth. "We'll take care of Gregory. But you leave. *Now.*"

They looked at one another, their expressions hard, rigid with anger and pain, but they turned and limped their way into the woods, obviously deciding to cut their losses while they still could. Riley watched them leave, while trying to wrap his mind around what had just happened. The vision…it had started to come true, his fury and grief over the possibility that she might be dead nearly destroying him. But Hope had said that life was all interpretation…perspective, and in a way, she'd been right. He now understood that it'd been the rage of thinking he'd lost her that pushed him into the dark, seething madness he'd seen during the "vision" ritual all those years ago—but he also knew that Hope's faith in him had been powerful enough to pull him back out again. That it had given him the strength to have the hope that he would find her. That the bright, breathtaking future he'd never allowed himself to dream of might actually be theirs.

He looked around for Gregory, while sending up a continual silent prayer that the bastard had been lying, but he couldn't see him through the heavy rain. Driven by desperation, Riley knew he had to find the Casus, and destroy him, before he was able to make his cruel words a reality.

"Where the hell is he?" he growled, turning toward the place where Ian was standing with Shrader and Winston.

His brother's expression was haggard with strain from the scene he'd just witnessed, but Riley could tell that he was trying to pull himself together. Shaking his head, Ian said, "We've taken down most of the Casus that attacked us, but I never saw Gregory."

"Spread out. Find him," he grunted. "We can't let him get away. He knows the female Casus, which means he can get to Hope. If he gets his hands on her, you know what he's going to do."

Without further discussion, knowing time was working against them, they split up, running into the woods. Riley lifted his nose, struggling to pick up the bastard's scent, but the rain was too heavy, the storm making it impossible to sniff out his prey. As he narrowed his eyes against the downpour, he caught a glimpse of Gregory's leathery gray skin through the trees. Muscles burning, Riley took off running, not stopping until he found himself standing in the center of a small, familiar clearing that ran along a portion of the cliffs. The clearing bordered the area of land that they'd spent that morning searching over for the Marker, and Riley had been struck by its incredible beauty. No fence bordered the cliffs here, and he'd walked to the edge at one point during the day, staring down at the crashing fury of the waves, the air thick with the salty scent of the sea.

Riley had just turned in a full circle, distracted by the strange sensation that he was no longer alone, when he looked over his shoulder to see Gregory's monstrous body stalking toward him.

"I'm going to cut you down first," Gregory growled, his eyes burning with hatred and hunger, "and then I'm going after that bastard big brother of yours. I'll eat him with the taste of your blood still hot in my mouth, Merrick."

Before Riley could respond, a throaty female voice called out Gregory's name from the edge of the woods, and they both looked toward the sound, watching as a tall, green-eyed brunette came into view. She had her left arm curled around Hope's throat, and Riley's heart nearly burst from the staggering wave of emotion that slammed through him. Terror that she was in the female Casus's grip. Blinding, breathtaking relief that *she* was alive. And a powerful, fierce determination to do everything that he could to get her out of there.

"She's dead, huh?" he grunted, cutting a quick, snarling look toward Gregory.

"Oops," the Casus drawled. "Looks like I lied."

With a gun gripped in her right hand, the brunette took aim at Gregory's chest, saying, "He does that a lot, Merrick. Ol' Gregory and I had a deal, you see? One that was meant to buy me exclusive rights to you, but which he obviously isn't planning to honor. I've been screwing around with the Watchman, waiting for you to finally awaken, as well as find that bloody Marker, and then, once you'd done both, I was going to use Kellan as bait to draw out that brother and sister of yours for Gregory here. It was a genius plan, really. But then I had a visit this morning from a Casus named Miles. He told me that Gregory was going to be taken down, so I did the smart thing and switched my loyalties. Your Watchman pal is currently drugged to the gills back at the motel, where Westmore's men will be picking him up any second now, and it looks like I've shown up here just in the nick of time to keep Gregory from taking what belongs to *me*."

"Don't get cocky," Gregory chided. "It makes you look cheap, Pash."

She flashed the Casus a sharp smile. "I should have known better than to trust you."

Gregory threw back his monstrous head and laughed. "Said the pot to the kettle. I've been keeping my eye on you, Pasha. I knew about your little meeting with Miles the second it happened. And with the eldest Buchanan arriving in town this morning, I can have both of them and don't have to give you anything."

She curled her rouged upper lip, glaring at Gregory as she tightened her arm around Hope's throat. Riley tried not to look at Hope, knowing it was going to kill him if he had to see the fear in her eyes. Though her hands were bound behind her back, she seemed to be unharmed, and he planned on doing everything he could to keep her that way.

"What exactly is it that you want?" he asked the instant the female Casus looked back in his direction.

"How about an exchange, Buchanan? You for the girl," Pasha offered, leaning down to lick the gentle curve of Hope's pale cheek. "Mmm, and she's so sweet. If you don't agree, I might go ahead and take a bite out of her right now. What do you say?"

As if those were the words needed to spark her fury, Hope struggled against Pasha's hold, screaming, "Don't you dare, Riley!"

He flicked a quick look toward Gregory. "If I trade places with Hope, he's just going to kill her the second you let her go."

"Not if I kill him first," Pasha purred, her gun still aimed at Gregory's chest. Riley could have taken the weapon away from her with the use of his power, but he held back, knowing Gregory would simply go ahead and attack before he could aim the gun at the Casus himself.

Taking a deep breath, he struggled to come up with a plan that would get him and Hope out of there alive. Though he'd never expected it to happen, he knew that he was being given a second chance at happiness…at the life that he'd always wanted and, goddamn it, he was going to take it. Take it, and hold on to it for the rest of his days. No way in hell was he going to let this bitch take it away from him.

But he had to do something—had to find some way to buy them more time. He wished he knew where the others were. Wished he knew how long he needed to stall before Ian or Shrader found them, tipping the balance in his and Hope's favor.

"Your time is ticking away," Pasha snapped. "Are you willing to make the trade, Merrick? Or do I tear her throat out while you watch?"

"You can't have him, you bloody bitch," Hope snarled, her body going wild as she fought to break the Casus's hold. "He's mine! You lay one finger on him and you're going to be so sorry!"

Pasha started to laugh, as if she enjoyed Hope's desperate struggles, until Hope suddenly threw back her head, slamming her skull into the Casus's face. Screaming, the woman lifted both hands to her gushing nose, and Hope dropped to the ground. Curling up on her side, she tried to work her wrists down her body, so that she could slide her legs through her bindings and get her hands in front of her. Riley had already started to rush toward her when Gregory used the distraction to make his move, throwing his body against him. They crashed to the ground, rolling across the clearing, stopping only feet away from the edge of the cliff. He could hear Hope screaming, as well as Pasha, who was hurling curses at Gregory for daring to attack what was hers, the gun waving wildly in her hand. Doing his best to keep Gregory from ripping his throat out, Riley knew that at any second Pasha could turn and tear into Hope, and the thought burned through his brain that he needed that third Marker.

If he could find it, Hope could use its protection…could use its power to keep herself alive. Ian had seen the powerful cross in his dream, and after everything that they'd been through, Riley believed in the power of his brother's gift. Which meant that the bloody Marker *was* out there somewhere, just waiting for him to find it. When he'd talked to Saige that afternoon, she'd been sure that the cross would be found there in the patch of land by the clearing, where he and the others had been searching. And considering the way he'd used his power to control the trees, Riley suddenly wondered if there was any chance he could somehow "pull" the cross to him. God only knew it was worth a try, but he needed to be able to focus, and it was taking everything he had to fight off Gregory.

Sending up a silent plea for a miracle, his heart about stopped when he heard Pasha give a sudden cry of pain. Cutting his gaze back toward the place where the female Casus had been standing, screaming at Gregory, Riley watched as Shrader quickly stripped her of the gun, then slammed his fist into her jaw, sending her sprawling onto the grass. Without waiting to see if she'd get up, the Watchman sprinted across the clearing, launching himself at Gregory's hulking body and pulling him off Riley…giving him the opening he needed to find the Marker.

Instead of moving to his feet, Riley closed his eyes, pouring everything that he had into pulling the Dark Marker to him. His body strained, the now familiar pressure building inside his skull, the intensity so great, he wondered how his head didn't simply split in two. He could just make out the low sounds of Shrader's fight with Gregory, and knew that no matter how brilliant a fighter Aiden was, he wouldn't last long against the Casus. After all the human feedings Gregory had taken, he was far stronger than the monsters who had come with the Collective soldiers.

Gritting his teeth, Riley rolled to his side and dug his right hand into the damp earth. His desperation grew, the pain in his skull like a great, snarling beast as the ground began to shake with violent tremors, the sky exploding with a blinding, stunning burst of lightning. It seemed like madness, but he could have sworn that he felt the Marker's heat…its power, vibrating up through the ground. He shoved his arm deeper into the moist earth, reaching…calling the Marker, demanding it come to him, and the shaking of the ground grew so violent that it knocked Hope off her feet as she tried to make her way to him.

Riley wanted to shout for her to stay where she was, but a deep, guttural roar poured up from the depths of his soul, and in the next moment, something slammed against the center of his palm. With his heart beating in hard, painful surges, Riley closed his hand around the object and ripped it from the ground. Looking down, he saw that he held a small velvet pouch, its original color indistinguishable from the muddy soil that covered it. Using both hands to rip open the knotted end, his breath caught as he felt the hot, metallic weight of the Dark Marker spill across his palm, its black velvet cord draping across the thickness of his wrist.

Cutting a look back at Gregory and Shrader, he blinked with shock at the sight of the Casus lying on his back, his throat ripped open with three deep slices, while Shrader stood over him, struggling for breath. Wondering if the Watchman had actually managed to kill him, Riley started to yell for Shrader to check the bastard's pulse, when a deep, chuffing noise pulled his attention back to Pasha, and he saw that while Gregory seemed to be down for the count, she had managed to pull herself back to her feet. Her hands and mouth had already transformed into their Casus shape, while the rest of her remained eerily human. She eyed the Marker he held in his right hand, then let out a chilling cry of rage as she charged him across the clearing. Riley gripped the Marker against the palm of his hand, in exactly the way Ian had shown him to do, and the heat of the cross began to spill up his arm, burning and painful, as he readied himself for Pasha's attack.

Just before she reached him, he twisted to the side, stretching out his arm and grabbing her hair with his left hand. Twisting the long skeins around his forearm, Riley jerked her into position with her back to his front, then drove his molten "arm of fire" against the base of her neck. His fiery hand broke through her skin, sinking into her convulsing body, and the sizzling burn of the flames spilled through her, setting her on fire from the inside out. Her pale skin began to glow an unearthly blend of orange and yellow and black, the colors melting together as raw, agonizing howls of pain tore from her throat. Despite the pouring rain, the intensity of the flames began seeping through the Casus's charred flesh, and Riley turned his head away, unable to stare any longer at the blinding light.

Trying to breathe his way through the stunning pain radiating from his arm, throughout his body, he focused on Hope. She stood no more than twenty feet away, taking in the violent, savage scene with a wide, worried gaze, while the rain poured down on her head and shoulders. Shrader came to stand by her side, his own amber gaze focused on the burning body of the Casus.

Riley was still locked into Pasha when Hope gave a jolt of surprise, a sharp cry breaking from her beautiful mouth as she stared over his shoulder, and he realized that Gregory must have regained consciousness. Knowing he wouldn't be able to break free of the dying Casus in time, leaving him wide open for Gregory's attack, a deep, piercing ache of regret poured through him at the loss of what could have been. The future he'd always wanted. The woman he'd always loved.

He opened his mouth, ready to finally shout out the words that he'd never allowed himself to say to her before, when she shoved her bound wrists into the bag draped across her body and pulled out the gun he'd given her before she'd left with Kellan. In the next instant, Pasha's burning body suddenly disintegrated in a violent explosion that sent Riley sliding over the rain-soaked ground, just as the blast of the gun rang out through the night. Hope had fired, the bullet slamming into Gregory's chest. The Casus's arms flew wide, and he lowered his muzzled head, staring down at the bright bloom of crimson that spread over his gray-skinned chest. When Hope hit him again, in the shoulder this time, his head shot up and he stumbled back, an outraged roar ripping from his chest as he plunged backward over the edge of the cliff…

And disappeared into the darkness.

SHAKING HIS HEAD, still unable to believe what had just happened, Riley took the velvet cord attached to the Marker and looped it over his head, then pushed himself to his feet and looked back toward Hope. They stared across the moonlit clearing, her beautiful gaze slowly touching upon the Merrick's face without a trace of fear. The rain finally mellowed to a soft, lazy drizzle as he began moving toward her. With the Merrick pulling back inside him, Riley fell to his knees in front of her and went to work on the ties that bound her wrists. Drawing in a deep breath of her sweet, mouthwatering scent, he thought about how fate worked in such strange, wonderful ways. It had been his belief that he'd lost her that had almost driven him into that dark, desolate hell he'd always believed was waiting for him. And yet it was the faith…the *hope* that she'd given him for the future, that had helped him make his way back to the light, crawling out of the pit and rediscovering his soul.

The instant her hands were free, Riley lifted her shirt and touched his mouth to the cool skin of her belly, before pressing a tender kiss against the thickest of her scars, finally able to face the pain of her past. Finally able to trust himself in a way that he hadn't been able to do in years. He had a second chance at life, and he wasn't going to waste it. He was going to do everything he could to show her how he'd changed. How precious she was to him. How crazy mad in love he was with her. With every perfect, beautiful inch of her.

"Riley, we're not alone," she gasped, trying to pull her

shirt down as he continued to kiss her scars, while Shrader snuffled a low rumble of laughter under his breath.

Staring up at her beautiful face, he said, "I sucked it up, took the blow, and walked away from you once. No way in hell am I doing it again. Whatever it takes, I'll keep you safe. Make you happy. Just tell me that you'll forgive me, Hope. Tell me that you'll give me another chance, and I promise that you'll never regret it."

She whispered his name, looking awed by his words while his fingers bit into her hips, his voice a husky, desperate scrape of sound as he said, "Even if you don't love me yet, you can…you can keep using me for sex. I don't care. Just don't leave me."

More muffled snorts came from behind her, where Shrader stood, and she tried to put her hand over his mouth. "Honestly, Riley," she whispered. "We're not alone!"

Moving to his feet, he cupped her face in his hands. "Damn it, Hope, I don't give a crap what Shrader hears. I just…I need to tell you that I love you. God, I've been in love with you for half my life. And I'm going to love you till the day I die."

Her chin trembled, and he watched as her mouth bloomed into a precious, breathtaking smile. "You never told me."

"I know," he rasped. "And I know that I've been such an ass, Hope, but I swear I'll spend the rest of my life worshipping you, proving to you every minute of every day how much you mean to me." He kissed her between the husky words, tasting her lips, her mouth, her chin. "I've *always* loved you. And I need you, for so many reasons. But most of all, because I can't live without you."

"You won't have to," she whispered against his lips. "I promise, Riley. And I love you, too. You probably already know that, but I'll say it anyways. I've loved you for what feels like forever."

A hard, shivering tremor of relief swept through him at her soft words, and he pressed his forehead to hers as he took a deep breath and said, "The light, Hope. It's still burning."

"What light?" she asked, her voice soft with wonder…with love.

"I'll tell you later," he whispered, wanting to be alone with her, to show her with his body how much he loved her. To make amends for everything that had happened between them.

He touched his mouth to hers, sinking into her, lost in her perfect taste. It was like warmth and sunshine spilling over his tongue. Like…happiness. And hope.

Riley could have kept on kissing her forever, lost in the moment, if Shrader hadn't cleared his throat, his voice dry as he drawled, "Should I…uh, cover my eyes here or something?"

A low laugh rumbled in Riley's chest, feeling strange in his throat—but then, it'd been so long since he'd laughed out of happiness…out of pure, blinding joy. And yet, as happy as he was, there was still a knot of dread sitting in his gut over Kellan. Riley was just about to tell Shrader what Pasha had said, knowing they needed to get to the motel to see if they could pick up a trace of the Watchman, when Ian and Noah raced into the clearing, his brother nearly sagging with relief to see that he was alive. His gaze moved between them, taking in their tender embrace, and before Ian could even ask the question, Riley said, "She's coming back with us."

"About damn time," Ian grunted, before slanting his gaze toward the pile of ashes that were still smoldering, its spiraling tendrils of smoke struggling against the stormy wind. "Gregory?"

Riley shook his head. "Pasha."

Looking around, Ian said, "Then where's Gregory?"

A proud smile curved his mouth. "Hope shot him and he fell off the cliff."

Ian blinked with a stunned look of amazement, then asked, "Do you think he could have survived the fall?"

Riley shrugged his shoulders, pulling Hope into his side, his arm wrapped possessively around her waist. "In his Casus form? Who knows? But I doubt it."

Shrader walked to the cliffs, staring over the edge. "There's no sign of him down there," he called out. "Hopefully the tide's pulled him under."

"Pulled who under?" a deep voice called out from the edge of the trees.

Everyone turned to find Kellan standing there with his shoulder braced against one of the towering cedar trees that lined the clearing. He was drenched from head to toe, as the rest of them were, his skin was chalky, and his eyes were red-rimmed and bleary.

Hope stiffened, giving a sharp cry of joy, just as Ian narrowed his eyes on Kellan and growled, "What in God's name happened to you? You look like hell."

"Feel like it, too," Kellan muttered, shaking his head as he pressed one hand to his stomach.

"I was just about to tell you guys that we needed to get to the motel," Riley said. "Pasha told me that she'd drugged him, leaving him there for Westmore's men to pick up." Catching Kellan's gaze, he asked, "How did you get away?"

The Watchman snorted. "Luckily, the drug she gave me must not have been dosed for a full-blooded lycan, because it started to wear off before Westmore's men even showed up. The bitch was stupid enough to leave my keys behind, so I was able to drive myself back here in the truck." Looking around, he said, "Speaking of the little green-eyed fiend, where is she?"

It was Ian who answered, saying, "Riley fried her."

Kellan's eyes went wide, his gaze lowering to the Marker that rested against the center of Riley's T-shirt-covered chest. "You found the Marker?" he asked, his surprise obvious. "How the hell did you do that?"

"Yeah," Ian added, pushing his dark hair back from his face as he swung his gaze toward Riley. "How *did* you do that?"

Lifting his free hand to rub the back of his neck, the

other arm still wrapped around Hope, Riley explained how he'd used his newfound power to somehow pull the Dark Marker to him. "We must have been right on top of it today," he added, "and just didn't dig deep enough."

Gesturing toward the trees that surrounded them, Noah finally spoke up, saying, "It might have even been trapped beneath one of those trunks, if the tree is young enough. You guys could have kept digging and never found it."

Kellan did a double take at Noah, as if only just noticing that he was there. "What the hell are *you* doing here?"

"It's a long story," Shrader rumbled, making his way toward Kellan. "He can explain it on the way back to the house. I figure we can warm up with some coffee, if the power's back on, then get started on cleaning up those bodies."

"How *many* bodies?" Kellan groaned, looking ready to collapse.

Shrader slapped the redhead on the shoulder as Noah joined them, while Ian remained with Riley and Hope. Riley could hear Shrader making some smart-ass comment, in a low voice, about the tree he'd used to kill Westmore's men, and then the Watchman looked at the three of them over his shoulder. "You guys coming?"

"In a minute," Ian replied. When the men were out of sight, Ian turned, meeting Riley's gaze. "If I were you," he said, "I'd get out of here. We got damn lucky tonight, but there's no sense taking any chances. You should head out of town, and get her someplace safe for the night. Then drive straight for Ravenswing tomorrow."

Knowing his brother was right, Riley agreed to do just that.

ONCE HOPE HAD packed a bag and they'd grabbed Riley's things, they loaded into her car and drove for a few hours, wanting to put as much distance between them and Purity as they could, before checking in to a hotel for the night.

It'd been a stroke of luck that before they'd even left the clearing by the cliffs, Seth McConnell had finally shown up with a small group of Collective soldiers who'd remained loyal to him after he'd broken ranks with the Collective Army. And while Seth had been pissed that he'd missed the battle, at least he'd gotten there in time to aid with the cleanup, helping the others to dispose of the bodies. Riley had quickly given the soldier a rundown of the events that had transpired, explaining about Westmore and the Casus, as well as Gregory and Pasha. As she listened to the harrowing account, Hope realized it was truly a miracle that they'd all made it through the nightmare alive. Then, once they were alone, Riley had told her about what had happened when Gregory had claimed she was dead, and it terrified her to know she'd come so close to losing him.

Shivering at the thought, she finished washing her face in the hotel's bathroom sink and opened the door to find Riley waiting for her in the center of the room. They'd only been there for a handful of minutes, but she knew that before another sixty seconds had passed, he would be inside her…covering her…reminding her that while things were far from perfect in the world, they'd somehow managed to find their own little corner of paradise.

Breathing in the rich, provocative scent of desire that warmed the air between them, Hope walked to him, not stopping until their bodies were touching, chest to chest. With a dark, intense expression of lust shaping the angles of his face, he lifted his hands, pushing her hair back from her brow as he said, "No more talk about tonight, okay? I just want to hold you in my arms, under my body, and know that you're all right. That you're safe."

She nodded and, with shaking hands, he slowly undressed her, his dark gaze lingering on each bit of skin as it was revealed. Then he laid her down on the bed, covering her with the hardness and heat of his body while he threaded their fingers together. Pressing their joined hands into the pillow beneath her head, he buried himself deep inside her, giving her every inch. "Nothing between us, Hope. Just you and me," he murmured in a deep, husky rumble of words that melted through her like hot, bubbling honey, while the dark, beautiful cross swung from around his neck, its polished edge catching the light. He filled her, enormous and thick, pressing hard against her womb, and then held there. It was a symbolic gesture. One of significance and intent. He was telling her what was going to happen. That he would fill her up…and give her a baby. And afterward, as they lay wrapped in each other's arms, he kissed her mouth, and said, "I'm sorry I didn't tell you everything sooner. About the ceremony. About how I feel."

As she stared into his deep blue eyes, her mouth twitched with a grin. "I'm sorry I lied and said that I just wanted to use you for sex."

"You mean you don't?" he asked, lifting his dark brows in a playful look of hurt surprise.

"Oh, I want to use you all right," she murmured, snuggling against him, "but I also want to love you. And I knew that if I told you that, you'd never have laid a hand on me."

The corners of his eyes crinkled in that sexy way that she loved, a slow, kind of crooked smile softening his ruggedly sculpted mouth as he growled, "I want to lay more than that on you."

She smiled at his sexy teasing, then slowly tilted her head, her smile slipping as she said, "It almost doesn't seem real, does it? I mean, so much has happened. Tonight was such a nightmare, and yet I'm so happy right now. Is that terrible?"

"No, honey, you deserve to be happy."

"So do you, Ri. You've lived with your secret for so long," she murmured, smoothing a fingertip over his dark brows. "Did you ever tell Elaina what you saw the night of the ceremony?"

"I tried, but she wouldn't listen. I think she felt guilty, and then I decided it was something for me to deal with alone. You'll never know how hard it was for me to do that to you, Hope. I've missed you for so long." His voice trailed off, and he studied her eyes for a moment, before saying, "Are you sure you're okay with leaving Purity and going back to Colorado with me?"

"I've loved it there, but it was never home," she told him. "The only thing that I'm not okay with is being away from you."

"Won't happen, sweetheart. We're always going to be together," he promised in a low voice. "I just hate that this is how it has to be. If I could stay in Washington with you, I would. In a heartbeat. But there's—"

She put her fingers over his lips to silence his troubled confession. "I know you would, Ri. But until this war is over, you need to be at Ravenswing. So I'll go where you go." She took a deep breath, then said, "And it's the right thing to do, for me *and* Millie. She's looked after me for so long, and I love her so much, but it's time she got to enjoy her own life now, without me around."

They'd gone by the hospital to check in on her aunt as they'd driven through Wellsford, bringing her up-to-date on everything that had happened. Millie told them that Hal had come out of recovery. She also said that he didn't remember anything about his attack, and they hoped it would remain that way. It had been strange saying goodbye, but Hope knew it was time for both of them to move on. After almost losing him, Millie had vowed that she wasn't going to let Hal out of her sight, and maybe together they'd keep the café going…or just keep renting the cabins. It was their future, their destiny, and she'd do everything she could to help them.

"Hal, he'll be good for her," she murmured with a smile. "But what about your job back in Colorado?"

"I don't know," he rasped, staring into her eyes as he rubbed his battered knuckles against her cheek. "I didn't think I'd still be around, so I hadn't planned that far ahead. But now that I've awakened, it's too dangerous for me to stay on as sheriff."

She nodded, understanding the troubles that still lay ahead for them. But she had no doubt that together, they could face whatever those assholes threw their way. After years of lonely desperation, they finally had one another, and nothing was going to take him away from her.

As he rolled her beneath him, his blue eyes smoldered with a breathtaking look of love and possessiveness as he stared down into her face, saying, "Here's the way it's going to happen. You can argue, but I'm warning you now, it isn't going to do any good."

"You're just telling me, huh?"

"That's right," he rumbled in a low, sexy slide of words. "And for once, you're going to listen."

"I'm all ears," she whispered, knowing instinctively that she was about to hear something wonderful.

"Our lives aren't always going to be this crazy," he told her. "And someday, when this war is over, we'll build a house, Hope. Wherever you want. Washington.

Colorado. Hell, I don't care if you want to move to the farthest reaches of the earth, so long as I'm there with you. And we'll have a family. The life we should have had a long time ago. The life we've always wanted."

She smiled at the exquisite vision of their future glittering in his dark, beautiful eyes, and as he kissed his way into her mouth, she tasted the breathtaking promise of his love…and a wild, wonderful forever.

Meet Joanne Walker, a regular Seattle beat
cop who also happens to be a magical shaman
with a penchant for saving the world...

Catch all three titles in the mesmerizing
Walker Papers series by

C.E. MURPHY

Available now wherever books are sold!

And don't miss the all-new tale
WALKING DEAD
coming soon in trade paperback!

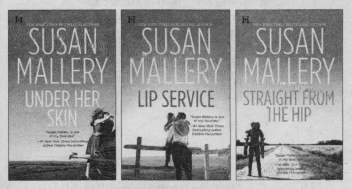

REQUEST YOUR
FREE BOOKS!

2 FREE NOVELS
FROM THE ROMANCE/SUSPENSE
COLLECTION PLUS 2 FREE GIFTS!

YES! Please send me 2 FREE novels from the Romance/Suspense Collection and my 2 FREE gifts (gifts are worth about $10). After receiving them, if I don't wish to receive any more books, I can return the shipping statement marked "cancel." If I don't cancel, I will receive 4 brand-new novels every month and be billed just $5.74 per book in the U.S. or $6.24 per book in Canada. That's a savings of at least 28% off the cover price. It's quite a bargain! Shipping and handling is just 50¢ per book.* I understand that accepting the 2 free books and gifts places me under no obligation to buy anything. I can always return a shipment and cancel at any time. Even if I never buy another book from the Reader Service, the two free books and gifts are mine to keep forever.

185 MDN EYNQ 385 MDN EYN2

Name	(PLEASE PRINT)

Address	Apt. #

City	State/Prov.	Zip/Postal Code

Signature (if under 18, a parent or guardian must sign)

Mail to **The Reader Service:**
IN U.S.A.: P.O. Box 1867, Buffalo, NY 14240-1867
IN CANADA: P.O. Box 609, Fort Erie, Ontario L2A 5X3

Not valid to current subscribers of the Romance Collection,
the Suspense Collection or the Romance/Suspense Collection.

Want to try two free books from another line?
Call 1-800-873-8635 or visit www.morefreebooks.com.

* Terms and prices subject to change without notice. Prices do not include applicable taxes. Sales tax applicable in N.Y. Canadian residents will be charged applicable provincial taxes and GST. Offer not valid in Quebec. This offer is limited to one order per household. All orders subject to approval. Credit or debit balances in a customer's account(s) may be offset by any other outstanding balance owed by or to the customer. Please allow 4 to 6 weeks for delivery. Offer available while quantities last.

Your Privacy: Harlequin is committed to protecting your privacy. Our Privacy Policy is available online at www.eHarlequin.com or upon request from the Reader Service. From time to time we make our lists of customers available to reputable third parties who may have a product or service of interest to you. If you would prefer we not share your name and address, please check here. ☐

BOB09